SICILIAN NOCTURNE

Creative Texts Publishers products are available at special discounts for bulk purchase for sale promotions, premiums, fund-raising, and educational needs. For details, write Creative Texts Publishers, PO Box 50, Barto, PA 19504, or visit www.creativetexts.com

Sicilian Nocturne: Profiles in Murder: Book 4
By Don DeNevi
PO Box 50
Barto, PA 19504
www.creativetexts.com

ISBN: 978-1-64738-038-0

SICILIAN NOCTURNE
1944, WITH BANDIT SALVATORE GIULIANO AND HIS PARTISANS FIGHTING THE NAZIS

CREATIVE TEXTS PUBLISHERS
Barto, Pennsylvania

TABLE OF CONTENTS

CHAPTER ONE 1

CHAPTER TWO 8

CHAPTER THREE 14

CHAPTER FOUR 22

CHAPTER FIVE 29

CHAPTER SIX 42

CHAPTER SEVEN 54

CHAPTER EIGHT 60

CHAPTER NINE 75

CHAPTER TEN 93

CHAPTER ELEVEN 107

CHAPTER TWELVE 119

CHAPTER THIRTEEN 134

CHAPTER FOURTEEN 143

CHAPTER FIFTEEN 157

CHAPTER SIXTEEN 165

CHAPTER SEVENTEEN 174

CHAPTER EIGHTEEN 185

CHAPTER NINETEEN 202

CHAPTER ONE

Four Assassins Disappear

"Ah…there you are!" exclaimed Captain Herman A. Spanagel with a faint, wry smile. Standing in the doorway of his administrative office in the lobby of the Del Monte awaiting Peter's arrival, he was cheerfully relieved spotting Peter enter the hotel through the side door foyer revolving door.

"So, Lieutenant," he called out, "nice to have you return to us. Did you enjoy your night's sleep at the Papa Largomarsino home? And, by the way, it's none of the business of the U.S. Navy whose room you slept in."

Peter blushed, "Sir, it wasn't the way you imagined. Not in a good Sicilian family household. If interested, however, I will share with you the contents of Pietro's seminar Mafia Lecture delivered on my behalf.

"Come in! Come in! There is much for each of us to catch up on. And, by the way, young man, although we knew precisely where you were, and with whom, we couldn't follow your movements because the shades were pulled!" he chuckled, genially.

With the morning's sun streaming through the office's large stained-glass windows, the Director/Head of the Naval Postgraduate School motioned for Peter to sit in front of his executive-style desk. With several small family photos on it, plus two telephones, one in vermillion red, the other in Marine blue, the gold-colored single-light bulb lamp over his writing pad was the only other object atop the desktop.

"The desk is as fastidious as the Captain's clean, meticulous mind. A perfect mind to run an important new postgraduate school."

As before, Peter was impressed with four same-sized framed under glass portraits of Pacific War heroes, each autographed. They were of President Franklin Roosevelt; Secretary of the Navy, Frank Knox's Admiral Chester Nimitz, and Fleet Admiral Ernest J. King. On the full-length wall opposite the large stained-glass windows were innumerable photos, a few in color, ranging from former Heads of the Naval Postgraduate Schools such as Capt. Act. E.M. Tillson and Capt. V.R. Murphy to ships named in honor of alumni since 1819, i.e., those displaying heroism during wartime.

As Peter relaxed in the surprisingly comfortable chair, Captain Spanagel ambled over to a padlocked filing cabinet in between one of the large windowsills and the stenographer's table in the corner half a dozen yards from the desk. Unlocking the fastened padlock, then the cabinet itself, he pulled out a thick manila file labelled in pitch-black, CONFIDENTIAL, and in lower letters beneath it by several spaces, the subtitle: Vito Genovese Crime Family. In the right was stamped with the official seal of the "United States Justice Department--Office of the Federal Bureau of Investigation".

Handing it to Peter, he said, "You don't have time to peruse it now. But interesting material accumulated by the Federal Bureau of Investigation. The Navy is fighting a World War, not American Italian hoods, mobsters, rats. But with you in the thick of it, all by accident, our brass at headquarters on Pennsylvania Avenue see a gift dropped from heaven. You and Mr. Antonello will be on a flight by special aircraft to Washington, if we get the matter cleared up by tonight. Two or three days of meetings, instructions, and preparations, and you two will be in Palermo 18 hours later with two refueling stops."

Peter heard this before. Nonetheless, he felt his heart drop.

"Really?" he asked in a muffled voice, hoarse and barely audible.

"As mentioned before, you two working together in subterfuge have the opportunity to shorten the war in Italy, perhaps getting the Germans kicked out altogether."

Glancing at Peter's heavy-hearted expression, the captain said,

"So, let me tell you what we know and it's not much, but important. After you tell me what you have, we'll escort you two over to the cathedral to plant you safety in the middle of the procession. Peter, we pretty much know what's going on."

"Yes? You do?"

"In the while between the breakup of our meeting and this moment, we, our Navy brain trust from our fleet staffs in San Diego to San Francisco have assembled a single team which Captain McCormick has been field commander. I'm out of it once I brief you and lead the escort in an hour or so to the assembling procession. While you slept comfortably, we've called upon plenty of lawmen for assistance. They have been quietly assembling in the parking behind the cathedral, ready to surround you two when the procession begins. It was last night's hours that we were helpless, isolated.
"

Peter cast him a swift glance of respect and admiration, as Spanagel's eyes, deadly somber, fastened on his postgraduate school's temporary lecturer.

"You know our Monterey Bay is a well-fortified estuary. Soon after Pearl Harbor, freeing a Japanese landing on our Carmel, Pebble, and Pacific Grove beaches to say nothing of those between Seaside and Watsonville we established defenses including submarine nets, mines, coastal artillery augmented by regular patrols, offshore Naval craft, and airborne patrols by military aircraft and blimps. Our area fishermen had to have special passes to sail through those defenses to fish, and upon completion of their work, reenter the Bay."

"But by early 1944, with the Pacific War closing in on our Japan, and the fear of Japanese invasion no longer an obsession or even remotely prevalent, our safety and security measures lessened. Hence, a small launch got through our ring of observers. Five men in civilian work clothes were observed by wharf restaurant workers and returning night fishermen noted them climb out of the boat and then up the wharf-end ladder carrying one bag each. With the final wharf workers headed home by 1:00am or so, the five were seen casually walking down the promenade to a waiting long, black Cadillac to accommodate that many and their bags. The car apparently disappeared up the hill into the Sicilian-Italian community."

"As soon as McCormick heard about this development, he dispatched several two-and-three-man teams to locate where they were taken. Within an hour, the house was located on Lausen Street and placed under secured observation. No one arrived or left after the five walked up the steps into the house. Shades were drawn. No lights were on in the front rooms of the house. All activity occurred in the back."

"At about 2:30am, three or four cars full of men, approximately 12 men in all, climbed out, and carrying sawed-off shotguns, Sicilian Lupara-style, hurried up the steps and simply rang the doorbell. All were allowed in after a few words with the man who opened the front door. No one knows what happened next, although four of the five visitors exited with their hands tied behind their backs. All were blindfolded. One man at a time was walked out the back door and placed in the last car as the four cars were driven up the driveway toward the garage. That last car, with three shotgun-armed men, two in the front seat, one in the back seat with their prisoner backed out of the driveway first, followed by the third back-up car with its prisoner, and so on. Then, they formed a tiny convoy, one after another, all four of them, to a slow drive back to the wharf where the prisoners were led down the boardwalk onto the wharf to its end and, surprisingly, placed on the very same launch that brought them through the defenses in the first place. Whoever owns the launch is obviously an Italian or Sicilian fisherman playing both ends against the middle. That's all we know. That was the officially report by our strategically placed observers. Their report was officially documented by Navy officials. And, that report was officially accepted by the Navy Department in Washington, D.C. Nothing further need be said or done. The assassins got through the perimeter, met with local residents, presumably of their own race and nationality, and escorted back out where they came from. As far as we are concerned, officially, the four went home, leaving one behind. And, he's the problem of local police. We've got plans for you, Lieutenant. Now, what's your story? What say you about the last 10-11 hours?"

Peter, at first leaning, then straining forward, began to lessen his fixed gaping, although his mouth remained slightly ajar.

"Did anyone in the household say a word, or hint, about any of this? Just asking to satiate my curiosity," Spanagel asked insouciantly.

Peter, with lips seemingly frozen, said nothing as he watched his captain fumble with his curiosity.

"Of course, this is unofficial, off the record, locker room gossip between friends, lieutenant. Being at war supersedes this thin incident. And, now that it's pretty much closed, it's become an issue of voyeurism. Mafiosos in Monterey, California? Whoever heard of such a thing? Unless the Sicilians around with their fishing boats start smuggling in saboteurs, none of this is our business."

Both men were silent for a long moment, gazing out the office window. The heavy clouds that reached the Monterey Peninsula a few hours before dawn had by now created a thick overcast.

"Rain will soon hit us, ruining the Festa, sadly," ruminated the concerned captain. "And it hasn't rained around here since last March."

"Well, it may hold off for a few hours so that we at least get the procession over with," said Pater, cordially, as if the previous questions hadn't been asked. Because he hadn't been asked a direct question yet, there was no reason to offer what little he know. Yes, Papa Largomarsino had provided him a thumbnail sketch of old-world Sicilian Mafia thinking. Certainly, the large Sicilian community, and one of their three impartial Italian leaders who mediated disputes and conflicts between the men of different provinces and districts in Italy using language dialects not recognized as standard. Certainly, his future father-in-law participated in deciding who among the Italian prisoners-of-war housed in nearby U.S. Army camps would be allowed access to Italian girls, including the Sicilian young women, of marriageable age. In short, Pietro was one of the leaders in the three-member commission overseeing the entire Italian community of perhaps 18,000 to 25,000 Italians, not only on the Peninsula, but the surrounding counties and communities. That he was the guiding head of the Sicilians was incontestable. Everyone knew it; state officials, local authorities, especially law enforcement, although not a single Italian had as of yet faced criminal charges of any sort. And, if such agencies, civic governments, and other authorized formal authorities knew it, so did the highest commands of the U.S. Navy, Army, Air Force, USMC, and Coast Guard.

If asked point-blank by either of his two current superiors, Captains Spanagel and McCormick to tell what he knew, Peter would be obliged to tell the truth. Namely, he felt an odd and singular presentiment assail him as he departed the Largomarsino kitchen early that morning and started walking down the front steps back to the Del Monty only to see Pietro, Pasquale, and Fausto climb out of a long, black Cadillac, each holding a small sawed-off shotgun. As if having worked, all three were disheveled in one way or another, i.e. partially water soaked, clothing rumpled, hair tangled or matted, and generally sour, rancid, choler, but more forlorn than anything else in their dispositions. All three walking up the driveway as Peter slowly descended the steps said nary a word to him. Uncle Pasquale carrying his shotgun and a small black medical bag cast a glance his way without a smile or a nod. Other than this, Peter knew nothing. He was already asleep when they departed and departing when they arrived home. Lieutenant Peter Albinoni Toscanini, USN, Medical Corps, Special Assignments, would not offer this information unless a formal question was asked by either of his two superiors including any future Board of Inquiry.

Just then, the red telephone on Captain Spanagel's desk rang loudly with two bursts.

Picking up the receiver, Spanagel answered, "Yes?", then listened. He responded, "We'll be in the driveway in less than a minute."

Hanging up, he smiled.

"Let's go…And by the way, you were saved from a direct question by more of a friend than you think you have."

CHAPTER TWO

With Saint Santa Rosalia Comes Death

As the staff car conveying Lieutenant Toscanini and Captain Spanagel from the Naval Postgraduate School to the Royal Presidio Chapel approached the parade's staging area, Antonello, dressed in khaki as a Navy Petty Officer, or yeoman, bolted down the steps of the small church.

"Hey, you! Welcome, welcome!" he shouted, wrapping his arms around his tennis partner as he and Spanagel climbed out of the four-door black sedan. "What do you think? Almost a thousand people here lining up for the procession!"

As the captain began a private, one-on-one conversation with Captain McCormick, who had also descended with his staff from the top step of the old mission building constructed in 1794, Peter, arm around Antonello's shoulder, whispered,

"Our mutual enemy, as far as we know, four of the five, are gone, no longer a threat. That is all I will say."

"Galante one of them?"

"We don't know."

"But one left?"

"Yes, we believe."

"Still coming to get me?"

"Undoubtedly."

"Yes, it would be an infame, a disgrace, not to kill me. Little Antonello by surviving will have defeated the entire Don Vitone clan, meaning the

Genoveses are stupid. They must kill me for self-respect. Did Pietro tell you this?" Peter turned and studied the large throng.

"I know. I know. And friend, Peter, I understand. You say one word about it and you lose Aliandra. Not because of her doing, but because Papa Largomarsino is 'honorable'. He tells you because he knows you are a fine man. But he needs to know if you talk. Sicilian men never tell women anything, nothing. Sonner or later, they talk, not to the policia, but to sons and daughter, to friends, to priests, to, sooner or later, anyone who listens. Papa Pietro tests you now for the future. Are you man enough not to talk, even to his daughter, the woman you love? If you do not tell her what you know, you prove yourself, not as an Italian, but as a Sicilian. Papa will know you can stand with Pasquale, Fausto, and himself."

"And, you too, Antonello?"

"Yes, Peter, me too. I stand with them, and I know for hard secrets you involve no family, nor the woman you love."

With that, Antonello clasped his shoulders and kissed him on both cheeks.

"Look around you, Peter. Isn't that wonderful. The starting point is right over there. We're on Church Street, 550 Church Street, intersecting with Cemetery Drive. What you see unfolding in the earliest stage is the Annual Santa Rosalia Fisherman's Benediction and Procession and Festival."

As the two walked halfway up the steps of the Presidio Chapel, they turned to better view the huge assemblage scurrying for their assigned positions in the parade. Antonello smiled, "Waiting for you for more than an hour standing up here. I scanned every face for Carmine Galante and every military vehicle that might be transporting you here when I saw the four-door blue staff car, I knew it was you! So anxious to see you, hear what you know. I overheard McCormick comment under his breath that after the procession and a few hours of Festa, we're to be put in that very car that brought you here and taken to the observation training runway north of Fort Ord to board a Piper, waiting, engines running, for a quick flight to the Alameda Naval Station to catch the flight to Washington D.C. Supposedly, we have a meeting with the Secretary of Navy at 10:00am tomorrow morning whether we shower, change our clothes or shave!"

To his amazement, Peter found himself caught up in the infectious spirit of exhilaration as the crowd grew to over 1,500 community residents, visitors, and off-duty military personnel.

"Look!" Antonello pointed. "The procession to the wharf to bless the fishing fleet is almost a mile long. There's Father O'Connor holding up the small Holy Cross to offer the first benediction, this one of the procession itself. At the wharf, he'll give the second, overlooking the fishing fleet."

"My goodness, there must be at least 30 or 40 little girls, all dressed in white dresses, holding candles standing in front of him. That alone is impressive," responded Peter.

"They represent Santa Rosalia's angels."

"And behind them, I think is the Monterey High School marching band dressed in blue and yellow."

"Yes, and behind it, the Italian style band from the Italian Catholic Federation of Monterey. Then comes Santa Rosalia herself. Count them; more than 20 fishermen dressed in their fishing gear, carry her on their shoulders, the venerated patron saint of Palermo who horrible plague," answered Antonello.

He continued, "And, behind the raised platform carrying the large stature adorned and embellished with flowers picked fresh this morning come the congregation and community, led by older Sicilian women dressed in traditional black dresses and shawls singing ancient Catholic hymns."

Just then, Captains McCormick and Spanagel walked up the steps to them, the Head of the Naval Postgraduate School adding,

"Something new in this 1944 annual procession. Because of the war effort, the Santa Rosalia Festa committee allowed us to include that beautiful float way in the back on Cemetery Drive, completing the parade."

"To celebrate the usually unrecognized work of the Navy Construction Battalion, the Seabrees, stationed in Aptos, the men held a contest to crown a young lady as the Queen of the Military Ball. She was selected from over a hundred senior girls from the high schools of Santa Cruz, Aptos, Watsonville, and Crow's Landing. The Seabees worked off-duty to create and ornate it in the showiest float I've ever seen. And, to support the Seabees, all the area's military men and women are marching behind it. The teenager the Battalion selected is certain to be a movie star someday."

As the head band concluded playing the National Anthem, and Father O'Connor concluded his benediction, Captain McCormick instructed Peter and Antonello to march in front of the 20-fisherman team carrying the statue unobtrusively surrounded by MPs in civilian clothing, some carrying bibles, rosaries, and various religious relics. No one suspected an attack on Antonello would be made in such a huge, congested procession, in some instances, 6 persons wide.

Slowly, with the band playing patriotic tunes, the elderly woman chanting, the procession marched the few blocks into the heart of downtown Monterey. All along the short route, side streets and alleys, families carrying colorful homemade bunting lined the parade route. From Church Street past Munras, a few blocks to the west, then over to Alvarado, then north toward the Bay, a left to Hartnell, back to Webster, over to Pacific and Lighthouse on the western entrance, to the parking lot of Fisherman's Wharf. The planners of the Santa Rosalia Fest, a committee of a dozen women, all influential, virtually all Catholic, seven of the twelve Italian and Sicilian, loved their Monterey County, one of the original 27 counties decreed by the King of Spain. In Spanish, Monterey translates as "hill or wood of the king". The main city was named in honor of Gaspar de Zuniga, count of Monterey and viceroy of Mexico.

With Peter marching side by side of Antonello, and Captain Spanagel on the right side of the lieutenant, and Captain McCormick on the left side of the target, the procession promenaded at a leisurely pace, at first, past more than 100 whitewashed adobe and wood-framed houses all labeled National Historic Landmarks in the Old Town Historic District of downtown Monterey.

"Sadly, the powers-that-be are beginning to demolish the magnificent houses for more modern buildings," offered Spanagel. "Sure, the city officials are doing more than most California cities to preserve the past, but yet the painted adobe walls in quiet unoffensive hues, the ivy-covered verandas with the year-round coastal flowers, the upper balconies with large vistas of the Bay and beyond the ocean, the iron-barred windows and walled-in rose gardens are rapidly being town down."

And, so it went, as even more joined the procession as it ambled along. Captain Spanagel, who loved the Peninsula so dearly, especially Mission San Carlos Borromeo, Carmel Mission, that his hero Junipero Serra founded. Unbeknownst to Peter, his superior loved the 5'4" Franciscan founder of the California Missions even more than the lieutenant. Later, he would explain, "That truly great, heroic, sacred man is my personal hobby. When the war is over, and I eventually retire, it will be in Carmel, which my wife and I adore."

As the perfect guide explained the nature and history of each and every historical structure the procession passed, now more than 20,000 strong, Peter and Antonello lost all interest in an increasingly decreasing assassination attempt. Peter, for one, was enthralled hearing about Portola's trail through Monterey in 1769, the establishment of the Presidio overlooking the Bay in 1786, the establishment of the fledgling city from 1815 through 1900, the historical significance of Colton Hall in the founding of California, the state's first convent school, California's first theater in 1843, and details about structure after structure when passed, including the birth of Cannery Row. The captain couldn't shut up, and Peter, even while leading the parade, barely took his eyes off whatever was being described. Antonello was almost equally involved, leaving himself open for death.

And, at the foot of Pacific Avenue intersecting with Lighthouse Avenue, in front of the most prominent building in California history, the Monterey Custom House, death was on its horrific way from none other than the Festa Italia's very own Santa Rosalia.

CHAPTER THREE

Chasing Galante

Although ominous black clouds were directly overhead, the mist and moisture which earlier had promised teeming thunderstorms had fizzled. The windy breeze of early morning diminished to a few whispy whiffs, while nary a sprinkle seemed intent, or even interested.

Festa, meanwhile, was off to a good start. All the marchers seemed fresh, eager, full of joy, just as the 12th Century devoutly religious Rosalia Sinibaldo, daughter of the Duke and Lord of Quisquina wanted all the Kingdom's people to be during excessive hard times. With everyone officially sanctified at the start, and heads bowed amid Catholic incantations, the throng approached the western gate of the Festa grounds. All were somewhat solemn except for the ever-invigorated Captain Spanagel, who pointed,

"To your left, gentlemen, is the old stone, wood-framed, adobe structure begun in 1813 under the King of Spain. But it wasn't completed until 1823 or so, by the then-Mexican dictator. Finally, in 1846, under the American government and its import and export laws, rules and regulations, all foreign and U.S. trading ships had to dock and enter the cargos aboard their ships and list on their sailing itemized manifests on the Monterey Customs House daily logs to pay the calculated duties. It was the only Customs House along the whole of the California Coast and whether ships for fishing whales or hunting sea otters and seals or trading for tallow and cowhides from the eight or ten nearby missions, had to drop anchor, declare register, and list what they carried. Furthermore, few people know that…"

Suddenly, in the flash of less than a fleeting second, a loud, single pistol shot whizzed past Captain McCormick, abrading the scalp of Spanagel, totally missing Antonello, nicking Peter's ear superficially as the .38 caliber bullet crashed through the curb onlookers and finally lodging in the entrance door frame.

With animal cunning, the would-be murderer had carefully chosen his location to instinctively whirled, blood engulfing the right side of his face, partially blurring his vision. Antonello, with lightning speed, also swiveled to face the source of the resounding noise. In spinning around, he found himself face-to-face with a dark-skinned, squat, broad-shouldered, still-faced, expressionless man brandishing a .38 caliber revolver in his face. To Peter, the man appeared ragged, dirty and treacherous-looking, obviously a fisherman of sorts with a small net over the shoulder of the hand that held an old-rusty harpoon. In the length of time of his first glance, burred vision and all, Peter recognized the man as the fifth of the five he accidentally bumped into a La Vecchia Cucina two days before. Only now he had abandoned his flamboyant Hawaiian shirt-sleeved shirt for the garb of a Monterey Bay fisherman.

Both Peter and Antonello screamed out, "The rotten _____!" He's part of the contingents, one of the 20, assigned to hold up the raised dais support of the Rosalia statue He's dressed like all of them, one of the Bay fishermen.

Having walked up to within 10 to 12 feet of Antonello, with the harpoon in one hand and the gun in the other, he slowly lifted the .38 to fire point blank. Antonello shouted,

"It's Galante! It's the hitman, Galente, Vito Genovese's favorite assassin!"

For less than a second or two, Galente's mocking face turned to a sneering flash of hatred, causing him to jerk his hand forward as he started to pull the trigger.

Peter, despite blood flying all over his face and shoulders, hurled himself into Galante, grapping his arm, just as the mobster fired, missing wildly over Antonello's head, as the two tumbled over, Galante got off a third shot, this one managing to rip the flesh off Peter's left shoulder. With the lieutenant down and quivering in blinding pain, Galante was still standing but shakily. Yet, he was strong and determined enough to ram the harpoon into the wounded naval officer, attempting to lift himself on his elbow as blood flowed freely from his shoulder. As any number of military police, sheriff deputies and others converged on the scene with guns drawn, the murdering assassin, unable to thrust his harpoon into his intended victim, he would at least kill his protector.

As the assassin raised the harpoon while Peter on the ground gazed nonchalantly up at the snickering killer about to thrust into him, Antonello, head down, rushed at Galante, the large assembly of law enforcers arriving four or five second later; Spanagel and McCormick right behind Antonello.

No one could delineate what happened in the free-for-all brawl that followed, since no one could determine who was Carmine Galante. It was a hubbub of flying arms and legs, a tousling melee with Galante the wildcat in the center, firing point-blank with one hand, handling the harpoon with the other.

Luck favored Galante.

In the midst of the carnage, with several military people wounded, their blood commingling with that of the others, a light rain started to drift down; more as a heavy mist than actual raindrops, the assassin managed to crawl from the center of the action that all told lasted less than 60 seconds, cast away the harpoon and fishing net over the shoulder, and slipped into the lines of sidewalk onlookers. Peter lost all sight of Galante after Antonello charged him in the middle of it, his throw of the harpoon which surprisingly hit close enough. Antonello glimpsed him running at breakneck speed down an alley, narrow and uncluttered, he must have scouted out as an important segment of his escape plan the day before the attack.

"There he goes, up that slope behind the Heritage Inn down the block here on Pacific Avenue," shouted Antonello to Peter, .45 in his hand, as Peter stopped his pursuit long enough to receive instant cleansing and anti-infectant cream and bandage coverage allowing resumption of the pursuit.

"Okay, you're good to traipse around searing for a killer," glowered a ruddy-faced aging nurse sardonically. "But not for long. You want to bleed to death; you just keep right on running over those yonder Presidio hills above Pacific Avenue."

"Hope your adhesive tape can hold the gauze, because I'll run until I catch or kill him."

As Peter replaced his bloody shirt with one Spanagel had removed from himself and handed him, with a dry, ironic half-smile, and the Captain ordering immediate search parties, Antonello said, as he hastily approached,

"I thought he was headed for the shortcut in front of the Presidio Army entrance to Lighthouse for an escape through Pacific Grove. But I changed my mind. He is probably thinking Cannery Row shoreline to get back to Fisherman's Wharf and the point of his arrival with his team to await the motorboat to pick him up for delivery to a larger ship in the Bay. So Galante is leading us to believe he's headed down Lighthouse, but instead dashing toward Palm Street leading behind the Canneries."

Peter, gazing in the direction of Galante's escape from the back alley to the lower slopes of the Presido Army Base, focused upon the same path he took after playing tennis with Antonello and Aliandra to La Vecchia Cucina.

"Uncle Pasquale was 100% correct when he said the attack would occur during the most unlikely event, the Santa Rosalia procession when no one was looking for it. He also predicted the assassins would come from the sea, not the road or highway, and wearing ordinary working clothes of the fishermen. They certainly wouldn't be wearing business suits or gaudy Hawaiian shirts. The only thing he couldn't predict was how the murderer would strike. Neither he nor any of us predicted he would be one of the twenty fishermen carrying the platform dais for the statue. In any case, I'll go find him."

As he hurriedly walked toward the escape alley with his .45 Colt automatic raised, Peter heard Antonello's voice call out,

"I'm right behind. We'll keep our distance lest he ambush us."

Peter, turning, and seeing his .45 Colt automatic raised, shouted,

"No! Damn you, Antonello, no! The Navy, America, needs you. You're much too valuable for the war effort."

"In my struggle to be polite, Lieutenant Toscanini, I say you're the one too valuable to lose. You stay. I kill him and tonight we can fly to Washington, then home to Sicily. I'm right behind you. Besides, you're hurt."

"NO! NO! NO! NO! You're in the way. You'll hinder my efforts and I'm wasting time yakking. Get back. If you follow, never again will I allow you to win over me in tennis."

With that, Antonello froze in his tracks, allowing the moment needed for Captains McCormick and Spanagel and several MPs to grab and bind Antonello.

"Sorry, friend," Peter shouted as he waved while heading for the paved trail leading to Lighthouse Avenue.

At Lighthouse Avenue and one of two side streets, Palm, that led unhindered directly to Cannery Row without stop sign or stop light, Peter had a critical life and death decision to make; follow Antonello's mafioso instinct to scramble among the four blocks of commercial fish-packing plants still at work, 24 hours a day, even on Festa Day, or his own hunch, as well as Antonello's first thought, Lighthouse Avenue, in order to mix and hide among live people rather than continuous moving belts with working women sorting dead sardines, solomon, and other fish. Even thinking as Uncle Pasquale or Mafia hitman Carmine Galante, Peter struggled. Which road would the pursuers opt to choose? In less than a few seconds, he weighed Palm, the obvious road and the larger area of building and industry in which to hide. So obvious that the pursuers would discount it out of hand. Hence, Lighthouse Avenue.

Yet, Peter hesitated in a rain that was beginning to pelt his borrowed oversized shirt, soaking the adhesive that was beginning to disintegrate. Furthermore, he was an open target as he stood erect contemplating in the heavily increasing raindrops, should Galante double back and shoot him dead.

Mind made up, he chose Palm Street and started to run toward it.

But at that precise moment, the hourly metropolitan bus connecting Monterey and Pacific Grove pulled up before the covered bus stop at the intersection of Lighthouse and Palm and an elderly gentleman, well-dressed and groomed immaculately, who had been sitting quietly reading the Saturday edition of the Monterey Herald, stood up, placed his eyeglasses in their small case and with folded umbrella, started toward the passenger entrance at the front of the bus.

"Sir!" Peter shouted as the gentleman reached the man, one foot on the bus stop to provide his fare. "Please! Need your help! USN Lieutenant Toscanini giving chase. Which way did he go?"

Seeing the Peter clutched his .45 Colt automatic at his side, he smiled and nodded to his left, toward Pacific Grove. Peter knew instinctively and intuitively Galante would hide in La Vecchia Cucina.

Although the bus was crowded, almost every seat taken, all quiet and respectful, Peter said to the bus driver, "I'd like to ride with you to the next bus stop. The whole area is being cordoned off. We have a single killer at large and he may board a ride like I've done."

"No worry, Lieutenant, my heart lives and breathes USMC, although a bad back injury classifies me as 4-F. Everyone else is fighting for our country and I'm driving a city bus. Tell me how I can help."

As Peter stood next to the driver holding the step railing, he said,

"Be on the lookout for anyone on the street looking unusual, in the garb of an ordinary fisherman, call the guy into the local police and/or the USN at 38086. Give the precise location seen."

"Got it," said the bus driver. "Because this is an intercity express bus, we'll be pulling up to Lighthouse and Forest Avenue. La Vecchia Cucina is only a few yards down the Avenue. Still open for lunch meals since not all local residents are interested in Festa. And, by the way, lieutenant," he began to whisper, "Before I stopped for the two of you, I picked up a fisherman near the Fisherman's Wharf entrance on Del Monte Ave running along the shoreline. Seemed to me the harshest, roughest fisherman I ever saw. I said 'Hello' and he simply stared at me. 'A man of death', I thought. So wet, so disheveled and rumpled, doesn't talk, all that enforced with the eyes of a dead man. As I still glanced at him through my rearview mirror, I say to myself, that sorry-look crud has just crawled out of some unknown penitentiary graveyard. He's not of this world."

Peter blinked.

"Where is he now? Did he get off before I got on?" Peter demanding anxiously, glancing around the crowded faces.

"Sorry," the bus driver said, wistfully.

"The light had just turned green and we're pulling in at Lighthouse and Forest. La Vecchia is just right over there," he said, pulling up and opening the bus door.

He continued, "No, the man has just gotten up in the last seat waiting for the two or three to get off."

Horrified, Peter found himself staring amid the crowded bus into the coldest eyes he had ever seen--the frozen facial expression of Carmine Galante.

CHAPTER FOUR

An Embarrassing Fade Out

What happened next were the most inexplicable few seconds of Peter's entire young life. There was only one explanation; one insight and understanding, but the odiousness of it left the answer inexpressible, especially among those in law enforcement.

As the bus driver pulled the crowded metro bus up to the Lighthouse Avenue and Forest Driver intersection bus stop, he quietly suggested the Lieutenant glance toward the back of the bus where passengers were lining up to disembark.

"He's the short, ugly guy; bareheaded, always staring as if he's deciding whether you live or die."

"I don't see him."

"Yes, the one with the soaked, filthy clothing. He's even staring at you. I see him at an angle in my overhead mirror. The cerebral-palsy young teen girl on crutches is right in front of him. He's staring steel hard and straight at you, lieutenant. I don't see a gun."

Just then, the driver opened both bus doors; one at the rear of the bus where Galante was last in line to step off. With both doors open and passengers lined up at the entrance to board, Galante raised his .38. Instinctively, Peter did as well. Not a word was uttered as screams and shrieks echoed and reverberated throughout the bus. Everyone who remained on the bus crouched behind their seats. Peter, seeing the young teen girl who saw the .38 caliber lift past her head and point was hysterical, considering one of her crutches accidently lodged in the step-down well at the door. Peter quietly studied Galante's face which showed no sign of life although his .38 was pointed directly at Peter's chest. With various forms of uncontrolled weeping, emotional tears, convulsive and frenzied moaning, groaning, lamenting, and bewailing, virtually all of it growing instantly subdued as Peter placed the .45 on a nearby vacated seat windowsill and ambled up the bus aisle to quietly place his arm around the 12- or 13-year-old, whispered a few words, then bent over and released the crutch leg from its stuck position.

Galante, less than six feet away, pointing the .38 directly at Peter, was stone-cold dead in any emotion or expression of feeling. Nothing, absolutely no sign of life, crossed his lips. Once the release was affected, Peter stepped aside and waited until the afflicted girl bravely descended the bus where her apparent father took her in his arms. Then, with a nod to both men, and an obviously heartfelt appreciative long glance at Peter, he hurried his daughter to a waiting car.

The entire incident lasted less than three minutes. Galante turned without killing Peter, walked down the aisle toward the driver, stopped at the vacant seat, retrieved the Colt .45, walked past the bus driver without so much as a glance and disembarked.

Peter rushed forward looking through all the windows for a sign of Galante, but he had vanished in seconds

"And, he's got my gun!" he mumbled to himself.

After instructing the bus driver to inform Captains McCormick and Spanagel, then local law enforcement, Peter began a self-imposed search of the blocks of businesses along Lighthouse. With the bus long gone, Peter decided to stop in at La Vecchia Cucina for a bowl of its daily freshly-cooked soups and daily-made pastas.

Even as Peter approached the famed and popular Italian-Sicilian restaurant, he could see the noontime lunch crowd had dissipated, that only a few patrons remained. As he entered, he was pleasantly surprised to find Maisie Lil' Lulu waiting for him!

"What?" he asked. "I thought you and Aliandra were going to meet at the Festa around 2:00. It's around that now."

"I was on my way when our last customer of the noon hour entered."

"And, you have to stick around until he finishes? That's not fair! And, no other waiter or waitress to handle this last-minute customer?"

"Not this one. And he's special."

Peter glanced over her shoulder in the dimly-lit restaurant and saw the figure of a broad-shouldered man hunched over eating what appeared to be a Caesar salad. With the luncheon hours virtually over, the front door was locked and the light dimmed.

"Why's he so special?" Peter asked, unconcerned.

"He's got a gun in his pocket. He looks terrible. He's obviously a mobster intent on killing Antonello and anyone near him. And, the fact that you're here without a gun in your pocket, looking as terrible as he, and don't tell me, searching for him Peter, Aliandra knows this about Maisie Lil' Lulu, I'm no fool. I knew you would be coming in after I observed him up close while seating ad smelling him. He said two words; 'salad' and 'wine'. I was about to ask how much he was planning to tip, then thought better of it. So, there's your man. Seeing you through the window, it was obvious you had no holster and the large cannon you always carry. So, quickly, I reached for my purse and here's my gun, six rounds fully loaded, plus a handful of shells.

No point in talking to you because you won't listen. So, go play big manhunter, and remember, don't do anything stupid and get killed. I'm now going to do something I never do to myself. I'm going to shut up without someone having to tell me to do so."

"Where did you get this?" Peter asked, fondling the small World War I Italian revolver. "Does it work?"

As Maisie Lil' Lulu started to respond, as both she and Peter were examining the gun, Galante, in the relatively empty, noiseless restaurant, turned and instantly recognized Peter. Angrily, he stood, turned, and .38 in hand, fired two shots in rapid succession, both hitting Maisie as she flung herself in front of Peter, who fell back. Galante then headed for the back door and the restaurant parking lot which led to Cannery Row without looking back.

Peter, unscathed, immediately attended to Maisie Lil' Lulu, as the remaining two cooks, one waiter, the manager, and four patrons rushed to aid.

Peter asked the manager to call the private number of Captain Spanagel to say he was going after Galante, who was headed down the slope toward Cannery Row, a bumpy, rolling mile of history begun on a pile of ocean rocks.

"Peter, I'm so, so sorry. I exposed us both, but you in particular. We took our eyes off him to look at this antique Italian gun, and attracted his attention without knowing we had. Go get him, Peter! I'm fine. Both bullets penetrated, both bullets exited. No bones shattered. Minimum loss of blood. Ambulance on the way, to say nothing of the whole world of military police. So, I'll see you and Aliandra later. Right now, go get him, Peter. Go, get him!"

As the lieutenant turned to go, she exclaimed, "Peter, don't forget! Aliandra is there. Watch for her! Don't let her get in the way of a bullet! His life means nothing. To let her get hurt while you're trying to get him would kill us, Peter. Be careful!"

At that very moment, on Ocean View Avenue, operating around-the-clock, Galante was already hiding or seeking a hiding place in one of 25 buildings carefully packing and colorfully labelling the best sardines in the Western Pacific. Of course, Carmine Galante had no interest that he was in the center of "The Sardine Capital of the World." He had worked hard, risked his life, but failed miserably in killing Antonello for Don Vitone. His only goal was to get back to New York to face the fact four top Vito Genovese were missing and presumed dead.

Carmine Galante had no idea where he was going as he dashed down the steep hill on a neglected city street pockmarked with potholes and neglected, crooked, well-worn paths across the railroad tracks spurring off to separate canneries. Everywhere he looked, he was surprised by the flood of smoke stacks, steam pipes, smoke, noise, pollution, and general disorder that abounded through Cannery Row.

Almost desperately searching for a cannery to take refuge in, knowing full well that Peter was right behind him somewhere, and troop carriers loaded with Army and Navy searchers were only minutes away behind Peter to seal off the entire area, Carmine spotted a side door to The Pacific Seas Fish Company.

He knew he had to enter it, especially since a low-hanging fog bank seemingly began to push away the rain. Crossing Ocean View Avenue as the piercing shriek of the 3:00pm cannery whistle. The vast machinery network he hoped to find and temporarily hide amid turned out to a huge, open, smelly hall of chit-catting yakety-yakking apron clad, brightly-colored bonneted and head-scarfed women seated at several parallel conveyor belts. The second of three shirts had begun and the hard-working ladies' second order of business had to be catching up with the gossip of the previous night's activities.

Since Carmine Galante was searching for a building containing a power plant, he exited as quickly as he entered. Even the huge flock of hungry seagulls hovering over the dock waiting for scraps from the sardine factory didn't impress the New Yorker. As he turned to leave that cannery in search of a more complex one with more of a maze of modern equipment, a horde of paisano, Spanish-Mexican-Californio, and Chinese fishermen began descending upon the dock as Galante stood in indecision. Fresh catches were due to arrive, tons and tons of sardines, a fourth of the tonnage for the factory Galante had exited, and the rest of the dozens of trucks jammed on the narrow Cannery Row streets and hundreds of refrigerated freight cars waiting on the tracks only two blocks above the row.

"No," thought Carine Galante. "I must hide in a boiler room or carpentry or metal shop of some kind. I'll have to find it If I can't see getting b ack to the Fisherman's Wharf where we landed, I'll go down to the water's edge, or this very dock and point my gun at him to motor me out to the waiting boat in the ocean to take me back to San Mateo where I can catch a train to New York."

Reentering the sardine factory door he exited, the workers totally oblivious to his presence, Galante walked to his left and began opening doors to see if any had steps toward a basement. The third door was lettered "The Chef". Quickly descending the steps, he found himself in the sardine cooking process room where a permanent boilerman was stationed to carefully monitor temperature and steam pressure gauges as the sardines cooked in their cans. Peeking around the corner, he spotted the boilerman conversing with a young woman holding a clipboard to her chest Both were engaged in friendly chatter, occasionally roaring in laughter or merely smiling and giggling.

On the opposite side of the huge cookers lined in rows of 25 each, 7 rows deep were a dozen reduction grinder-dryers that assisted in turning over more than half of the sardines landed at Monterey for fishmeal and fertilizer.

Galante hit paydirt!

Aliandra!

Here by sheer luck, he had found the perfect hiding place for an overnight stay. In the morning, he would exit to hijack any small motorized boat to take him out to sea. For now, however, he merely wanted to sit down behind one of these boilers and go to sleep.

As the boilerman and young lady were beginning to break up their conversation and returned to the exit door labeled "The Chef", Galante crossed the aisle and small office lobby and walked behind a screw-cooker that squeezed cannable sardines into liquid content. The remaining pulp was dried at high temperatures in the reduction grinder-dryers then reduced by hotter cooking for heavier consistency that was marketed as poultry feed additive.

Little did Carmine Galante know that…

CHAPTER FIVE

"Four times in four hours today I could have put bullets into your face…"

And so it was that Carmine "The Hair" Galante believed he found the perfect hiding place from pursuing Lt. Peter Toscanini, holding Maisie Lil' Lulu's antique gun.

Fleeing the resolute young Naval medical officer on special assignment jogging slowly and steadily to overtake him, the squat, powerfully built fugitive, ungainly and out of breath, noticed as he scurried down Cannery Row on Ocean View Avenue a half-opened side door of the main Pacific Seas Canning Company sheds, one of more than 27 "fish factories" and their hundreds of cannery storage shelters, abuts, and lean-tos.

With Peter less than three minutes behind him, the terror-sticker assassin dashed across Ocean View Avenue, past parked cars, small trucks, and pickups, directly into the lot across which was the abutting door. Flashing lightening momentarily streaking the on-again, off-again storm sent an entire boat crew sitting on empty wooden boxes and crates mending huge cotton fishing nets scooting and scampering for cover. Reaching the door just as a female worker from within was about to slam it shut, the first sheet of sweeping rain struck amid the overhead rumbling of thunder.

Without so much as a glance or word to the interloper, the cannery worker relinquished the door handle and Carmine Galante entered. Searching for the nearest exit in the event of being discovered, he glanced around, amazed. Standing or sitting upon stools before noisy conveyor belts were countless grey-uniformed, white-aproned, hair-bundled and netted women of all ages packing fish. Operating in three 8-hour shifts, the women of the second shift happened to be packing "talls", one-pound tall, round cans of sardines from the morning catch. The cans on the belts were fed to high-speed sealing machines. The impact of noise and the stomach-wrenching smell left the New Yorker momentarily staggering.

Meanwhile, outside, bearing the brunt of the initial onslaught of the thunderstorms teeming heavy rain, Peter entirely missed the now-closed side door of the Pacific Seas Canning Company. With the downpour, pedestrians and workers alike vacated Ocean View Avenue, allowing the lieutenant to jog down the middle of Cannery Row, gun still held at elbow level, unimpeded. Reaching the avenue's high Cannery Row crossovers that shuttled empty cans over the roadway to the slew of canneries and full cans back over the street to their warehouses, Peter realized he had lost his enemy.

"How did I miss him? My fault. Will not blame it on thick rainwater."

Full drenched and in considerable pain, he smiled as he noted numerous Army jeeps entering the eastern mere from Palm Street, each carrying four full-armed MPs.

"No time to coordinate," he told himself as he waved to follow him.

Retracing his steps, he concluded Galante had to have entered the large Pacific Seas Canning Company through the front entrance. Upon reaching it, and about to enter it, the fishermen who had been mending the large net in the lot on the side of the corrugated paralleled grooved thin steel structure starting yelling. Huddled in the doorways of several commercial businesses awaiting the storm to diminish before returning to their boat, they noted the officer with the raised pistol when he passed and now that he returned, concluded he was tracing someone significant.

Clamoring for the lieutenant's attention, more than a dozen pointed around the building, shouting,

"Side door! Side door! He went in by the side door!"

Peter waved in acknowledgement and gave chase. But upon reaching the steel-framed door, he found it was locked!

With no time to waste pounding on it, perhaps without result, he returned to the entrance, stopping to shout at the huddled fishermen.

"If he comes out, stay away! He's extremely dangerous. He will shoot to kill, whether trapped or not. He's an assassin."

And with that, he turned and entered.

Meanwhile, back inside the 'fish factory', Galante, regaining his sense of balance upon adjusting to the din and odor, stumbled toward the nearest exit, which happened to be a stairwell obviously leading to the basement and most certainly the maze of machinery he so desperately sought to take refuge amid.

Sinking and slipping down the steel stairs, Galante found himself at the basement door with a one-word sign painted in red, "CHEF". Opening it, the fugitive frantically glanced around. It was indeed the boiler room and "Chef" was the boiler room supervising engineer.

Looking about as he walked in, the mobster found himself in a small lobby before an office, well-lit and door open. Two huge boilers were centered in the room, partially surrounded by a forest of steam pipes and smokestacks leading through the ceiling to what had appeared to be newly-installed cookers, grinding machines, reduction-dryers, heavy screw-cookers and rotary kilns.

Galante smiled to himself. Here, he was in a world unto itself, especially if he could make himself comfortable on wooden planking behind one of the massive boilers, or within the labyrinth of varying sized piping, regardless of how cramped.

In awe of how sizeable the boilers were, how large the basement was, every inch of it was stocked, orderly, and well-managed, the fugitive stood openly in the center of the lobby fingering his .38 pistol as he gazed upon stacked sacks of smelly fishmeal, fertilizer, and offal consisting of fish heads, tails, entrails, and various remaining pulps. Having been born in Sicily to a fisherman family, the Mafia figure knew all too well the dozens of 100 lb. sacks were more profitable than tons of canned sardines.

It was then that Carmine Galante noticed at the extreme end of the basement standing before the temperature gauges of the second floor-to-ceiling boiler two individuals in deep, serious conversations. The male was obviously the boiler engineer, holding a large wrench, and the female, dressed in loose trouser overalls and holding an oversized metal framed clipboard, an engineering monitor recording the hot and cold boiling point temperature gradients. Instantly, he recognized her as Aliandra Largomarsino, Antonello's would-be fiancée.

"What?" he must have thought. "She works here? By accident, I happened into the canning company she works at? Even on Festa Day? No time for nonsense. Must hide, because the other one will surely come down here."

With that, Galante hastened across the lobby, past the engineer's office to hide at the end of an apparently rarely utilized walkway behind the two boilers and the back wall of the building. The walkway led to a barred exit door with a small window. Next to the door was a dusty, dilapidated chair. Several Sicilian lampara fish nets were on the walkway leaning against the wall.

Since he could hear Aliandra and the boiler engineer talking over the basement's continuous confusing din, the Genovese Crime Family's No. 1

killer removed his shoes and hurried down the walkway toward the exit door as quietly as possible.

Reaching the exit back door unobserved as Aliandra and the boiler engineer had moved to the No. 1 boiler recording various temperature gauges. Since the door was blocked and locked, he quickly noted how three .38 caliber shots could disintegrate the metal bar, debarring the escape route. Glancing through the small window in the door, he saw the vast Monterey Bay and Pacific Ocean before him. The back door stairway led to wooden stairs leading not only to a small landing dock, but also the rocky coastline underneath the Pacific Seas Canning Company. Despite the murder in his eyes, and the unmistakable facial expression of the desire to kill, he sat down on the rickety chair and pulled one of the lampara nets over himself. A second net he placed at his feet, which gave the illusion from a distance that a few nets had been heaped and left for eventual removal. A certain wildness he could not explain seemed to consume him for some inexplicable reason. All he could think about at that moment was that he was in a perfect position to shoot should someone decide to inspect the piled-up lampara nets.

As Galante wearily sat back on an aging chair near collapse, gun drawn and pointed down the walled walkway, and one of the two cotton nets pulled up to his neck despite the heat generated by two active boilers, he began weighing a variety of issues, mainly how he would return to his waiting motorized skiff only 500 yards offshore. A studied glance through the backdoor window at the Monterey Bay panorama reassured him. There were at least 150 swift "wolves at sea, the "purse-seiners" boats, anchored or docked at each cannery hopper where every night's catch was disgorged into a wooden pen.

Since sardines were tracked and caught at night, the entire fleet was strangely idle at mid-afternoon. However, on that particular day, most of the crews were attending the Festa despite the thunderstorms. Finding a captain or mechanic to motor a powerboat may be difficult, although seeing the front end of his .38 should be enough persuasion to behave as ordered.

"But there's not a match in the world rivaling the tough Sicilian fisherman in catching, packing, and selling what comes from our Mediterranean," he smiled, reflectively. "Our innovations, our skilled boiler-makers, engineers, carpenters. And, no one can beat how we use the leftovers of fish after we pack their main fish bodies in cans."

And, with that, hidden under the net, and in the thick of "fish factory" debris, the murderer's thoughts returned to the deadly events of the past 90 minutes beginning with his risky, thoughtless decision to hide in a far, dark corner of the La Vecchia Cucina, the Old Lady's Kitchen restaurant. After being discovered, and the shooting of the waitress with two .38 caliber slugs meant for his pursuer, his sprint out the back door into the graveled parking lot, floundering for an instant in a pool of mud and rainwater. Extricating himself, seeping in muck and mire, he was disoriented.

Which way to the rocky seawall of coastline and the Bay harbor?

In that second, the back kitchen door of the restaurant swung open, and, seeing Peter hurriedly but cautiously emerge, he, in a mixture of panic and consternation, fired two successive sots, both narrowly missing Peter's head and shattering the windows of La Vecchia's lavatories adjacent the kitchen. Peter, bending almost waist-level, aimed Maisie's gun at Galante who had pivoted and began to hurl himself, literally, across the rest of the lot to the side street leading down to the start of Cannery Row and Ocean View Avenue.

"Darn, too much traffic to fire in," he thought, hesitating, then lowering the revolver. "And, he almost clipped me too, having felt the heat of the two shells."

In the afternoon's dim overcast scattered sprinkles and showers, Galante managed to maintain a three to four minute lead as he bypassed Wave, Davis, and Irving Streets and the so-called "Chicken Walk" and its planks down the embankment from the railroad tracks to the corner of Irving and Ocean View Avenues. A few blocks later with the Cannery Row nearly vacant of pedestrians, he spotted the half-opened door.

Now, leaning back somewhat comfortably, his adrenaline dissipating, the cotton lampara net pulled up and over him, allowing sufficient space to see and breathe, the young killer drifted into a sound, solid sleep, despite the commingling noises of the steaming boilers and continuously monotonous grinding reduction dryers. But what caused him to slowly emerge from either an instant of slight drowsiness or hours of heavy slumbering snoring was the reverberating graveyard silence that engulfed the basement. Repeatedly, he blinked. Was he dreaming? Where was he? In the hell he knew he deserved? How long had he been out? Was anyone coming to kill him?

Deadly silence.

Impossible, he thought. But true. Not a sound, even a smidgen. Inside or out. Above or behind. The end of the life on Earth? His swarthy face paled under the net, as his nose protruded forward, quivering, his jaw clenched, fists knuckled.

Suddenly, Galante's eyes widened, focusing plaintively upon three figures approaching him from the basement lobby down the narrow walkway. The young woman with the oversized metal clipboard in the lead was followed by the tall, heavy boiler engineer, his long heavy wrench in its open trouser leg socket, and the pursuer bringing up the rear clutching an old gun, his arm dangling at his side. Obviously, Aliandra and the engineer were escorting the Lieutenant to the barred, locked door which she, in the lead, held the key.

The fugitive froze, although his hand-held .38 rested on his leg pointed at the first of the three approaching in a swinging, hurried walk, joyful, gentle and delicate. She was happy that Peter had arrived, and, once she unlocked the door and removed the steel bars, she would hasten upstairs to join the other women evacuating the fish factory under the supervision of the military police who were also now picketing sentries around the entire Pacific Seas Cannery.

Within 25 feet of the backdoor, Aliandra slowed her pace as she began to study the two cotton nets that were stacked atop and at the foot of the wooden chair near collapsing. She hadn't noticed the unusual dispositioning of the heaped nets earlier that morning when she recorded the temperature behind the two boilers from that wall walk-way.

Suddenly, Aliandra, who had been personally requested by the owner of the Pacific Seas Canning Company to work on Festa Day, halted, raising her hand to stop the two behind her. Leaning forward, she stared hard at the hodge-podge of black netting, then issued a raw shriek. Instantly, she stepped back horrified by what was so obviously hiding under the hand-sewn and carefully stitched Lamparas. As Galante cast the main net aside while holding his .38 waist-level, standing erect, Peter pushed past the chef to position himself before the woman he loved. The tension of the silence was insurmountable. Hurried movements and sensational melodrama were senseless.

Peter, partially paralyzed from surprise, murmured,

"Leave the girl along. She knows not who you are or why I chase you."

"We make no war on children and women," Galante responded in a low voice, maintaining his stoical composure.

By now, loud voices could be heard upstairs in the main canning room as its working women, many no more than 18 years of age, were forming single-file lines to evacuate to waiting army trucks and jeeps lining up Cannery Row and Ocean View Avenue.

"We're sealing off the entire vicinity," Peter continued. "Don't hurt anyone. You can't get away."

As the assassin studied Peter without comment or demeanor, he levelled his .38 at him, seemingly to the lieutenant, to wound, not kill. But as Galante extended his arm to fire, the elderly engineer skillfully wielded his wrench so adroitly in a singular twist that it struck the murderer's hand, knocking the gun away while simultaneously misfiring. Somehow in its twisting movement, the single slug deflected off the tip of the heavy steel wrench, causing it to carom in a circular streak within an inch of Aliandra's upper thigh beneath her hip. She recoiled, wincing, but refused to collapse or flee.

Seeing his brave Aliandra lean towards him in a shielding manner, Peter, so uncharacteristically of him, went utterly berserk. In a violent rage hitherto unknown, he managed to get off a single shot, which ricocheted obliquely off one of the metal bars of the back door. And then Peter was atop him, fighting wildly; the two in mortal combat. It was a thunderous wrestling whirl, so fierce and rapid that the body and head blows were ineffective. The bits of rubbish and refuse at that end of the walkway flew and scattered as in a whirlwind. Although trained, Peter had never engaged in hand-to-hang fighting. But, miraculously managing to hold his own, he was no match for Galante, a gutter-fighter since birth who depended upon his powerful physique for survival. Even Peter's fury could not overcome Galante who was atop him, pounding Peter across the head and face with the butt of his .38. Even the engineer, inadvertently knocked to the floor of the walkway, was helpless. Shaken to her core, Aliandra managed to grasp the wrench laying a few feet from the overwhelming struggle, but could do nothing, being confined behind Peter on the narrow walkway. Her fear maddening screams, as hoarse as they were, in addition to the sounds of gunshots, had managed to summon a host of MPs, who suddenly burst into the basement lobby, automatic weapons drawn to kill. In less than a moment, they began carefully creeping down the walkway. Battered, bruised, and in considerable pain, Peter, now unarmed, pulled his feel up slowly and tried to raise himself. Meanwhile, Galante managed to ride. Peter, somewhat in shock, started at his adversary as he stared in return, not at the downed lieutenant, but at the swarm of armed MPs inching their way down the walkway, their weapons drawn.

"You win," muttered Peter. "Go ahead and kill me. I'm defenseless. But the girl and engineer; they aren't chasing you. They have no idea who you are why you're here." He paused, then asked inquiringly, calculating, "You're not going to hurt them, are you?"

"Four times in four hours today, I could have put bullets in your fac," Galante said in his thick grating voice as he lifted and aimed his .38 at the lieutenant's head, "but we don't kill uselessly. I am paid to kill, and I kill well when I am assigned to kill. You and the two there are not on the list to be killed today. So, go in peace and wait for me on another day."

And, with that, he turned away and fired his final shots into the backdoor lock and bar support hinges, then kicked out the door and seemingly catapulted down the stairs, three or four at a time, to the water's edge, just as heavily armed MPs hurriedly turned the corners of the Pacific Seas Canning main building. A that point, Carmine Galante glanced back, offered the slightest wave, and disappeared into the shoreline rocks which spanned under all of that and the entire length of all the neighboring canneries.

Within seconds, the MPs were gently stepping past the boiler engineer, and over Peter lying prone on the walkway adjacent the fish factory's wall, his head in Aliandra's lap as she waited for urgent first aid and an ambulance to arrive.

As a slow darkness began to overcome his withering consciousness, he looked into Aliandra's eyes.

"I had no idea when I entered you were down here. I should have been more alert, more cautious. I lost him and put you in his line of fire."

Aliandra's tears were repressed as best as possible by remaining silent, other than when stroking his hair.

"He says four times he could have shot me to death. Three for sure. Here, just now, the restaurant's parking lot. The restaurant itself. The bus. And at the conclusion of the procession. It's true. I'm no hero in combat. I can't even fight. Heck, I don't even know how. But I went for his throat when he aimed at you. Oh, no! I wouldn't allow him to get near you."

"Shhhh," pleaded Aliandra. "Here come the medical people with a stretcher. We must get you to a hospital."

As Peter began to fade as medical hands lifted him onto a stretcher, Aliandra refusing to let go of his hand, he heard Captain McCormick say,

"He can't be found. We know he didn't get into the water. He's still in the rocks under one of these canneries. We'll get him."

Then, it seemed he heard Captain Spanagel say, "The plane is idling on the Del Rey Oaks tarmac. He'll be attended to in the air on the plane to

Alameda where an 8th Air Force B-24 is waiting to fly him to Washington and then Palermo. Antonello is already on board with Peter's suitcase. Within 48 hours, the two will be in Palmero."

Turning to Aliandra, Captain Spanagel said quietly,

"Come to my office tomorrow at 1:00pm. There is much to share with you. I'm not supposed to, but I will since your only way of communicating with him until war's end will be through me."

"Until war's end?" Aliandra exclaimed, panic-stricken through her tears, trembling, her voice quivering.

"Yes, dear. I'm sorry."

"Sicily?"

"Yes, then Italy. Underground with the partisans, accompanied by Antonello."

"Is he going there in pain?"

"Yes."

"Will he come back to me?"

"We are at war. There can be no promises, no guarantees about life, especially in one as bitter as this one. But, it is likely he will. His favorite world is 'nonpareil', which he most certainly sees himself, in high intelligence, in imagination, in courage and bravery, in a man's love for a young woman. We see his head and face and understand my cat 'Silly' can fight better than he can in hand-to-hand combat, the sorry intellectual. So it will be his mind that will see him through, that will return him to you."

As the two Navy corpsmen lifted the stretcher to quickly exit the basement boiler room walkway to the waiting ambulance, Aliandra rose, still clutching his hand. The blanket of the disabled lieutenant was pulled up to his nose, a towel draped over his eyes and forehead. She could no longer control her loving tears. A quick look at Spanagel led her to look upon her motionless man.

"Oh Peter, squeeze my hand. Please, please squeeze it hard. Let me know you'll come back. You must, must come back."

With that, Aliandra's sobbing became uncontrollable. Then, as the two medical stretcher-bearers began maneuvering through the small assemblage blocking the narrow walkway, a muffled voice from the swathed officer was heard whispering,

"Wait, wait…"

Instantly, Aliandra leaned down,

"Oh, Peter…"

"How can I not come back to you? Galante had no murder in his eyes. And how can the armies of Hitler and Mussolini stand up to Junipero Serra? I will be back, my Aliandra, and we will pray our thank you at the altar of Mission San Carlos Borromeo del Rio Carmelo. I swear it…"

Captain Spanagel placed his arm around Aliandra's shoulder and said softly,

"Evil may bring Peter close to death many times before he is returned to you. God gave your future husband life, Frey Junipero Serra of our beloved Monterey Peninsula, our spiritual father will protect him as he did this very day, four times, because we need men and women to fill the decisive roles in the future roles of our country, our people, all our people, our children, your children together. No, dear, sweet Aliandra, Junipero will bring Lt. Peter Albinoni Toscanini back to you."

CHAPTER SIX

Landing in Sicily

Far beneath Peter, by more than 4,000 feet through the clear, cold, gloaming sky, the rolling, grassy plains and hills of western Sicily loomed before the B-24, 'Liberator'.

"My God," reflected Lt. Toscanini, USN, Medical, on special assignment, "How exemplary these seasoned pilots are! Once they spotted the landing strip, they started their landing procedures because time and distance are so critical at this stage lest we overshoot the runway and crash into that nearby mountain."

Suited in appropriate heavy fur-lined flying suits, including vests and life preservers, Peter and Antonello, the only two passengers to have boarded since Monterey, California, had flown belted onto bench seats, their legs stretched out on the floor of the empty cabin.

Nudging Antonello, who was sound asleep, his head on Peter's shoulder, to awaken, the lieutenant said over the tiresome, unvarying turbosupercharger radial Pratt & Whitney two-row piston engine reverberations,

"We're here, you're back home in Sicily. Wake up, Antonello! Imagine, 6,475 miles, cruising at 215 miles per hour, 1,600 miles without refueling, all in 72 hours with four stopovers, if my math is right."

Just then, as Antonello began to blink, then stretch, the co-pilot emerged from the cockpit, smiled at Peter, and announced,

"Marsala's Carcitella Airfield in sight. Within 20 minutes, we'll be on the ground, safely. Tower's final landing instructions tell us no gusty winds.

No turbulence, including any at low level. Our grueling, long-duration flight is over and the airfield from our descent, I'm certain, will be a welcome sight. Once we park on the tarmac, you'll hop off and we'll continue on another 45 minutes to join the 489th Bomb Group based at Palermo's Punta Rinaldi Airfield. I might provide you with a tasty tidbit of gossip. None other than Col. Ezekiel Napier, the Commanding Officer of the 489th is waiting to greet you with your official assignment from the Joint Chiefs of Staff back in D.C. Our guys on board; pilot, navigator, radio operator, nose turret, top turret, two waist gunners, ball turret, and tail gunner, bid you two V.I.P.s 'good luck' in whatever you've been endeavored to do. And, when I refer to you as Very Important Persons, you must be. Very, very important men to command your own B-24 'Liberator'!"

Peter and Antonello smiled and waved, gratefully.

"We're touching down in a moment. I've got to return to help pilot one of the Army Air Force's primary bombers safely to earth. How embarrassing if we should catapult because I was chit-chatting."

As the powerplant of the aircraft slowed the two-row by two-row engines, causing the B-24 to spit and sputter crossing the port city's vast open anchorage, Peter marveled over the golden shimmering twilight on the calm harbor waters.

"Nothing hairing about coming down in the reliable 'Liberator'," Peter chuckled softly.

At about 300 feet above the ship's loading and unloading cargo, and 200 feet short of the runway, the pilot cut the power and touched down with minimal skidding. Antonello, now fully awake, smiled,

"I'm home, my friend. I'm home."

Although he smiled, Peter bit his lip. For some inexplicable reasons, a sudden surge of homesickness overwhelmed him. Certainly, he was glad to be on the ground. But this was not a happy time. He was nauseous. Not once during the past year while tracking down military men who murdered multiply did he feel a sick feeling in his stomach, with the impulse to vomit.

"At least the weather isn't bad," he reflected, deflecting the lurch. "I don't have to walk through mud and rain everywhere I go."

But his dejection persisted.

With ample space to spare, the pilot had perfectly placed the B-24 squarely on the intersection of two runways, the co-pilot emerged again from the cockpit and ordered,

"Suits off, boys. Leave them on the bench you've been sitting on. I'll disembark you both personally. The moveable stairs are on their way. So is Colonel Ezekiel Napier, the commanding officer of our 489th Bomber Unit. He'll be here in about 15 minutes to escort you to your night's lodging with orders for tomorrow. Oh, and it's too bad you won't be able to R&R here on the base. As you can see, one of our waist gunners is dropping off a large black handheld case carefully strapped down. In that case are three 16mm reels of 'National Velvet' starring Mickey Rooney, Elizabeth Taylor, and Jackie Jenkins. In the Army Air Force, we see all the Hollywood features before the city theaters get them, because we own the whole of the world's skies. We show it tonight, then tomorrow night they show it at the base at Birgi Airport in Trapani, and the night after that, at the Punta Rinaldi outside Palermo, and so on."

"Yeah," Peter said, managing a smile. "It's not out yet. It's the story of a girl who rides the horse, National Velvet, I think, in Britain's Grand National horse race and is the underdog. I don't know the ending. But the film is supposed to be the breakout role of a young teenage girl named Taylor, Elizabeth Taylor. I'd love to see it tonight after supper."

"Well, the commanding office may have different plans for you two. If you happen to be here at 8:00pm, the showing begins at 8:10pm in Hangar 7."

Standing on the tarmac in front of the 'Liberator', waiting for the colonel, Peter commented in a tone of sadness,

"Well, Antonello, we're down, the bouncing upon landing reduced to a minimum. It's so good to feel the earth, even Sicily's, under our feet."

"Yes, Peter," responded Antonello, "but tell me, my friend, how can I help you from this despondency?"

Gazing upon the numerous men on the field, hurrying, strolling, and ambling every which way, Peter remained silent, the barest hint of a tear clouding his eye.

Suddenly, he exclaimed,

"Here comes a three-jeep convoy. It's got to be Colonel Napier. And, he's coming up to us pretty fast."

After a pause, Peter said quietly, as he watched the three jeeps, one after the other, speeding headlong toward them,

"Tonight, when there's plenty of quiet time, I'll tell you all you want to know. There are no secrets between us, Antonello, no matter how personal. Right now, I'm thinking how Marsala and Trapani, Sicily's two Western port cities, obviously important, fabulously beautiful, have a climate similar to our Monterey. Warm, delicious every night at dusk, even during the winter, so golden as the sun sinks and disappears, who can resist watching that at day's end? Then, at dawn, a morning fog, probably thick and moist, burning off by early afternoon; my goodness, what a place to live!

Surrounded by the vast Mediterranean Sea, to Mussolini Il Duce, 'Mare Mediterraneo Nostrum', 'Our Sea', by Europe, Africa, and Asia, an exciting array of cultures and subcultures, Sicily is essentially a stepping stone to the whole world, as I see it, Antonello. If you return after the war, maybe Aliandra and I will join you."

With that, three U.S. Army diminutive amphibious jeeps, each capable of transporting five men, roared straight toward them, forcing both Peter and Antonello to instinctively step back with bated breath, as if breathing could halt a small convoy of multipurpose cross-country vehicles.

Screeching front wheelbases, all jolting to rubber tire-burning halts, halted within feet in front of Peter and Antonello as heavily-armed MPs jumped from the second jeep and surrounded the surprised two arrivals. From the lead vehicle carrying only an armed driver and an officer passenger, an officer, relaxed and with a sense of dignified stateliness stepped out of the jeep toward Peter and Antonello. To the wide-eyed Lieutenant, the Colonel approaching him, hand extending, cut a fine-figure of the high-level "brass"--immaculately uniformed, urbane, pleasant, with gentlemanly manners, albeit all official.

Jovially, the obviously highly-intelligent officer, perusing the dress of the two men, noting Peter's uniform and rank, asked,

"Ah, Lt. Toscanini, I presume?" shaking Peter's hand heartily, then Antonello's cordially.

"I'm Colonel Ezekiel Napier, the Commanding Officer of the 489th Bomber Group. From all the transatlantic wires, telegrams, and, yes, telephone calls, I understand the two of you are going to win the war for us in Italy!"

With that, he grinned from ear-to-ear, causing Peter to blush.

"Maybe him," smiled Peter, pointing to Antonello, who was grinning.

"Well, I heard you two together make up this superbomb we've been hearing rumors about. Full of atoms, I hear."

After a moment of friendly hand-clasping, Colonel Napier said somberly,

"Hop into the last jeep. We're taking you two to your lodging for the night. After a full, sound sleep, and a hearty breakfast cooked by Mama Anna Matta herself, we'll arrive and explain your first assignment, code name 'Sicilian Nocturne'. Nothing in writing, Lieutenant. Only whispered words form me, to the two of you. For now, hear me out now, in the engine racket of takeoff."

As Marsala's Carcitella Airfield maintenance personnel with their tools, kits, bags, and assorted engine upkeep and support equipment, decamped 'The Liberator', mechanics and workmen scampered across the runways, tarmacs, and fields into the hangars, the colonel hovered closer to Peter and Antonello and said,

"Here, at the beginning of night, late November 1944 in the noise of noisy turbosuperchargers, and swirling debris and airfield ground trash from twirling 10-foot fully feathering propellers, I say, as ordered to say, the following epistle. So, damn it, listen up, heroes-to-end-World War II, lest I come down with a sore throat repeating myself."

"You now are both under the strict jurisdiction of the United States Joint Chiefs of Staff and some odd committee whose name I've already forgotten. You will, at all times, awakened or asleep, be governed under the rules and regulations of the U.S. Army. Your missions, and instructions and orders to fulfill, will be issued verbally when the code name, Lexi, is announced. You will not know any other thing, other than the terse, sententious three or four sentences spoken. There will be no questions. If asked by you, they will not be answered. If caught and tortured, the less known, the limited possibility of endangering other sub Rosa stagers, operators, and agents. Your journey's destination and its route will be told you both once, and only once, upon arrival at the mission's first encounter. There will be no rest other than whatever sleep you can edge out from your assignment. Your lives are at enormous risk since spies and saboteurs are shot on sight. Now, that formally stated, and there can be no questions since I am under strict orders to not answer any, we will drive you to your flight, debriefing, then wait until you're prepared to be deposited with Mama Anna Matta."

Rumpled, each screaming for a warm shower, then a simple meal, the disheveled travelers, now in trench coats and boots, began combing their hair and using canteen water to scrub the grime from their faces.

The few minutes needed for debriefing were uneventful but necessary. Both Peter and Antonello expended nearly all their remaining strength and energy to fill out their flight questionnaires, then respond to sit-down inquires. The final interrogation by two 489th Bomber Group and a Sicilian Carcitella Airfield official was conducted in the presence of Colonel Napier. Emerging from the debriefing hut, Peter and Antonello were driven the short distance to the airport's mess hall where Red Cross workers, teenage Sicilian girls from Marsala, awaited them with coffee, tea, chocolate, and donuts. It had been almost 15 hours since breakfast, and the two relished what was so kindly provided.

"Well, men, I see you're both ready to lie down, even without bathing first. We're off, so climb in the backseats. Make sure you have your bags. You'll soon enjoy real blankets, not GI blankets."

Amid the continuous droning sounds of half a dozen of returning bombers after bombing missions over central and northern Italy, the three jeeps roared down the runway past the two-story control tower, maintenance hangars, workshops and heavy light and beam poles, and crossed the elongated rectangular airfield. Just as the initial four-engine "flying beast" was touching down in the near-perfect weather on the opposite landing grounds, Colonel Napier turned and addressed his two arrivals.

"Pilots, glad to be home. Six went out this morning, six returned, after bombing railroads marshalling yards in Milan, harbor installations at Laspezia, and assorted factories and troop concentrations. Always good to see our boys home safe."

It was nearing 9:00pm that night as the colonel's lead-jeep pulled into a wide circular lightly pebbled driveway.

"There you are boys, your overnight quarters. Well-lit, high atop a knoll in all her majesty and grandeur, welcoming you to walk up those ancient medieval steps of chiseled and sculpted rock and place those worn-out heads on soft pillows, beckoning, then fulfilling, at least 24 hours of uninterrupted authentic snoozing."

Lifting their heads and gazing upon the façade of the brightly illumined mansion ornament in the architecture of Gothicism, Peter and Antonello, who knew the mansion and site well, were in awe of the panoramic view from far away Trapani to the southern villages along the southern Marsala coast. While the mansion's country estate was pitch black, the west Sicilian coastline was little more than a beautiful string of lit-up golden pearls. On the outskirts of Marsala, the knoll was less than five miles from the southern tip of the Carcitella Airfield.

"Must be trillions of sparkling stars smiling down on us, this my Sicily. If time permits, my dear friend Peter, during or after the war, I'll show you where I grew up, played, and cherished all that was so sacred to my parents and their parents and their parents. Just over the hills to your level. The road where my father and mother, and our chauffeur were ambushed, either by Il Duce or the Mafia, and slaughtered like animals," whispered Antonello in the back of the jeep.

The lieutenant nodded solemnly, "Yes. I want that Antonello, and, if I survive these remaining months, fetch Aliandra and return to honeymoon on these back roads, every one of which leads 10,000 years back to the emergence of a rich island people; their culture, their history, their continual survival amid enemy people from all sorts of regions in this part of the world who landed to murder, enslave, and loot."

As Colonel Napier walked hastily up the steps of the mansion under the bright starlight, and the M-1 rifle-bearing MPs leaping form the second and third jeeps to post themselves as sentries around the residence perimeter, Peter, Antonello, and the driver, carrying their bags, followed.

Greeting the colonel at the top step was a middle-aged woman of medium height and a physique that could easily be referred to as "pleasingly plump".

"Neither burly, nor pudgy," Peter whispered, scrutinizing her from the bottom of the steps in the dim front porch light.

Then, a moment later, he added in a low tone, "With a whole lot of wrinkles surrounding deep-set, cool, watchful eyes drowning in twinkles."

"Mama Anna Matta," whispered the driver carrying in the bags behind Peter and Antonello and following from behind. "The name translates as 'Mother Anna Crazy' because everyone loves her so much. She is, as you'll soon see, even this late at night, spunky, vivacious, and endearing as all get out."

"And, boy, is he right," thought Peter upon being introduced to her, shaking her warm, friendly hand. Antonello, she knew, kissing him on both cheeks, but with a quizzical look. As weary and exhausted as Peter and Antonello were, it was astounding how personally electrifying it was to meet such an open, uninhibited, loving woman."

"A whole gallon's worth," reflected Peter as she laughed and giggled with the colonel and his driver, occasionally resting her glances on the young lieutenant. "She's no half-pint." Yet, Peter's studied eyes sizing her up, concluded, "This once raven-haired beauty, capturing years before photographically what true Sicilian womanhood was all about is something of the prim and proper schoolmarm, high integrity, honorable, dignified, even in speech and posture. But most of all, this woman, like my Aliandra, is indomitable. She is so archetypal the 'ma' and 'grandma' you can tell she will never fade. She is as radiant as the sun."

Then, somberly, she turned back to gaze into Napier's eyes, and asked seriously,

"Perche cosi tanti Soldati? I Tedeschi non sono piu qui." (Why so many soldiers? There are no Germans here.)

As the colonel responded in near-perfect Sicilian dialect rather than the polite patrician tongue, "Toscana in bocca romana," a paunchy, gray-haired, amiable elderly gentleman, obviously the house porter, exited smilingly and walked over and took hold of the bags patiently waited by Mama Anna's without comment.

She giggled as she again glanced at Peter and Antonello,

"Tutta La Sicilia sa che vengono dall America per vincere la Guerra per noi. Domani visiteranno Salvatore Giuliano! Al Montelepre." (All Sicily knows why they come from America to Marsala. They visit Salvatore Giuliano to end the war! At Montelepre.)

Colonel Napier was aghast, reeling in dismay. Antonello was so stunned, he clutched Peter with his left hand. He uttered in a barely audible sound,

"Fantastic! If true, fantastic. My friend, Salvatore!"

Napier, equally unnerved, almost to the point of disbelief, except he knew that if Mama Anna Motta knew, it had to be true, simply stared.

Peter, glancing at all three, had no idea why such a secne should unfold before him at the mention of the name 'Salvatore Giuliano'.

Without skipping a heartbeat, Mama Anna smiled,

"Li lavo. Dormond nei miei letti migliori. Quando si sueglieranno domani mattina, mangerannola mia casa." (I wash them, now. They sleep in my best beds. When they awaken tomorrow morning, they eat my house down.)

"Well," offered the colonel, "I won't dare ask how you know that. Their orders, sealed and partially coded, are being flown into tonight. I don't even know that! How on earth would you possibly…"

She smiled, placed her forefinger at her lips, winked, and yielded no response. Meanwhile, Antonello turned to Peter and said,

"Later I tell you all. Salvatore is a good friend, Sicily's greatest bandit, but a good, good friend. This is very, very wonderful, Peter, beyond belief."

Smiling at Antonello, Mama Anna Matta said quietly,

"Quando vinci la Guerra per noi, allora uccidi la Mafia." (When you win the war for us, then kill the Mafia.)

Antonello responded after a pause, almost in the quiet softness as Mama Anna spoke,

"La mia famiglia ti ha essempre amato, specialmente la mama." (My family always loved you, especially our mama.)

"La mio dolore," responded Mama Anna, "non canosoe. Limiti quando no Saputo che li hanno uccisi." (Antonello, my grief knew no bounds when I learned.)

"Now come with me and take all your filthy clothes off. The steaming hot water for baths is cooling down. Dirty men are disgusting. Clean looking naked men are tolerable."

CHAPTER SEVEN

Mama Anna Matta

Although usually giddy, Mama Anna Matta, standing rigidly in between the beds of Antonello and Peter without clutching a broom handle, hatchet or rolling pin, was uncompromisingly stern. As she leaned over and rubbed each sleeping head roughly, she hollered,

"*Destarsi!* Awaken! *Risvegliarsi!* Wake up! *Sono le otto meno un quarto.* It is quarter to eight."

"*La sera?*" asked Antonello, drowsily.

"No! No!" she scolded, yanking the blankets off their beds. "*Sono di mattina.* It is morning! It is *tardi.* Late. They come for you soon. You want *colazione alla Siciliano?* Breakfast Sicilian style?"

"*La ringrazio della Sua ospitallita,*" Antonello said, as he sat on the edge of his bed, rubbinb his eyes.

"Si, si," he continued. "Thank you, Mama Anna Matta, grazie, grazie."

Turning to Peter still in a deep slumber despite his hair and head being hand-scrubbed, Antonello bellowed earnestly, "Up, Peter, up! We have for us, God Bless Mama Anna, a light, fast, sweet breakfast before they come to get us. Think of it, caffe and espresso. Sicilian-style croissants filled with chocolate, or honey or Nutella. And, maybe, brioches."

"*Mama Matta, che orae,* what time is it?" Peter asked with a muffled voice, barely audible, in the Genovese dialect. "Excuse me for speaking Northern Italian, but I don't speak, understand, or know the Sicilian dialect."

"*Sono le otto e cinque.* It is five past 8:00 *la mattina. Presto! E tardi!* Hurry! It's late."

"Si, si, facia presto! Yes, yes, we'll hurry," responded Peter.

Fully aroused, eyes still partially blurred and blinking, then adjusting to the contents of the high-ceiling bedroom, Peter, despite feeling energized, even a tad ebullient after 10 hours of sound sleep, could only recall from the night before standing a distance from the B-24, propellers twirling, in a twilight breeze.

After a hurried shower, then an equally swift, but sumptuous, first meal of the day, Peter and Antonello with their small traveling bags next to them, sat on the mansion's front porch in the morning day. Mama Anna Matta joined them as they awaited the arrival of Colonel Ezekiel Napier, the Commanding Officer of the 489th Bombing Group. The sky was tranquil, the air warm, the hilltop breezes cool.

"What a glorious "Mare Mediterraneo' morning! Mama Matta, again in Genovese, 'Le sono molto grato' I am very grateful to you as Peter is, too, I'm sure. My promise to you is this. When this war is over, and I return for my Aliandra, together we will return to honeymoon, I don't know the word for it in Genovese, Sicilian, or even Italian, here in Western Sicily, here in your home, for your cooking, for your kindness, your laughter and giggles, for your whole wonderful personality. Then, when we return to Monterey, we'll want you to return with us, and hopefully Antonello, to meet her family. And, since you are an unmarried woman, you may be interested in some of my future wife's uncles."

After Antonello translated Peter's heartfelt gratefulness, Mama Anna howled in laughter, clapping her hands. But, in an instant, she silenced herself, allowing a flood of tears to stream down her lovely, aging features.

"Si, si," she whispered hoarsely. "Aliandra, I need a daughter with the beautiful Sicilian name Aliandra. So, I come, and if you like me, Mama Anna Matte, I stay until your children grow and marry."

Antonello laughed so heartily he almost toppled from the top step where he sat next to Peter. Mama Anna sat next to Peter, as well.

"Tell her, Antonello, I've only known her for mere minutes. Yet, I see so clearly how huge and golden her heart is. She is pure sunlight. And being so jolly, so mirthful and even frolicsome at the same time, makes me, and most certainly Aliandra and her family, want her busy nearby and under our feet. Translate that into the Sicilian dialect."

As he did so, with Mama Anna listening, her bowed head, gently bobbing in agreement, Peter gazed across the country estate, reflecting it was beyond description. He wondered if it had a name as English, Scottish, and Irish estates have, since he had heard none mentioned. As far as he was concerned, it was feudal, the mansion being the castle. When the Germans occupied Sicily only months before, Mama immediately turned it into a hospital for the Italian and German wounded rather than see it used as "La Pensione", boarding house, or hotel, L'albergo, for officers on leave. During those four years she retained one of a dozen or so guesthouses. Although the estate was not as well maintained while the war raged all around and over Sicily's cities, ports, and airfields, it was obvious to Peter that it had most certainly been maintained.

As for the mansion itself, the interior had been built with the finest Mediterranean woods, and cloth, all pre-war. The walls throughout the structure had been covered with silk, and the balconies of each bedroom and the doors were obvious works of art. The bathrooms were the best rooms of all, Peter smiled, since a 24-hour furnace provided all the hot water needed.

For a feeling moment as Mama Anna engaged in an animated Sicilian dialect conversation with a giggling, jovial Antonello, Peter flashed on the remnants of a most vivid dream he experienced only hours before. For whatever unconscious reason he found himself boarding a Santa Fe streamliner in South Stockton, California, for Primary Flight School Training when he first entered the service in 1942. Arriving at the Maxwell Air Force Base in Montgomery, Alabama, he disembarked, stepped into a waiting army bus which deposited him for duty in a pilot pool on the Tarrant Airfield. One look at the AT-17 training plane, he began to cry and begged the flight surgeon to change his orders for transfer to the medical orders of the U.S. Navy. "I want to study how the mind comes to murder," he remembered pleading with the officer. Nonetheless, he found himself in the cockpit taxiing down the runway without the usual instructions, briefings, and orientations. He clearly remembered, even long after awakening, the beating, banging, and clanging of the AT-17 as it attempted liftoff. As terrifying as it was, the noise was bloodless in comparison to the loss of his life as the training aircraft crashed into the Tarrant Airfield control tower.

Suddenly, Antonello exclaimed in Italian,

"Guardi Laggio," Look down there, pointing to the convoy of three jeeps. *"Accidenti! Darn! Fai Presto!* They are making it snappy!"

Peter's attention was instantly drawn to a single narrow dirt road running along the rim of the horizon off the main two-lane highway connecting Palermo, Trapani, Marsala, and Mazara along the coast of Mare Tirreno adjacent Mare Mediterraneo. Indeed, three speeding vehicles, small and open, were rocketing toward them. Although the fields through which they traveled were barren, the weeds of Western Sicily grow tall, providing the illusion of a convoy of three jeeps, the last occupied by five Military Police bearing their M1 Garand semiautomatic rifles, each employing standard .30-caliber magazines, were floating atop the five-foot late fall wild vegetation.

"Yes," Peter mused. "They should be here in about 10 minutes. It's enough time, Antonello, for you to explain I refuse to refer to her as Mama Anna Matta any longer. In my Genovese dialect, Matta translates as crazy, mad, insane, lunatic, wild, and loony. Whomever named her saw her genuine happiness, joyfulness, gayety, joie de vivre as madness. Mama Anna is no nutcase, wild card, madwoman. Yes, she's jolly. And she's feminine, kind, and good. Matta is insulting. So ask her how she feels. Does she want us to continue that stupid degrading nickname, or a new one? Or, better yet, why not be called by her endearing real name, Mama Anna, which I personally like?"

As Antonello nodded in agreement, whispering, "Ever since I was a boy, I remember her being called Mama Matta." He turned to her now holding Peter's hand firmly in hers. As she bent down and kissed it lovingly, she said in astonishingly solid English,

"Grazie, Peter. Thank you, almost all my life I hated that 'Matta'. I am not crazy, just happy like my mama, full of excitement to be with my family and loved ones. Si, Peter, change it. As I care for my Aliandra's babies, your little ones, the children of your blood one with Aliandra's."

Peter put his arm around her and hugged her gently,

"From this moment on, Mama Anna, you are Mama Anna, nee Toscanini."

In less than an instant split in two, even before the 12-word sentence was concluded, Mama Anna's eyes illuminated brightly, the sky opened more deeply and wider, as the sun suddenly erupted into a hitherto unseen blazing ferocity. For a moment, her heart and vision of the future were illimitable.

As the three rugged military vehicles rumbled noisily into the mansion roundabout with Colonel Ezekiel Napier standing straight up on the passenger side of the jeep's driver, he waved while smiling continuously.

"Good morning, everyone. We'll keep the motors running while my escort relive themselves prior to our long journey. You two are ready, I presume? Mama Matta, did they behave themselves when you took them to shower?"

"*Si, si, vigile!* Yes, yes Signore policeman!" Pointing to Peter and Antonello while winking at the Commander of the 489th bomb group, she divulged in a lushing whisper,

"*Passa ogni limite,*" That's the giddy limit, such a silly question. *Che spaventa passeri,* this Peter! What a guy! Simpatico, *meraviglioso,* likable, nice."

"*Bene inteso. D'accordo,*" responded the Colonel. "Agreed. Okay. He is splendid."

As Antonello placed his bag on the back seat of the lead jeep and climbed aboard, Peter took Mama Anna's two hands and gazed somberly into her eyes.

"There is no time to struggle in Italian; let alone English. I will talk to Commander Napier and explain we have decided your name is Mama Anna, not Mama Anna Matta, and should he or any man in his presence use that nickname, he will be denigrating a beautiful woman. No one in our Monterey community, neighbors or friends, will ever refer to you that way."

"I have no idea whether I will survive the final months of the war. But, I swear, Mama Anna, on my mother's eyes and heart that I will return for you, either alone or with Antonello, or my Aliandra. So help me God, I vow that. So, I will return for you. Our future family needs you."

CHAPTER EIGHT

"Peter, meet Salvatore Giuliano,
Sicily's famous Robin Hood Outlaw-Bandit"

Engulfed in a variety of vexing thoughts and emotions, Lt. Peter Albioni Toscanini, USN, Medical Corps, Special Assignment, struggled to maintain a semblance of dignified forbearance as the Sicilian countryside slid by.

Sitting in the backseat of the speeding convoy's lead jeep, Peter offered Antonello in the adjoining seat a weak smile. With the early morning coastal fog gradually dispersing, Colonel Napier shouted for the three drivers of the escorting guard to accelerate at the near-maximum level of 60 mph.

Antonello, meanwhile, having noticed that upon Peter's adieu of Mama Anna, his friend withdrew into a depressed funk. Unable to phantom its cause, the Sicilian-born friend attempted a brief introduction to the physical features of the region.

"Peter, as we speed past, over, and through my lovely Western Sicily, allow me to familiarize you intimately with my playground so that you have an acute sense of place when you and Aliandra visit after the war."

Casting a knowing glance down at the small town of Mazara from Highway 115 which would lead past the side road to their destination, Castelvetrano south of Prizzi, Corleone, and Calatafimi, Antonello, over the engine's hubbub, and related short, sharp noises of rattling, clattering, clacking,

"My village of Montelepre is over those hills in those mountains from here you can see. It's only 17 miles from Palermo. As you know, Peter, the best friend I've ever known, my real name Antonello Audisio, not Antonello Zolli, the name I used in New York and Monterey. Vito Genovese knew it, as well as every member of his crime family. I explained to you during my open, honest revealment. My father, Guido Audisio, was a true hero of the republic. Some, especially the corrupt gangster mafia, called him a traitor. But he was not. He was a true '*maffeuso*', a well-to-do land proprietor, as were his unimpeachable aristocratic ancestors, then his father, my grandfather, whom I loved so dearly. When we drove away from Mama Anna's, we crossed the lonely side of the road, Papa was driving with my mother sitting alongside of him when they came upon a hastily built roadblock outside Montelepre and when he fearfully but politely pulled up to inquire, the two assassins stepped from behind the barricade and machine-gunned them to death. A farmer walking through the fields on his way home that sunset saw six men--two with U.S. Army automatic, rapid-firing weapons--fire until they had no more bullets. He told my uncle that night that they were certainly low-life mafia gunmen."

After a pause, as he glanced across the barren hills toward the high mountain range of his home, he said quietly,

"If we have time, say, a day or two, before our first mission with Salvatore, I will visit my people, who will be shocked to see me since they believe I am safe with Vito. But I must learn why the mafia murdered them, most certainly with Genovese's approval, because Papa and Mama's deaths had nothing to do with the war, or the thefts of America's aid to help the Sicilian war victims, as nice, old Vito was known to do."

"Do you believe he is somewhere on the island, or the American sector below Rome, or even German occupied Northern Italy?" Peter asked.

"I don't know. But when I find out, I will leave you, my friend, and go to see him. They will allow me in, and after we talk, and I gain his confidence, I will kill him."

"The Sicilian way, with as much pain as possible?"

"Yes, if there is an opportunity."

For more than a half-hour, the two sat without words as the three-jeep convoy raced along the Mare Mediterranean coastline towards Castelvetrano via the sideroad below the small port of Sciacca. Occasionally Colonel Napier would turn from the front seat and offer a lump of recent battle information.

"On July 23rd of last year, 1943, we kicked the Germans out of this tract of west Sicily. You can see all war debris alongside the highway. We have much to be proud of in our Sicily Campaign. Our boys of the 1st and 9th Infantry Divisions began the Invasion on July 12th and less than five weeks later, the last of the Germans, both Wehrmacht and SS, were gone on August 12th from Messina and across the two-mile stretch of inlet to Reggio di Calabria. After our landings down the coast there on the beaches of the Gulf of Gela, Gulf of Noto, and Gulf of Catania. The enemy tried counterattack after counterattack, to no avail. We and the British pursued them over sunbaked hills until the island was ours. In 38 days, we and our British colleagues killed or wounded 29,000 enemy soldiers, capturing 140,000 or more. In contrast, we lost 2,240 with 6,600 wounded. The British suffered 13,000 casualties, but only 2,700 dead. Not bad, indeed, a great victory for U.S. Allies."

At that point, Antonello interrupted,

"Ah, but I must share this. Something I saw with my own eyes, something Salvatore Giuliano also knew better than I, but was able to do something about."

"The Axis, as you know, consists of Germany, Italy, and Japan, three objects rotating on an imaginary straight central line. Well, the German troops, about 30,000, were fighting side by side with our Italian and Sicilian men, between 200,000 and 300,000 of them. But since our troops were considered less fierce when it came to fighting, they were given the worst weapons, worst food, worst positions to defend. General Alfredo Guzzoni was in overall command. He saw most of the Italian soldiers were tired of Musso's catastrophic war and ran away every time the Germans of the 15th Panzer Grenadier Division and the Herman Goering Division weren't looking. They hid in the island's rugged topography."

"Giuliano told me later, just before Papa and Mama were gunned down that he and his roving band of elite brigands watched from a hidden spot on the clifftop the thousands of landing craft that hit the beaches below on invasion day. Once word got out the Americans and British had landed successfully, the Italian troops vanished. Whole Divisions simply walked off. There weren't any Italian soldiers wearing uniforms anywhere!"

"That's right!" roared Colonel Napier in laughter, slapping his leg while seated in the front seat. "They buried their military attire and borrowed civilian clothes. Their defections left whole sections of the front lines unmanned and our boys had no trouble making huge strides across Sicily. Marsala fell in three hours, Trapani in two. Palermo took 72 hours to fall because the city was protected by the rugged Caronic Mountains. Heat exhaustion brought on by Sicily's 100-degree temperatures knocked additional Germans and SS troops out of the ranks."

Antonello added, "Don't forget only four narrow roads trisect the Italian, only two circling the entire thing, and we're on one now, the Highway 115. When the Italian soldiers fled, Salvatore called all good Sicilian men to fight the Germans side by side with the Americans and British."

With the crossroads off the highway to Castelvetrano still more than an hour away even at the breakneck speed of 65mph, the maximum for Willy's 4-wheel drive command reconnaissance jeeps, Peter leaned back with the sun almost overhead to gaze out to the calm, dark-blue Mediterranean.

Yes, he reflected. He would return after the war with Aliandra to escort Mama Anna back to Monterey. Meanwhile, he would introduce his new wife to a beautiful new country, the origin of her ancestors; their heritage, and culture. In short, her very blood he felt when he hugged her hard, when she pleaded for him to squeeze her. She would see for herself that her race was most rare, an unusual mixture of so many origins being only 90 miles off the coast of Africa and a mere two miles off the "toe of the Italian boot". Peter would take her to Messina to show her up close.

Noticing how alert and obviously reflective his friend was as he quietly surveyed the fishing hut and hovels, as well as occasional docks and piers all along the edge of the sea, Antonello tried conversation.

"My land, Peter, my people, my way of life. I love my roots, my Sicily which since Man began was a natural bridge between the lower African continent and upper Western Europe, an imposing impediment dividing our vast sea for invading armies in search of new territories to conquer. Musso, Italy's and Sicily's Fascist premier and dictator, certainly not mine, claimed his Navy advised him not to construct costly aircraft carriers like your country has in abundance since Italy has four of the biggest in the world, and in place ready to launch our air force in defense or to invade other countries in the Mediterranean. They were the rock-anchored islands of Corsica, Sardegna, Trinacria, and Sicilia. They are unsinkable bastions that can also interdict American and British shipping and Navy battle lanes."

Peter, nodding his appreciation of his friend's effort, began to notice the ravages of recent battles. Shell-pocked concrete defenses and bunkers, burned out enemy trucks, artillery pieces, and SS tanks off Highway 115, portions of the thoroughfare's asphalt ripped away and hastily repaired with rocks, sand, and dirt, countless unfilled small potholes, and abandoned German and Italian unopened creates and boxes. In and around the major scars of war were makeshift shacks still occupied by the random Italian soldier, despite more than a year's passing since the last shot was fired.

"Look, Peter!" Antonello smiled, pointing to a small town at the sea's edge. "There's Piana di Lucca, originally an Albanian settlement. That tiny community has the reputation of making the finest macaron in all Italy, let alone Sicily."

"Which reminds me, gentlemen," interjected Napier, "I hope Giuliano's cooks prepare some for lunch. We're about half an hour later, but should be there in about 45 minutes, in time for his noonday lunch."

Peter barely smiled, so alone was he with hitherto unknown emotions he had been struggling to repress all morning. It had only been less than a few days since boarding an aircraft on the Monterey tarmac.

Nearing the main crossroad to Castelvetrano, the convoy slackened its speed on Highway 115 near Sciacca due to the intensifying animal-driven cart and wagon traffic emanating from the Pto. Empedocle beach villages.

Meanwhile, as the minutes flowed by, and the traffic grew heavier and heavier, the silence between Peter and Antonello deepened. With his thoughts drifting aimlessly, a nervous restlessness seemed to be devouring the lieutenant. Antonello was worried. Something was slithering over his closest friend and he somehow had to pierce it. Idle chatter, and even tidbits of Sicilian war efforts or island surface features would hardly interrupt Peter's inner struggle between mind and heart.

"Aha!" he exclaimed loudly, causing Napier to twist around in the front and Peter to awaken from his stirred depths with a quick glance.

"I see now the reason for the earlier single tear that ran down your cheek as we drove past Mazara an hour ago," Antonello giggled. "You sincere fool. Overcast and melancholy? Your heart is riddled by a feverish demon and the incubus, the burdensome encumbrance is named 'Love'."

"Huh?"

"It goes without saying that you are brave, undeniably so. If you were to burst into the den of Musso, old womanizer Mussolini himself, the cockroach, while he and young Clara Petacci, his mistress, were engaged in, say, pleasant titillation, you would have no regard for safety, or your life. Simply put, dear fellow, you unconsciously long for Aliandra!"

Eyes narrowing, Peter turned to his friend. Flushed with a hue as reddening as a rising sun, he stared in disbelief, then, ever-so-slowly, a thin grin began to creep across his lips. As her vague extraordinary beauty and girl-next-door demeanor slowly converged upon a sharply focused Lissome, near-black chestnut-haired, innocent. With Peter's only show of emotion was a shifting of his legs on the jeep's backseat floorboard. Glancing back out to sea, and his broken, harassed spirit beginning to revivify, Peter admitted,

"Yes, Antonello. You're right. I can reflect on her kindness, her honor and loyalty, her gentleness and generosity, her courage, all day long with intelligent objectivity. But what's throbbing and pulsating throughout me is yearning to see her smiling, her gentle ways with the children of the neighborhood when we walked, her genuineness without a smidgen of the fake, artificial, pretentious, and affected. And, yet, all tied together with a healthy, absolute assurance which she would explain by saying with a glow in her eyes, 'It comes from Mama.'"

"Oh, Peter, you are so clear to see through. If not for you, she would be mine. So mine will come from somewhere on this island I love. And, your Aliandra and my 'Eleonora' or whatever her name will be, will be sisters to raise truly heroic sons and daughters."

"Thank you, Antonello. Yes, I fear no man on earth, no dangerous predicament, no God. But I tremble as I stand before her."

After a pause, he concluded,

"Now, here, bouncing along this dirt road in the utter reality of death and destruction, of World War where a sniper, landmine, or stay bomb can launch us into eternity's oblivion, let's get on with it, get it over quickly so that we can go home."

Then, after a pause, he added softly,

"Her warm call to me just at this moment has to go unanswered. I have work to do, not just for me, but for all good men and women who, too, have loved ones waiting and want to join and hearing their voices again."

To reach their destination, Castelvetrano, the jeeps had to traverse the stark, forbidding terrain for more than an additional 30 miles, much of it over the hard, impermeable black lava beds from millions of years of Mount Etna's 3,263 foot high volcano located in the eastern region of Sicily between Catania and Messina overlooking the port of Taormina and the Mare Ionio. Peter said to Antonello,

"I remember clearly what Aliandra's father said, 'As beautiful our island terrains, hills, and mountains are in the Spring and Fall, it is still a land of treachery and intrigue, where it has been for 3,000 years. It is a country where killing is allowed for anyone perceived to be plotting to take possession of one's property. Killing in self-defense is permissible on one's word alone. Such laws make the vendetta inevitable. Thus, the rise of roving bands of brigands for hire to do one's killings, the cowards. Yes, the government's carabinieri are present everywhere. They even police the high mountains. But, the Mafia is in control. Never forget the Mafia is not men, or a single man. Mafia is the Sicilian character, Sicilian honor, Sicilian principles. It is an idea, not an institution. It is a spirit, a system of values that makes it possible to govern Sicily. Yes, there are secret societies with the capacity for extreme cruelty, especially with those who deceive or betray Mafia in the 1930s before the war, the Mafia sending to him in Rome the heads of those prosecutors and secret police sent to reform Sicilian Society. A note was wrapped around each head which spelled out, 'You have no idea of what is waiting for you here when we are aroused.'"

Entering the ridge road along the north western rim of the Villarosa River basin, the small party encountered increasing numbers of donkey carts and laden mules being led to the markets of Aragona and Agrigento, an hour's walk from Pto. Empedocle and Favara. For a long hour, traffic was reduced to a crawl, causing Colonel Napier to curse,

"Forgot Fridays are the main market days in this part of lower Sicily. Yet, had to get you two up here and back by sundown."

Approaching the outskirts of Castelvetrano, the pounded earthen road merged gradually into a newer, wider thoroughfare of sand and crushed rock passing through sloping fields of ploughed earth. Vineyards and melon patches, most less than a half an acre in size, dotted the beautifully groomed scenery. Larger tracts followed, mostly of carefully lined olive trees bordering corn fields and sheep pastures.

"I smell the Giuliano clan," Antonello grinned. "He's up here, above Castelvetrano somewhere among the mountain caves. A perfect hiding place, well-known to outlaws for centuries. Plenty of food, a valley pleasant to gaze upon, and true Sicilians notorious for keeping their mouths shut. If Musso himself drove into the village and asked the old men sitting around the plaza, the public square and its small ancient fountain, directions to the village up the road, they all, and I mean every single one of them, would look at each other blankly, and shrug his shoulders. This is the one area in all Sicily the carabinieri will never enter."

"Well, responded Peter, glancing behind him, you can see through the mountains the long, white sand beaches and wide dunes we passed on the Sciacca seaboard. Aliandra will love this place. I wonder if her family members born over here know of this demi-paradise."

"All Sicilians do, as they know of the painted houses and paneled doors of nearby Prizzi and Corleone."

After a slight pause, Antonello pointed, "Look, Peter, to your left where the sideroads elevate toward the bluffs. Those ancient appearing houses and churches are the villages of Santa Ninfa and Partarina."

Suddenly, the three-jeep convoy found itself on an obviously historic rock-paved, cobbled, narrow street, barely wide enough for single trucks to negotiate.

"Venerable, Peter, archaic and venerable. Must be at least a thousand years old. When the early, first true Sicilians left their towns on the coasts because of the constantly invading armies by non-Italian nationalities, they flocked up here for residence. No force of arms was strong enough to penetrate these mountains. One or two men alone could hold off whole armies at any given pass, or time of day."

On varying angled slopes, to the left, high limestone mountains, to the right, glimpses of the sea, were rows on both sides of the main road of low stone houses, most sordid, some simply but rustic, as if unchanged from centuries before. In front of some were vegetable gardens mingling with fruit patches accentuated with occasional almond or pear trees. No matter where Peter glanced, hives of children and the elderly dominated the scenes, even on the main road or the narrow backstreets, life seemed to be lived outside the house during the daylight hours, and, when darkness descended inside. For a fleeting moment, he felt he was in the heart of a charming time long past.

Approaching the district on the edge of the village, the Lieutenant, thoroughly enjoying the panorama, noted the stone houses were fewer in proximity, and beginning to thin and scatter. Where in the center of the village, nary a fraction of an inch separated the structures, they were now separated by alleys, lean-to's, and single, or even double animal shelters, storage attachments, and add-ons.

Less than a quarter of a mile later, the colonel stood up in the jeep and pointed toward a side road on the left leading to the mountains.

"In ancient villages like this," explained Antonello, "all is designed around a central plaza within a grid of parallel narrow streets. The grid is really a huge square area of maybe four narrow streets on each side of the thoroughfare. The square, or grid, encompassing the center plaza, has four corners. The northwest corner of this grid, the one that faces the mountains has the residence we're going to. It's the house of Giuliano's uncle and two sisters who hid from the Germans. His father and mother occupy the house across from the corner house, two houses down, if I recall correctly."

As the drivers slowed to less than 20 mph rebounding off the frayed cobblestones, Peter was relaxed sitting back in the warm winter sun listening to Antonello's enthusiastic narratives on the social, economic, cultural, and criminal histories of western Sicily. As Peter was fascinated by the shabby, threadbare domiciles of festive villagers despite the poverties and hungers, family deaths and tragedies, at the hands of German and Fascist troops and police, Antonello smiled,

"Not much greenery in these parts about now, making Giardinello, just below Montelepre, where the Giuliano family originated, and Partinico, Borgetto, Alcamo, and this Castelvetrano, is Salvatore's stronghold, his territory, his home, his heart. The men of Hitler and the bastadaro, Musso, would not come looking for him, or downed pilots, or the partisans, up here because each of those villages is a blind pitfall where troops are easily lined up by their commanders to enter the narrow passageways, niches, nooks and crannies cut and carved from the stones by my Sicilian ancestors, to be cut down en masse. Each village was, is, and always will be a vast silent army ready to fight, men, women, children, the young and old. After all, they are Sicilians, and will always be true to the source and taste of their island blood."

Pulling up to the last house that formed the corner of the square grid layout at the end of the row that ended before the mountain cliffs, Colonel Napier turned to the driver of the lead jeep and ordered,

"Sergeant, pull on into the front yard next to that cacti garden and the chairs and tables next to the clump of pear trees."

"Peter," Antonello called out, "This is Salvatore's uncle's house. His two nieces, Giuseppina, Salvatore's oldest sister, and Mariannina, the youngest, live in safety here, as they have throughout the war. The middle one, Cassandra, joined the Giuliano bandit-partisans when the Germans started occupying Sicily in 1940."

Isolated from the last houses of two rows facing the narrow cobblestone, Peter noted not a single engine-wheeled vehicle was to be seen down the street, and that the unusual cacti observed in the front yard extended all around the flat-roofed two-story stone house and along its sides and up the slopes leading into the higher elevations.

"Why so?" asked Peter in a low voice.

"To help in a small way of keeping unknown assassins away. No man of importance, criminal, political, or law-related, ever has any bushes, large plants, and other shrubbery for the evildoers to hide in next to his windows. The prickly pears and spiky sisals make it painful to enter."

As the occupants of the three jeeps clambered gingerly from their seats, Peter stood in amazement as to what was before him.

The unusually tall residence, certainly the highest in Castelvetrano, was engulfed by two building protuberances, a veranda and a balcony with 19th century handsomely curved iron railings. Coupled with light-blue, grayish washed stucco surfaced walls, large bunches and bundles of evergreen myrtle and colorful periwinkle flowers of blue, white, and pink, the façade was, to Peter, a photograph of pure pastels.

"Adding to it," he whispered, "are the 20 or 30 people, especially the children, surveying who just arrived. What a scene!"

Antonello chuckled. "The first question is whether we're enemy or friend. Are we German, SS, Italian, Black Shirts, or Americano?"

Then, in the ensuing moment of silence with more than 30 staring at them, and as Colonel Napier began striding forward up the walkway toward the assembled tables and chairs as all were now standing, apparently to flee if the newcomers turned out ot be hostile, a booming voice from behind the thick vines of the veranda shouted,

"Buon giorno! Good morning! *Avanti! Avanti!* We wait for you! Venga presto a vedere the cooking of *bitecca alla Siciliano.* Then, *si serva!* You help yourself!"

Suddenly, Antonello bellowed,

"Salvatore! Come *sta?*"

The young man, with a holstered pistol at his hip, stood in utter amazement.

"Antonello, you! They no tell me, you!"

As the two grasped each other in a holding embrace, hands fastened to hands tightly aid laughter and exclamations, Peter had a long moment to measure Salvatore Giuliano, a 22-year-old, perhaps the handsomest man he had ever seen.

"Ci siamo molto divertiti!" Giuliano chortled gleefully. "We had such a very good time together when you were attending the University degli Studi di Palermo, learning the basic courses for law and medicine while at the same time learning English."

"And you, Salvatore, the most intelligent of all the altar boys at La Cattedrale, the Palermo Cathedral. You were my favorite placing the thin, flat, gold metal plate under my chin when the Monsignor served us communion before the altar in the nave. We will catch up when time permits, my friend. But, no, Salvatore, *permetta che la presenti* a Lieutenant Peter

Albioni Toscanini. We were told we three will work together behind the German lines.

"Si, si," Giuliano beamed, reaching over to shake Peter's hand. With a broad smile, he said,

"Cosa dice mai! You don't say. *Mi e parso maraviglioso.* I think it wonderful."

Antonello, also glowing with joy and pride, turned to Peter and said in English,

"Peter, meet Salvatore Giuliano, Sicily's famous Robin Hood outlaw-bandit."

CHAPTER NINE

A Delightful Garden Lunch

For Peter, the ambience of the pageant unfolding before him was astonishingly reminiscent of facing Aliandra's parents and extended family, perhaps as many as 30, waiting to meet him on the Largomarsino front porch the week before.

The unusual hollow lethargy that devoured him on the three-hour journey to Castelvetrano dissolved as he amusingly gazed upon the surrounding environment, the totality of moods of guests and neighbors commingling or seated at numerous tables across the front yard, and unrestrained emotional affection heaped on Salvatore. And, all in the cool breezes of a near-perfect warm November Mediterranean temperature!

Pointing to several elderly persons standing on the top step of the front porch, Salvatore smiled and said,

"La Mamma and Papa. Come say hello. Papa was a brick and mortar carrier on his shoulder for 20 years in New York. He returned just in time for me to be born. I was conceived in New York! With the money he earned, he and Mamma returned to Montelepre near Palermo, in the Palermo province, where he bought a little farm in the mountain region. We know Lucky Luciano who was born a few miles from us."

Focusing upon Salvatore's immediate family, Peter had to smile.

"My God, I'm meeting in Aliandra's family all over again. Papa Pietro has a gentle and gaunt face. Like Mr. Largomarsino, he is medium-height to tall, grey-haired, quiet-eyed, and sober-looking, obviously a leader within the village community, especially since he's Salvatore's dad."

Antonello whispered,

"He's prematurely aged by hard work. Even in lower Manhattan where he and Mama lived in a Little Italy tenement building on Elizabeth Street, he was well-known and considered brave, honourable, and with a work conduct and morals that put others to shame."

Shaking Peter's hand enthusiastically, while smiling a kindly smile, he said,

"I know English. We talk."

"Yes, sir. Would love to."

Salvatore stepped between the two, gently steering Peter's shoulder and elbow toward a small peasant woman standing between two younger women slightly behind Papa Giuliano. Peter sensed the two were Mariannia and Giuseppina, Salvatore's two older sisters. But his attention was drawn to the most important on earth for the Bandit King, "La Mamma", as he referred to her.

Maria Lombardo Giuliano personified the ultimate mother-figure because her adoration of 'Turridu' as she called him all his 22 years to distinguish him from Papa with the same first and last name. She referred to him as 'Turridu' after the hero of the Sicilian opera 'Cavalleria Rusticana'. Peter reflected,

"Maria, and Aliandra's mother, Catarina, nicknamed Concetta after her mother, are rather plain in features. Like Catarina, Maria was born to bear babies. Look at those thick-knuckled hands and burley body. Just standing there smiling at me shows her heartiness in manner. Precisely, Catarina. Black Sicilian eyes, a thin mouth, less than 6 feet tall, yet old rustic values and countryside, virtuous morals. A pure backwoods farmgirl with all the world's love to give overflowing from heart. Her entire being oozing kindness, generosity, all that's matriarchal."

Recalling Aliandra's mother, Peter, without thought, instinctively bent over and kissed her cheek. After all, such a good-hearted peasant woman was his mother, too. The entire Giuliano family, including the extended family standing and seated quietly observing the scene, applauded, Peter endearing himself to everyone present forever.

"Come, this way," Salvatore waved to Peter, Antonello, and Colonel Napier, including escorting M.P.s.

"We go through the house to get to the back porch where we eat and talk."

As the party walked across the porch and through the residence's entrance, Antonello pointed to a shiny plate of metal fastened to the doorway bearing the initials 'PG', Pietro Giuliano, in the center of the design. Surmounted by a semi-circle of open wrought-iron design, it was cast perfectly, and attached professionally, proof of the owners' wealth and prestige. Adding to the dignity and distinction of the residence was its incongruity color in contrast to the melodies and mélanges of white, pastel blues, yellow, red green and purple hues.

Within the house, the entry passage, a small foyer, for coat and assorted clothing racks, and a large mirror, in addition to the two 19th century photographs of Giuliano patriarchs, led straight down the hall, past numerous rooms, including the formal dining room and kitchen, and straight out the back door to the terrace garden.

Where virtually all the Castelvetrano homes were crowded, smelly, and without electricity and sanitation, the Giuliano house was exceptionally clean and dominated by the customary Catholic religious objects. Antonello whispered,

"Note how the image of the Virgin dominates this interior, as all interiors of good Sicilian families that can afford the prints, candles, and terra cotta pieces. As in Aliandra's home back in Monterey, the Mediterranean Goddess is Mama, or, as the true island Sicilians say it, 'Mamma'. Replicas and effigies and even a small shrine in the living and waiting rooms of the Virgin Mary outnumber those of Jesus Christ."

"And, I see that candles are kept lit throughout the day," Peter whispered back as the party treaded loudly down the hall. "Yet, I see a number of saint reproductions on the walls, but not one of Junipero Serra."

"Serra was a Majorcan Spaniard, certainly not Sicilian, let alone Italian," giggled Antonello.

Nearing the backdoor leading onto the terrace, Peter commented,

"Pure stiff Victorianism, including the richly ornamented framed photos and portraits on all the walls of the family dead. Reminds me of my own Nona's home in Stockton, California."

Striding out the backdoor onto a clean, well-curried terrace, Peter found himself under a wide, shady trellis topped with tangled grapevines. In addition, he was greeted by a variety of plants, herbs, and miniature cacti in varying-sized pots. Aromas and scents coupled with open natural fresh breeze whiffs, all under a blinding warm Sicilian sunlight made the encounter with the Giulianos all the more gratifying.

"So hospitable, the scene, the villagers, the great family, the Giulianos, and now it's time to know Salvatore and our mission together."

As the bandit king, Colonel Napier, and Antonello, followed by the M.P.s headed for a large round table at the corner of the trellis overlooking the southern hills sloping toward the sea, Peter paused to return a heartfelt smile form a white-haired lady, perhaps in her mid-to-late 90s, dressed in the traditional black funeral frock, although the bereft may have been deceased for more than half a century. Seated on an ancient wooden bench, leaning back on the backwall of the residence, with a large ceramic bowl on her lap as she pulled open strings of pea vines, allowing the legume pods to drop into it. Recognizing Antonello, she beamed in delight as he walked over and without a word, bent over and kissed her on the cheek as Peter had kissed 'Mamma' Catarina only moments before.

"She may well be over a hundred years old, no one knows for sure. What we do know is that she is the Nona, the grandmother, of everyone in these hills and mountains. In truth, she is Salvatore's grandmother, his father's mother, who lives with the Giulianos here. She and my own Mamma were related in a distance."

Glancing up, and, for a fraction, beyond, Peter was pleasantly surprised to face a stunningly painted donkey cart in every imaginable color. Atop its rear bucket was a wood-framed flat screen with more than a thousand halved figs, recently cut, drying in the sun.

"Peter!" boomed Salvatore, "...*Prego, si accomodi*, please sit down. *Viene! Viene! Desideriamo mangiare subito!* We want to eat at once!"

"Indeed, Peter!" echoed Antonello, "You won't believe the size of the steaks being served! It's their specialty in these hills."

And, so it was. As the M.P.s positioned themselves around the terrace, their machine guns raised, four sat around the round table, Salvatore in the middle of Peter and Antonello, Colonel Napier across from the three.

With Sicily's western sunlight beating down on the trellis shading the terrace, and several chickens scratching around the grass at the foot of its steps, Peter stared in utter wonderment at the spread of foodstuffs on the round table's pink tablecloth. Although the setting was well-shaded by the thick grapevines, the freshly cut winter flowers, silverware, and rare antique china dishes, cups, and glasses seemed to glitter despite lack of direct sunlight.

"My goodness," Peter muttered, "No family in Monterey, including Aliandra's, can equal this!"

As he continued to gaze upon the variety of "delicacies, viands, victuals, and esculents," as Antonello whispered, Salvatore could barely contain himself from giggling. One of the itchy chickens boldly mounted the terrace steps and, continuing to feel a tingling of the skin, scratched as it ambled aimlessly, lightly, and happily across the plank flooring and settled on Peter's left patent leather shoe.

"Elegant!" Peter laughed, along with Salvatore, Antonello and Napier. "Including the cheery chicken. Save him, my friend, and after the war, Aliandra and I will fetch him with us to California. Like Antonello, and the colonel, I'm sure, I am hungry."

Three young women still in their teens attended the table, carrying trays back and forth from the kitchen, replacing used dish plates, refilling water and wine glasses, and simply watching for needs of the four.

The side dishes were especially fulfilling; the attendants handling the stirrings and spooning of antipastos, risottos, and small bowls of either minestrone, spinach and rice, or meatball and vegetable birodi soups, all of which were wonderful.

"Not much of a menu," commented Antonello under his breath, "but certainly, how you say it? a potpourri, a hodgepodge of 'who-cares-as-long-as-it's-good' appetizers and homemade wine. For me, the 'birodi', the blood sausages, are to die for. All you can think to say to Salvatore and the girls,

"Molte grazie!"

Meanwhile, no one was paying much attention to how fine the weather was, the western mountain was. "Our November up here is a repeat of our May," Antonello explained, "despite how advancing the early afternoon shadows are."

Peter, unaware, could only comment, "All I know is how embarrassed I am that an obviously young hen has fallen in love with my left foot."

"Or, more like the smell of your shoe's hard, glossy shoe finish," giggled Antonello as Salvatore barely contained his near-raucous laughter.

As each of the four gormandized on his soup, hors d'oeuvres, antipastos, and canapes, Peter continually glancing under the table at Miss Domesticated who was eyeing him lovingly, the cry rang out from Antonello,

"They come! *La bistecca alla Sicilia!*"

Suddenly, Peter, diverting his attention, was consumed by the aroma of grilling steaks floating across the open terrace in the warm air.

"And, two fingers thick. So thick in fact, grab your sharpest knife."

"The aroma reminds me of the Carmel Mission Ranch Restaurant. Since 1882, its kitchen has cooked the best steaks on the entire Pacific West Coast."

"In Roma and Milano, the restaurants serve chops, boneless thin fillets."

As the teenage girls began forking two steaks onto each man's plate, atop the appetizers, Salvatore commented,

"Ours is an art of cooking, only young beef, less than 18 months old, always served rare, like the English T-bone steaks. These were captured by my men in upper Italia only four days ago, sent to Mazara then brought up to these villages. The Germans in a 10-truck convoy of live cows, the special white cattle from Tuscany's Val di Chiana province where as early as the Etruscans got their beef, were ambushed, the cows captured, placed on one old boat and within the night, shipped past Corsica to us. From Mazara, 100 or more of them were driven to Prizzie where then butchered and rationed to all the villages around these high mountains. What we eat is our family share. Mamma and Papa no longer eat meat and give you their shares."

"So, you see, Peter, we are enjoying the meat destined for General Kesselring and his staff!"

"And what do the neighbors say around here, those watching us from their windows? They must be as hungry as we are on this postwar island," Peter questioned sincerely.

"They sure are," Antonello shrugged indifferently. "But, Peter, even the entire Giuliano family. No one has seen the Giulianos eat more than they do. All the villagers share what is grown up here, raised here, driven up here. And, by the way, that includes any pasta that finds its way up here, such as spaghetti. The cows, pigs, even chickens were hidden in the mountains, their crevices and hallows so the Germans wouldn't find them. The rabbits, they put in cages, then shoved the cages under their beds. The chickens were stuffed in the ceilings and behind walls. Salvatore's father heads a committee that dispenses the food, as they did the unexpected treasure of two and three finger-wide steaks. These, that we are now eating, are the last, the very last, and they go to the last one on the committee to receive such a gift. Everyone eats, all is shared, and all is used to feed the poorest villagers. After cows and pigs are butchered, the women take over and save the lungs, stomach linings, brains, and scraps and bits and pieces for soup cooking. Sounds excessive, Peter, but it's wartime and we must save everyone. No one goes hungry."

"I think that's wonderful, Antonello," Peter nodded, as Salvatore nodded as well, smiling.

"Si, si, the bandit king offered. Every Sunday after twelve o'clock Mass and communion, Castelvetrano gives a feast and again every morsel of food is eaten. Other villagers also come to partake, families and friends, to gather and enjoy each other, and eat."

Gnocchi and Sicilian raviolis were served next and consumed as readily as the initial appetizers and antipastos. Only when the desserts, cialdes, waffle cookies, biscotti, apple pie, and hot coffee was served that the four leaned back in their chairs.

"Over the coffee we get serious, Salavatore. Your departure time is midnight, which means we will depart in less than an hour. Much to discuss before then. Now, that the MPs are fed, Salvatore, fed first and as much as ourselves, please see to it that small boxes of rice and zucchini tortas are packed in the middle jeep for your journey."

"Si, si," Salvatore nodded. "I told the girls who told Papa who is gathering them. But now I have two questions to ask before I accompany these two gentlemen to Italia to kill Tedese; the first deals with one of your American airmen, Colonel. Please tell me if the story is true. If it is, I want to make the pilot an honorary member of my gang."

"Ah, Salvatore, I know who you mean even before you tell me the story. That's why I was late to Mama Anna's house this morning to pick up these two. We had a big meeting what to do at that time about your hero or our maverick."

"Si, si," responded Giuliano, wryly. "Huh? Did I hear something while in New York about an American telling the British air command to *Va gagaw* when ordered to bomb Sicilian women and children?"

"What?" Peter perked up, somber, almost glaring at Colonel Napier. "I want to learn all about this!"

"Well," the colonel said somewhat pridefully, "all Sicilians have heard about it. Before the invasion of Sicily, which began during the night of July 9 and 10 of last year, 1943, an air raid had been planned on Palermo itself. At that point, Allied planners, mostly British, were charged with picking the best targets in the major enemy cities. Other than the planners, no one was allowed in the briefings. It was definitely a 'hush-hush' decision. Why? Because it was to take place on innocent Palermo on a Sunday morning! And, Palermo without a tittle or jot of military significance! Hundreds and hundreds or elderly, women, and children would be at Catholic Mass about to take or taken the Eucharist. And the young kid planner commenting, 'Well, so what? They are enemies, aren't they? Our American planner was defiant in saying, 'No!' The Sicilian people don't even like Mussolini, let alone Hitler and his air force. Not one of the Sicilians, not one woman, not one child said, 'Let's hurry up and go drop eggs on the British kids, women, and old people.' Yet, the planner said, 'It's our show, so stay out of this. A lot of the Sicilians will be killed coming out of church, if we schedule the arrival of our Lancasters overhead at twelve noon when Mass concludes. A handful of B-17s would be included in the mission.'"

After a pause, at which time Peter leaned over and scratched the back of the head of the chicken nestling comfortably on his shoe, Colonel Napier, continued,

"Well, we told our boys they had the opportunity to bomb churches on a Sunday morning. About 30 or 40 of them met, led by one bombardier from Texas. Most of the fliers had more than 50 bombing raids from our Trapani and Marsala over occupied Italian territory. That Texan met with the fliers for about 30 minutes with none of their supervising officers. I'm in charge of our U.S. contingent and the Texan, whose name and rank will not be divulged until after the war, politely asked to meet with them alone. When he exited from the hangar lounge, he said,

"Colonel, simply put, we did not train back home to kill the elderly, women, and children, all church-going people who are pro-American, pro-British. We may be reprimanded, perhaps confined, even jailed. I said, 'No, Lieutenant, get up there. I'll see your flight group goes first, then over Palermo drop your bombs, which will be diffused in the hangars prior to take off in the harbor. The British aren't kill-crazy, ruthless, vengeful.' They say, 'By bombing an Italian city once, killing civilians, no matter how many or how few, the Itais will get a helluva scare that should once and for all blast them right out of World War II. That one bombing will do 'em in. They'll be rushing to us for a separate peace.'"

The bombardier smiled, "Their way means blood on all the streets and in the gutters of a great city. And, as you know, Colonel, blood on pavement and stone is hard to wash clean. Our way, a few harbor fish will be frightened out of their wits. The harbor is good enough for us all."

"Well," continued Napier, "The boys went up in five B-17s and bombed the Gulf di Castellammare off Punta C.S. Vito, far enough from the harbor shipping to hot hurt anyone. We heard of not one casualty, and we know not one ship or boat was damaged, let alone sunk. When the B-17s returned, the crews lined up for doughnuts and coffee served by pretty West Sicilian girls in Italian uniforms, even though by then every Italian male who had been called to duty by Mussolini had vanished into the hills. Everyone was happy. No one hurt. The bombing of Palermo was cancelled by the British when the planners learned of a near-mutiny by the Americans. By the next day, the whole episode was forgotten, and the only mention of it since that fateful noontime was just now. Salvatore, once there is surrender, I will have the bombardier who led the revolt to you as a show of respect to the Sicilian people on his way back to America."

"*Si, si,* Colonel. I will speak in appreciation for all Sicily when I meet that man of courage."

As Peter bent over to stroke the chicken under its beak, gratifying it to the point of clucking delightfully and Antonello, gazing with a grin of discernment past the terrace through the bamboo thickets to an olive grove at the foot of the 2,000-foot high Madonie Range, the minutes-long silence was virtually deafening.

"*Che spaventa passeri!*" Salvatore suddenly exclaimed, still reflecting upon the bombardier.

"*Si,*" responded Colonel Napier, "'What a guy!' is right. I promise you, our friend of America, you will meet him, either by you coming to us at the airfield, or me walking him up here."

"*Per caso,* by chance, can you also arrange for me to meet Lucky Luciano? Is it true what they say about the air dropping everyone is talking about?"

With the mention of Charles "Lucky" Luciano's name, Antonello jerked into an erect position, full attentive. The sudden movement did not go unnoticed by Peter.

"I know all about it, my father having told me right after it happened. But you go ahead Colonel, and I'll follow."

Peter leaned forward, barely, but certainly noticeable.

"Well," Napier began, "with the mass defections of the Italian armies overnight at the beginning of the invasion last year, and Italian and Sicilian boys borrowing peasant clothing, the lines they were supposed to defend simply vanished and the American and British made huge strides toward Palermo and Messina from the southern invasion beaches."

"Luciano, the king of La Cosa Nostra 'this thing of ours', who was in the New York's upstate Dannemora Prison on a 50-year prostitution conviction, somehow, probably through our military, got word to the Mussolini generals to release, even encourage, the troops to bury their war clothes and run. He was supposedly the chief architect, the reason for the desertions. One version, which, indeed may be the most credible of all, has Lucky sending a coded message to Sicilian Mafia leader, Don Calogero Vizzini, persuading him to assist the Allies in all manners possible. If so, Lucky said, the Americans would turn a blind eye to all his illicit criminal activities he wished to engage in postwar, war-torn Sicily. Ironically, it was old Musso himself who eradicated the Mafia in the late 1930s since he saw it as a rival to his own power. He boasted, 'I kill 10,000 Sicilian men to destroy 1,000 Mafiosos, so what? You have a growing cancer on the arm that will kill you, you cut the arm off, no?'"

"Astounding!" breathed Peter, hoarsely. "An American gangster serving 50 years in an American penitentiary has that much power?"

"Mafioso, not gangster," corrected Giuliano, more stone-faced than expressionless.

"Sorry, Salvatore. In America, we have both, plenty of them. It's not that Lucky wasn't quiet and reserved, shunning photographers, publicity. But no Mafioso in America sold drugs, was a bootlegger, controlled prostitution, or tried to take over specific industries, such as the garment industry. Old world Mafiosos were, and still are, disposed to extortion, as their fathers and uncles were in the 'Black Hand'. Extortion, loansharking, fraud, hijackings, gambling protection, etc., the lesser crimes so they wouldn't be targeted as hard or harder than all such criminals. The police know the difference between a 'gangster' and a 'Mafioso'".

Antonello added, "He's still in prison. After the war, the U.S. government will undoubtedly export and ban him back to Italy. For life, never to enter America again. Meanwhile…old world Mafioso Vito Genovese, whom I know well, is in charge of the crime family that Vito Genovese runs. Lucky the gangster murders at will or when hard-pressed, or his crime family is threatened. The Mafioso rarely murders, even if threatened. When we have time together, I will tell you the whole story about the Americans and how they interpret Mafia."

"Si, I want to lean about the Mafia in America before I go there someday. Now, Colonel, tell me the rest of the story of Luciano's influence in Sicily."

"So, Salvatore, our report, which is official and the type that usually makes its way to the President's desk, says unequivocally that Luciano's message was placed in a pouch, then dropped form one of our fighters at the Marsala airfield next to Don Vizzini's mansion over there between Alcamo and Calatafini a few days before the Sicilian invasion. The P-38 had a black initial 'L' for "Luciano' or 'Lucky' painted on its side in black on a yellow background. The pouch, some say a 'wallet', was wrapped in a yellow shawl, some say 'handkerchief', with a big black 'L' on it. Our report also said

Lucky and Don Calogeru had been communicating all the time before the war and that Luciano, even after going to Dannamora, did 'favors' for the Sicilian Mafia in general and Don Vizzini. When U.S. reporters got hold of this story, wrote it up, and started to send it to their respective newspapers, our Army censors killed the stories which would have made all the big American papers across America. The censors, I'm certain, got orders from Washington, D.C. to stop the news. But the censors explained, 'We won't send your stories because they give aid and comfort to the enemy. Your articles would tell Hitler and his kind, as well as the rest of the world, that America and its heroic men are successful in Italy, having easily overrun Sicily within days, because of the Sicilian Mafia and a request from the King of the American Underworld.'"

"When will I ever meet him?" asked Salvatore.

"If he's still in Dannemora Prison at war's end, and you are in New York, I personally will drive you up there an introduce you. And, if he's in the territory we've reoccupied from the SS, I'll take you to meet him wherever he is staying or hiding. Chances are he will settle in Naples for helping to save thousands of lives, American and British."

Glancing at his watch, the Colonel exclaimed vehemently,

"It's nearing 3:00pm! And, I haven't broached a discussion of your mission. Well, gentlemen, that will have to wait until later, when the four of us are in the Captain's cabin of the destroyer."

"Huh?" blinked Peter, startled.

"Accidenti! Damn!" snapped Antonello, equally surprised, but a bit testily.

Salvatore simply glared at the colonel with the bad news.

"Scusi," Antonello continued, partially in Sicilian, but mostly in English.

"I beg your pardon. Questro si che e troppo. That's going too far. Destroyer? Dove Andiamo? Where are we going? We only arrived last night! Sono arrivato il…"

Peter interrupted, "Colonel, what can you tell us in just a fraction of a moment since I see you're in a hurry to get us someplace?"

With somewhat of a perplexed expression on his face, albeit a smiling one, he said,

"Gentlemen, we leave for Trapani in 30 minutes. Wash up; I'll be in the lead Jeep with the motor running. By short cut, we're crossing over the southern portion of the Madonie Range down to Calatafimi and on to Trapani. A destroyer from New York with a very important Army man will be aboard. The boat will arrive by 9:00am, pick you three up, along with provisions, and sail by 11:00pm. In the morning, the three of you will find yourselves and the destroyer anchored off the port of Livorno. With orders for your mission in hand, you'll be picked up and by a Toscana unit of partisans and driven to either Viareggio or Pietrasanta where you'll be under an SS command crossing the Gothic German line extending from Pisa to Remini to a villa outside La Spezia to confer with none other than Field-Marshal Albert Kesselring, one of der Fuhrer's three still-living military strategists. Of all the Nazi war bigwigs, he is the least brazen, blood-thirsty, and obedient to the insane dictator. Your mission orders which will be presented to you on board within an hour after setting sail spells all out, I'm sure, including Kesselring's personality profile, and what he wants. That field-marshal is the German true authority in Italy. Between us, I can speak a bit freely since I am not privy to your sealed instructions. Personally, I think he wants a negotiated peace, first a cease-fire, then the evacuations of his troops to POW camps until war's end. The war is lost for Hitler's

Germany, but the lunatic will fight to the bitter end, and believe me, it will be bitter since his whole murdering machine cares not about civilians, about the innocent. Old Albert, the antithesis of the Antichrist, wants to cease pointless bloodshed of all our boys and his, our civilians and his, our innocents and his. That's what I think your mission is all about."

Peter and Antonello, leaning forward, their elbows on the table, were so flabbergasted their mouths dropped, literally slumped visibly.

"Why us?" Peter asked so weakly he was barely audible.

"I supposed Antonello in his case because he knows the area up there above Rome, having gone to school in Tuscany. You? I have no idea. He can serve as interpreter and guide. You must have demonstrated your ability in some way or another. In Salvatore, even though only 22 years old, is already known for his exploits in both Sicily and Southern Italy, especially in Napoli and throughout Basilicata's Calabria and the Campania regions. The Giuliano name is known by every child, every man and woman in Sicily because he is a 'Robin Hood', a 'Billy the Kid'. He is not Mafia, although like Antonello, he is the son of a famous Mafioso. But both father and son have a special status among all Italians because they shun the traditional and new Mafia of Sicily like Don Vizzini and others, and they vomit before Mussolini and his Black Shirts. The Giuliano name is known all the way to Svizzera, Austria and Yugoslavia, and all points Italia del Nord. So, in his company, no one hurts you. You both are safe. Everyone who speaks our Italian will kneel before him. The Giuolianos want no power or profit. They must have complete faith in you, whoever you are, because you, single-handidly with your high intelligence, patience, intractability, intuitive sense, and who knows what else. All I know about you is what I observed on the drive up here, a grown man, a lieutenant no less, who appeared more lovesick than studying his immediate surroundings as all real leaders are taught to do."

Giuliano, who had remained silent during the colonel's discourse, finally voiced a thought,

"Me, *n'infischio*. I don't care a fig. Tedesci are Tedesci, no matter how you look and see then. I go get my dentifricio toothpaste and brush. Then say a word or two to Mamma and Papa when I return, you tell me all about Aliandra."

"Aliandra?" Peter uttered in a shout.

"I am anxious to know about such a Sicilian American, how different or similar she is to our Sicilian girls."

"How…"

"I see her all over your face. And, si, si, we also have a friend or two in Monterey, California, like the poltroon cowards of Mafia who came to kill Antonello last week."

"HOW DO YOU KNOW ALL THIS, SALVATORE?" Peter demanded angrily.

"TELL ME!"

CHAPTER TEN

*"Gentlemen, Meet General Mark Clark, Commander of the Fifth US Army.
Sit Down, He Has Your First Assignment, Working Together."*

Roaring away from the patriarchal house of the Giuliano clan on the edge of Castelvetrano, more than a hundred extended family members, neighbors, and village onlookers gathered in the front yard among the creeping shadows of dusk to wave their ciaos, adios, and *arrivedercis*.

The three-vehicle convoy swung north to the Calatafimi crossroad some 35 miles away. From there, a paved road shortcut would lead them past high mountain precipices onto the Salemi grade, then straight down to the sea and the Trapani harbor and docks.

"If you hold your breath as we bounce and jostle on the way down, we can make the jeeps lighter," Antonello winked at Peter, repressing a snicker.

Although anxious for answers to his myriad of questions, Peter had Salvatore's promised word he would reveal all his knowledge of Aliandra and the Largomarsino family once the trio was comfortably sequestered in peace and quiet. There would be much to tell, and Peter was in store for the shock of his life. Further reassuring was Mama Giuliano's personal vow to assume responsibility for the safety and security of the romantic hen that had fallen in love with him, or more precisely, his left foot. Antonello translated her Sicilian dialect promise as,

"After the war, you come back up here and take the poultry who loves you. She will be fat and sassy, ready to make new friends in San Diego."

It was nearing 5:00pm when the group slowed to a stop on a narrow, winding cobbled thoroughfare leading through the dismal Sulphur mining village of Capuana. Smoky, sour-smelling, and crowded with workers in muddy work clothing, some actually wearing trench coats in the humid heat, the scene echoed a coal-mining town in Wales, England.

Peter's initial glimpse told him this indeed was the poorest environment and habitation in all of Sicily, possibly the entire Mediterranean. The stone structures that faced the main street appeared feeble, virtually in a state of crumbling decay. There was nothing here, all the buildings, as the clothing of the workers tramping toward their hovels, were covered in a thick yellow soot, or grimy thin dust. All stopped in their tracks and gaped, some in terror, recalling how the SS often entered the town suddenly, unexpectedly, grabbing any male hostages they could find.

Antonello whispered, "The insides of their houses are as suffocating, scanty as their food plates and house exteriors."

"Si, si," echoed Salvatore, "See the yellow crystals in their tangled hair? The asphyxiating odor clings to the miners' bodies even out of the minds, their wives, their children. Sulphur is Sicily's soul and civilization. The Palermo Mafia controls the industry, mining, profiting, and killing the workers who resist. Everyone knows this, no one cares. All these people here also have nothing to eat. Sulphur mining barely keeps them alive. No carabinieri are ever seen up here. Up here, honor demands murder, and even decent, law-abiding people commit it. Yet, among these Capuana villagers a certain 'gallismo', cockiness, is present. Poor, yes; defiant, always. Want to be killed? Look sideways at someone in a bar and when you leave, he will be waiting to plunge his family's stiletto, handed-down from one generation to the next, into your neck."

Antonello nodded in agreement, as Peter studied the villagers and workers scurrying down the street to their simple abodes.

"Si, Peter, like all the elderly on our island, they believe, 'Quid est enim novi, hominem mori, cujus tota vita nihil alud quam ad mortem iter est?' That is Latin for 'What new thing is it then for a man to die, whose whole life is nothing else but a journey to death?'"

"Who said that?" Peter quizzed, frowning.

"Seneca, the ancient Roman. Lucius Annaeus Seneca, a statesman and philosopher."

With that, the convoy exited the village, pulling away with no one glancing back, or at the Sulphur mining district on the nearby mountain slopes. Speed again was increased to its maximum as the road now led straight and wide to the Calatafimi crossroad and down to Tropani.

No island twilight in the world could match that amber-colored evening of Western Sicily. Peter was silent as he sat between Antonello and Salvatore in the backseat of the lead jeep. Consumed by anxiety over the bandit-king's promised revelation of the source regarding the mysterious information about Aliandra and her family, he drowsily gazed upon the Largomarsino homeland as it rolled by at more than 60 mph. He murmured softly to himself, "This sun-drenched island of olive groves and sulphur mines, where loyalty is paramount, a bond of blood, and insult and infidelity demanding murder, is truly fascinating. With Aliandra, I will return to Sicily, first to retrieve Mama Anna and the new addition to our lives, the cackling hen Aliandra will name, then to study the history to know the land, to love its people. Look at how dazzling the landscape, especially the rocky terrain."

"Well said, Peter," smiled Antonello, a slight smile dancing across his sleeping lips.

"Si, si," echoed Salvatore. "No Sicilian can say it better."

"You two heard what I said to myself? Above the knocking, jolting motors?"

"I even heard you," Colonel Napier smiled as he turned to him from his front seat. "But always remember, Lieutenant, and I'm certain you are sensitive about it, Sicily, including little Capuana back there, were ravished last year as the Germans retreated to the Messina straits, then Italy's mainland. This part of Sicily was at the bottom of the list for food priorities, causing the civilians the cruelest sort of revenge by the laughing German SS, and by Musso for them allowing him to rule so long. Starvation was rampant. It was awful, as us allies came across children with bloated bellies. It made many of even the toughest of the tough of our troops cry."

Antonello said quietly, "At our estate, Mama emptied all the cupboards to share what we had. Papa and I went out every morning to buy, even steal from the Germans, what foods we found, knew about, or could buy to feed the families nearest us."

"We know, Antonello, we know, and because the Mafia of Palermo profited from the black market, they began to kill the leaders of the organized village groups who helped the starving. This was why your parents were gunned down on the road on their way home."

After several tedious minutes driving in the early evening shadows, the convoy finally reached its destination, circumventing downtown Trapani to enter the Ansado yard and port where several destroyers and a minesweeper were berthed.

By then, dusk had darkened black and as usual in late November evanesced into a bewildering starlit brilliancy. Antonello smiled, and, nudging Peter, pointed to the center of the wide harbor.

"Oh how I love this time of night when the cold evening mist thickens into the coastal fog that always envelopes the western seashores, tidelands, and beaches of the Gulfo di Castellamore, then floats across Palermo to the south, all the way to Mazara. On all the islands of Mare Mediterraneo, the country people sit in the hills on the western side and watch the invasion of the cooling fog."

Upon recognizing Colonel Napier and his MPs, the Gate Control Officers waved the three-vehicle convoy through the heavily guarded razor-wired, high fence entrance into the vast Trapani Allied Naval Base. More than 100 machine-gun-bearing sentries mingling about attentively observed the jeeps accelerate and press toward the harbor piers as the wind freshened, intensifying the air's chilly nip. To Peter, more than a few miles from the waterfront, all seemed peaceful under the bright illumination of the starts and port lights.

"Battles are still ranging north of Rome, colonel, shouldn't the harbor be blacked out?" Peter shouted over the din of the jeeps.

"Not really," Napier responded, again turning towards Peter. "The last German controlled airfield capable of launching bombers to reach us is in Southern France, above the seaport of Marseille near Montreux and Lago di Ginevra. They can barely reach Northern Corsica, let alone Western Sicily. Proximity is too far."

Trailing a long 50 Army truck convoy that had minutes before preceded the Napier party, the jeep drivers were forced to slow to less than 30 mph, allowing Peter to further study the Trapani Naval base and harbor.

First to capture his attention was the removal of permanent Italian Navy batteries. Napier turned again, "Installed by Mussolini when he was in his heyday, the late 30s when the Itie ships were in the best of health, vigor, and prime domination of his 'mares', seas Ligure, Tirreno, Mediterraneo, Ionio, Adriatico, one of the batteries had massive 16-inch guns, another 12-inch, and two 6-inch."

"Very impressive," Peter acknowledged.

"Soon," he continued, "the 21st Coast Artillery Regiment will arrive to deploy mines at the harbor entrance and provide heavy antiaircraft guns. In addition to the mines, we plan for our underwater harbor defenses to include Navy magnetic loops and hydrophones for the detection of submarines. Radar and searchlights will provide additional detection resources. Our combination of coast and harbor defenses are known as the 'Harbor Entrance Control Post Sicily' (HELPS)."

"Why are these installations needed? The Germans are almost defeated and the war sure won't see any more ships because they don't have any more other than U-boats. There's no need for all this."

"Oh, yes there is," chuckled Napier as the two convoys, truck and jeep, rode toward the piers and docks, only moments away now.

"What country are we taking flight for next?"

"La Russia with all their millions of Soldati," answered Salvatore, with a laugh.

"Huh?"

"He's right," the colonel agreed soberly. "Everyone, especially the brass, are talking about it. If the Russians take Berlin before we do, they'll continue over the Alps and grab Rome. And, since Palermo belongs to Italy, the commies will be right down here in a jiffy with their Black Sea Navy coming around the bend at Cape Passero."

Like us and the Germans, the Reds know the importance of the deep-water Trapani access to the bay and its important wharves."

As the convoys began pulling up to anchorages, the well-illuminated port provided a series of memorable Naval images Peter would call upon during the rest of his life. First and by far the most impressive, was the scene of the destroyers, two American and one British, lying at their buoys with steam up, wires slipped, and beginning underway maneuvers. Behind them, all sorts of boats and crafts, including 40-foot Italian trawlers, were zigzagging or sweeping the harbor waters for mines. Lying at their buoys were two large white U.S. Hospital ships, huge red crosses painted on the side of each. And, in the night starlight, a destroyer was limping in with a heavy list, spattered with splinter holes.

"She had a duel with a coastal gun at La Spezia in the Gulfo di Genova, was wounded as you can see, but sailed slowly, bleeding all the way down here under her own steam. A miracle, but easily achieved. She did that in less than 10 hours," said the colonel proudly.

All around them as the jeeps pulled up to the minesweeper, ships were being loaded, some unloaded, some both loaded and unloaded at the same time. Peter saw clearly supplies were coming in from the states in bulk lots. They had to be dumped on the dock, sorted, classified and reembarked. Even under the bright lights, all the docks of Trapani seemed in disarray. It was all a military man or jeep could do to walk or inch a way through as soldiers and sailors worked at double time. In the harbor behind these shadowy figures exercising their brains and brawn were several Sicilian-style sloops slipping, sliding, and gliding across the calm, glistening night waters. Further out, a flotilla of deep-water vessels, small and loaded with nets and hooks, sped west to work the early morning catches. For Peter, all, including the high cliffs of the Salemi Range to the east, and the islands of Egadi, Marettimo, and Favignana to the west with their engulfing sea, including the black sky with sparkling glitter, seemed to blur into each other. The garlic odor of the wharf upon which the jeeps parked was stronger than the smells of its lubricants, oils, and gasoline. Since stevedoring was at its peak, no one seemed to notice.

"Well, boys," exclaimed Napier, "we've arrived in the heart of the beehive. And, there she is, the pride of the old Italian Navy, the 'Mario Sonzini'. Isn't she a beauty, illuminated by the lights and stars? I haven't forgotten I told you it was to be a destroyer which would sail you to your destination. By the way, your sealed orders will be presented to you after you board. But isn't she a princess?"

For a long moment as those in the lead jeep sat back and studied the 7,600-ton light cruiser, "Mario Sonzini," converted in 1940 into a minesweeping, minelaying gunboat. With eight 152mm forward 6in guns arranged in four twin centerline mountings, two forward and two aft with turrets whose maximum range extended to 17,000 yards, the ship was still one of Italy's most formidable fighting boats.

"Che barca!" exclaimed Antonello, wide-eyed with surprise. "What a boat! And painted in camouflaged whites, blacks, and light matt greys, 'grigio cenerino chiaros'. She is so beautiful in the bright light. Is she just as brilliant inside?"

"Yes," responded the colonel. "But the disguised scheme in greys, blacks, and whites, identical on both sides of the boat, impresses me more than her big guns."

"Well," Antonello agreed, "she is certainly neither a zattera, a raft, or a canotto canoe! I'm just happy she is Italian and not German."

As a Trapani Naval Base Control Officer hurried down the ship's main moveable gangplank to greet the convoy party, Napier commented,

"Boys, get ready for pure springy buoyancy. Less than a minute, I'll be turning you three over to Major Contantino Zaino, the Sicilian-American born in Brooklyn who serves as the AFHQ Chief of the Allied Forces Headquarters of the Commander of the Fifth U.S. Army, General Mark Clark. I can tell you fellas now that you were to receive your orders directly from General Clark himself in my office at the airfield. But when we pulled up there, if you recall, I was called to the interbase telephone and, without comment, listened for a full minute, then hung up. I was being informed to bring you here. I also learned it wasn't the H.M.S. Hursley of the British Navy that was to deliver you to a secret rendezvous on the mainland below La Spezia. It was to be this cruiser, 'Mario Sonzini'. Also new to me, General Clark was to be on board! The German High Command in Berlin knows he is in Sicily, and, of course, wants to assassinate him. Putting him on the Sonzini is a brilliant, important supersecret deception. The three destroyers we watched depart simultaneously undoubtedly fooled the Germans into believing he was on one of them. Their aircraft are already in the air to bomb all three in hope and belief they might kill him and his AF command, if they sink all three. Now, he will be with you all the way."

With Major Zaino scampering across the dock toward them, the four climbed out of their seats in the lead jeep as he shouted,

"Greetings, gentlemen! Come, come with me aboard! The commander awaits! We depart the moment you step on deck. The Germans search for him now. We must get out to the open sea, pronto!"

As the major vehemently shook Colonel Napier's hand in appreciation for a job well done, followed by various arrivedercis and hands clasping hands and shoulders, including the officers of the Military Police security escort, Peter, Antonello, and Salvatore were led up the ramp and on board.

Zaino was a pudgy man, gray-haired, obviously highly able and intelligent, yet affable, suggesting a whimsical, loveable nature. Peter smiled as he whispered to Antonello,

"He may hint having a heart of gold, but beneath that cheerful paunchiness, I'm sure he's an officer with a solid steel pot belly capable of taking on and subduing a whole SS division. He has to have one if he's the Chief of Staff to the Commander of the Fifth Army. It's up to him to make all the lesser decisions of handling a whole army and initiating operations. We let him live instead of shooting him. Originally before the war, like so many Italians, he loved Musso. He is not Sicilian, but from Cosenza in Basilicata. Up there, they grew the filthy fascistas like rotten Calabria figs. Bit in 1941, even at the most dangerous time, he spied for us and provided my Papa with German and Italian documents he photographed. Only God could have helped him had the Gestapo or SS caught him doing it here at the Trapani Naval base."

"A good man," nodded Peter.

"Unquestionably," echoed Antonello. "Now he wears the uniform, shoulder sleeve and cuff insignia of the Air Transport Command, US Army Control Officer, and, when General Clark is on grounds in Sicily, serves as both his temporary adjutant and Chief of Staff. After the Armistice of September 3rd last year, Zaino came out and revealed he was at heart a partisan. The Palermo faction underground had him against the wall to execute him until one of my men intervened. Now he wears the 'gladio' insignia of Roman hero with 'Italia' inscribed."

"Well, men," Zaino smiled as he led the way up the gangplank past sailors loading the final crates into gangway bulwarks onto the deck's main passageway, "Listen to our men down there in the cargo hold singing the popular song, 'Funiculi Funicula'. They are very proud of their little 'Castello', a castle on the Mediterraneo. Of all the ships once in the now-defunct Italian Navy, the 'Mario Sonzini', by the way, assigned the name of the leader of a mercenary band of military adventures in Renaissance Italy, was always ordered to engage in the hardest, most dangerous assignments, especially that of the leading costal convoys. Because she is so fast, her performance records are glorious. But, at the same time, she takes on the heaviest casualties. Because she has 18 torpedo tubes and can launch a scouting airplane for anti-submarine attacks, she is also used as a training vessel. Mussolini once poured half the Italian treasure into maintaining her because the 'Castello' is capable of sinking capital ships, cruisers like herself, destroyers, merchant ships, and small Naval crafts. On July 30th, 1943, after the fall of Fascism, she was instantly confiscated by the German Navy and renamed UJ2111. Then, anchored in one Trapani harbor when the Allies invaded Sicily down the coast, the Germans forgot all about her! They had placed mines all over the boat to scuttle her. And, here was a ship capable of 37 knots with sufficient range to run around and shoot havoc in the invading forces! And, the stupid Germans left her alone!"

"No! No!" Salvatore spoke up vigorously as the group continued along the deck, walking past Turret 2, the Armoured Gun Director, the accesses to the boiler room, crew accommodations, and the forward magazines to an unmarked hatchway adjacent the walkway. Pulling up the lid, Zaino led the way down the narrow passageway wall rungs.

"In case German sea commands come aboard looking for the boss, they would have to climb down this way. To get out in case we're sinking, there's a secret ramp upward from his suite. And, Salvatore Giuliano, what do you mean 'No! No!'?"

"The Germans are not stupid. It was our Partisans who saved the 'Mario Sonzini'."

"How so? Never heard that before."

"*Si, si!* I sent my representatives to meet General Patton, General Truscott, and Colonel Gavin at the important Piano Lupo crossroads to tell them to slow down their invasion of Sicily because we had our partisans in talks with Field Marshal Albert Kesselring at La Spezia who wanted to retreat, first from Sicily, then up the 'boot' of Italy to Austria. Kesselring told Hitler the war was lost and there was no point in wasting German lives. Because the Field Marshal is too popular with the German armies, Hitler has not shot him. The American generals agreed to slow down but insisted that the 'Mario Sonzini' stay anchored here in the harbor of Trapani. If she came out to fight the landings or escaped to Genoa or La Spezia or was blown up and sunk to the bottom, the agreement was over. Kesselring agreed. The generals of America and Great Britain agreed, and my partisans then sought the help of General Alfredo Guzzoni of the Italian VI Army in charge of all six of Sicily's coastal divisions. Almost all Italian troops hate the Germans. As you know, not one wanted this war. Almost all were and are sympathetic to America and England. 'Sonzini' was not scuttled because the Germans forgot to sink her or were too busy running away to sink her. She survived because the great American generals, the realistic Kesselring, and our pro-American, decent, General Guzzoni worked together to save her. Now, this big boat fights with us against the Nazis."

"I heard rumors to that effect," responded Major Zaino, "but nothing official. Now I know. And, if anyone saw the happening first-hand, up close, it was you, Salvatore Giuliano. Be sure and share all you know with General Clark. He'll be very interested and happy to know these details about the ship he is now on and will disembark from at Livorno to meet with his fighting troops up there."

Having descended from the platform deck to the upper deck, the group made their way down the long galley between the day and sleeping cabins of the Chief-of-Staff and Captain, the sizable officers' briefing room, to halt before the day and sleeping cabins of the Admiral. Beyond these cabins were the officers' pantry, galley, and refrigerated food storage units.

Peter noted at least a dozen heavily armed MPs stationed at various strategic defensive points throughout the upper and lower deck areas, especially near the officers' day and sleeping quarters. He sensed others were on the main deck, although so well concealed they were invisible.

As the Trapani Naval Base Control Officer raised his knuckles to tap on the Admiral's day cabin door which the Commander of the Fifth US Army was temporarily occupying for the quick two-day voyage, the double half-doors of the adjacent officer's small pantry swung open. A personable-appearing officer of medium height in a freshly ironed short-sleeved Army shirt, holding a large cup of steaming coffee, walked through and upon seeing the four, smiled broadly, a shine with quick intermittent gleams in his eyes as he greeted,

"Well, gentlemen, just in time! Go on in and help yourselves to freshly brewed cups of java flown in last night form a North African coffee plantation. I've been waiting for you all afternoon. Feel the boat pulling away from the pier now that her lines are in? We'll be underway before our second sips. Go back down the corridor to the ship's briefing room and wait for me. I have two short calls to make to London from my apartment and will join you before you finish your cups. My G-3, Brigadier General Donald Brann, is the only one in there. He just arrived only an hour or so, just about the time you hit the airfield, from the island of Egadi aboard one of our Naval Patrol Torpedo (PT) boats anchored in the harbor there. Egadi is our rear echelon headquarters, but we're both in transit to Anzio, then Rome for permanent residence near the Vatican until the war is over, which I'll have orders for you three helping to achieve. I know all of you, but you don't know me."

With that, Major Zaino stepped forward and exclaimed, "Meet General Mark Clark, Commander of the Fifth U.S. Army. He will issue you your first order working together."

CHAPTER ELEVEN

"...your mission is behind enemy lines."

As for Peter during those minutes that seemed so tumultuous, he was hard-pressed to define, especially to himself, the emotions he felt upon not only embarking on the light cruiser, but also the pending sit-down with the only Allied officer Winston Churchill, British war leader, referred to as "...enormously intelligent, a man of high ability and powerful drive, a true American eagle."

Also intimidating was that Lieutenant-General Mark Wayne Clark, commanding general of the US Fifth Army, was known to succeed General Harold Alexander as Commander of the Allied 15th Army Group.

Earlier, when escorted up the "Mario Sonzini" midship gangplank by Major Costantino Zaino, with Antonello and Giuliano trailing, Peter had reflected,

"For such a short sail, and God only knows where to, there's little combat loading. Yet, it appears intense, with a sense of urgency. What's the rush? I supposed if I were eight or ten years younger, I'd be filled with the 'pick up and shove off right now!' attitude, too. But with Aliandra now an integral, intrinsic part of me, it's a whole different story. I have a new responsibility--to survive and get back to her, our future and begin our family. She and her parents, especially Papa, would be so proud of me if I accomplish whatever I'm assigned to do."

As a "Sonzini" steward opened the Briefing Room door to Zaino's soft knock, Peter, the second admitted, took in every detail, recalling the ancient

Italian adage, "Turning points in one's life have a way of stamping on one's mind the small concomitant details'.

Barren other than a dozen or so aluminum chairs, each with a soft green cushioned seat and backed with a blue and gold embroidered fabric depicting a hand grasping a red Roman sword superimposed on a wreath of oak, the room's only furnishings including four long, highly polished mahogany tables were stunning. Oversized portraits of Hitler and Mussolini, and photographs of their immediate admirals, and historic Naval heroes who donned the walls across from the ship's side portholes were replaced with sizeable maps of the coats of Italy and Sicily, including Golfo di Venezia, Golfa di Taranto, the Straits of Messina, the Golfo di Genova, and Corsica and Sardegna.

"The pride of the Italian Navy before the Armistice and the removal of Musso, now distinguished by maps!" whispered Antonello. "The 'Mario Sonzini' had the honor of leading the surrendered Italian fleet into Malta in September of '43. She is so obviously maneuverable; she'll sail us right up to the front door wherever we're going."

G3, Brigadier-General Donald Brann, had put down the stereoscope through which he had been combining two aerial images simultaneously of the remaining fleet of German controlled Italian torpedo boats and small convoy escorts to gage and solidify their water depths. Anchored off Rapallo on the Riviera di Levante north of Chiavari, they were all the enemy the Allied Navies could expect to encounter afloat in late 1944.

"Come in, boys," he greeted, a welcoming grin on his face, as he leaned back in his chair, hands clasped behind his head. "While all the attention is aiming our might north to rout the Huns out of Italy, we mustn't neglect the threat to our shipping lanes. Troops and supplies, boys, supplies and troops. That's what wins wars!"

Peter relaxed, telling himself, "I'm going to enjoy this pleasant, friendly officer." Well over the age of 50, white-haired, somewhat impressive with powerful shoulders atop a medium-sized solidly built body, his wide eyes in a once-handsome face suggested a good-natured, gentle personality.

"Well, well, the three crypts in tow have finally arrived," he chuckled as he stood up and extended his hand across the reddish-yellow hued table in an enthusiastic manner.

"You, I know, Major Zaino of Brooklyn. But of these two cryptic, I supposed the hefty, good-looking Sicilian-complexioned one is the Salvatore Giuliano one everybody is talking about. The other Sicilian-skinned one has to be the Mafioso son and best friend of gangster Vito Genovese, and you, young Lieutenant, have to be the chaser and catcher of those soldiers who go around killing fellow soldiers!"

Everyone nodded good-heartily, as the G3 beamed laughingly in delight. "Yes," he concluded, "the Three Crypics!"

As Antonello, Giuliano, and Zaino enjoyed a moment of trifling chitchat, Peter in contemplative thought, looked past the four and gazed through the string of window portholes along the hull size of the Sonzini briefing room.

Having cast off from her berth, and inching starboard, the light cruiser's slow momentum yielded a rare star and moonlit view of Trapani in utter tranquility. Neither starvation nor German attack from the air or sea was possible as the area's population looked forward to the new year of 1945. Early-to-bed Sicilians were grateful of the absence of burning buildings, vehicles, and bodies, in addition to the faint echoes of gunfire heard from across the Mare Tirreno's Stretto di Messina in Calabri.

For a long moment, it seemed to Peter he was observing the harbor, port, and city in the darkness through numerous eyes. It was as if he was simultaneously staring, listening to the sounds of the ship's movements, and calculating impressions commingling with his emotions. Mesmerizing were the barely distinguishable forms of sailors and tars silhouetted in motion by the tiny beams of deck lights aboard the small vessels of a flotilla on its way in from the sea. He flashed on a passage from one of his favorite authors, John Dos Passos, who wrote in the mid-1930s,

"So shattering was World War I that its tragic blast, still felt to this very moment, blew out the light of Diogenes' lamp. Millions of soldiers, sailors, and volunteers never returned home. I feel the fiery breath from the inferno on my neck as a more ferocious one approaches."

Looking past Antonello, Giuliano, Zaino, and Brigadier General Brann, then the small fleet of ships beginning maneuvers to anchor, Peter pondered the future of safeguarding Aliandra, her mortality in a postwar world of enduring peace. Would he be alive to ensure her safety and security, stalling her inevitable submission to eternity?

Suddenly, the briefing room door swung open and Lieutenant-General Mark Clark, commanding general of the U.S. Fifth Army, hurried in clutching his cup of coffee, obviously replenished, evidenced by its obvious steaming vapor. Under that arm was a large folder. He greeted, as the five pulled the silvery metallic chairs back and sat down. Peter, nearer the side portholes, sat the most distant from the head of the tables. Brann chaired himself between Clark and Zaino, followed by Giuliano, Antonello, then Peter. The commanding general half-waved a greeting, then sat down with the somewhat weary, rumpled-clothed travelers.

With his folder and cup of coffee in front of him on the table, the general leaned back, looked up, and smiled,

"You three men of daring deeds deserve a better welcome than this. Granted, hardly have you arrived from a long day's journey through Western Sicily when you're confronted with communique to board a boat for passage to inevitable danger, if not almost certain death. But I assure you the official, confidential envelope in that folder is of the utmost importance from the Allied highest-ranking military body in the European body."

After pausing a moment to study the three arrivals, he focused upon Peter,

"You, sir, I presume are the Naval Lieutenant Toscanini Secretary of the Navy, Jim Forrestal speaks so highly of. Somehow, in his new position as secretary after Frank Knox's death this last April, he dispatched me a copy of an official memorandum submitted the Joint Chiefs of Staff, their eyes only, of your work tracing and tracking murderers who multiple murder in wartime their own troops. He wrote you are deeply interested in probing the deepest layers of the human mind, the so-called psyche, to collect insights, maximum insights to help local police better understand and therefore track and capture such multiple killers. The Secretary of the Navy, upon the recommendations of so many in the medical services, feels you can 'read' personalities so well that your mind should be put to use in helping end the war sooner. Upon discussion among themselves, I understand the Chiefs decided upon your first assignment. Your orders are in this unmarked envelope take it. And, the body tape I brought. You are to tape it to your chest and read it tomorrow at noon as the ship approaches the Island di Capraia. I am to say nothing further. The orders detail all. These two men next to you are under your command and will obey any or all orders assigned. Both are known where you are going. First, they will serve as your bodyguards, protecting you at the costs of their lives. Furthermore, they are known to all members of the resistance throughout Italy. The resistance has its areas' partisans ready and available to support, if necessary.

In short, your mission with two able assistants is secret and behind the lines. Now, unbutton your shirt and allow me to watch as you tape the envelope under your neck hidden by your winter clothing."

As Peter immediately began to remove his sweater and unbutton his shirt, Clark went on to address Salvatore. While doing so, the Lieutenant had a few moments to observe the Lieutenant General.

"Being in the Pacific these past few years, I have to admit I don't know much about this General Clark. Antonello and I heard on the flight over the Atlantic that Clark was a West Point graduate, a wounded combat veteran of World War I. We heard that his close friend is General Eisenhower. We also heard that British Prime Minister Winston Churchill considers him one of America's three best generals."

"As I look at him, I see a tall, slender man with a handsomely shaped head, hands strong and unblemished, immaculately groomed, including polished shoes, overly so. In these few seconds as he settles himself and considers us, I see an officer devoid of any impetuosity whatsoever. There's an unmistakable air of breeding about him, a southern gentleman type. Soft-spoken, with an innate kindness. I like this man and would gladly serve under him, any day, any time. He's good, no question about it."

Addressing Salvatore Giuliano sitting quietly, leaning forward on the table, hands clasped, the farm boy from the hills who not only became a grown-up Robin Hood stealing from the rich and feeding the hungry hardworking peasants of the field, but also the most disrepute bandit in

Italian-Sicilian history. Good thing you agreed to help us by serving as Peter's aide and bodyguard. Thus far, you haven't killed any of the people you kidnapped and held for ransom; the politicians, the police officials, dukes and princes, never anyone in the clergy, but anyone else you can get money from. You are a man of the mountains who descends at will, sweeping toward the rich of the cities, robbing, robbing, robbing. In all Sicily, only the villagers in your hometown of Montelepre have any regard for you. Young, savage, violent, an idealistic elusive who believes Sicily belongs more to New York than Italy and Rome. But your hatred of Germans and Mafia endears you to all of us, and, perhaps, once the war is over, we'll see to your forgiveness, if you vow to atone your wrongdoings."

Salvatore, absorbing every word, weighing its innuendos and nuances for meaning, every inhalation and exhalation for subtleties of support, and any vellicating movements hinting the barest acceptance, smiled ear to ear.

"Si, si, generale. Si, si."

Clark then turned his attention to Antonello, who sat smiling warmly.

"You, sir, from the village of Montelepre, the same as Salvatore, I learn you, too, are a bandit, but Mafia-style. Correct?"

"Oh, no, *generale!"* responded Antonello, vehemently. "We knew each other as boys. I am six or eight years older. He followed everywhere, even in Palermo. I attended the Universita degli Studi di Palermo to learn English and study law. Because his family was so poor, Salvatore was sent to work in the fields to prevent his people form starving. He is my friend and I love him, am loyal to him, as I love Peter Toscanini, as I am loyal to him sitting next to me."

Perplexed, Clark asked more out of curiosity than in prying inquisitiveness,

"But are you not the son of a well-known Mafioso? Is Montelepre a village of criminals or heroes?"

Everyone laughed.

"*Generale,* when my parents were massacred one evening on the road driving home by either Il Duce or Vito Genovese and cohorts in the Camorra Unione Corse, the Stoppaglieri, or the Mafia in Naples and Palermo. I think Vito was asked their killing by Musso. Someday I will learn, and vengeance will be mine alone."

"*Generale,* only Sicilians know the meaning of the vendetta. And, I tell you now, Antonello, before we left Castelvetrano this afternoon, I asked Papa to try harder to learn who did that craven act. We don't ask Don Calogero Vizzini because he may be involved. But we have our people in all Sicily and Naples listening. Soon, we will know. And, friend, Antonello, I will stand behind you as the vendetta is fulfilled."

After a long pause in which everyone, including Peter, smiled to himself, Clark looked to Antonello as if to ask, "Continue".

"Well, *generale*, that very night, my people smuggled me aboard a ship to South America, then Texas, and New York where I became a driver for the beast, Vito, who had returned to New York undercover, also a ship to Buenos Aires, then New Orleans, and New York. I drove the car for the assassin Carmine Galante to shoot Carlos Tresca last year."

"Yes, I know the story from that point, Antonello 'Zolli' Audisio. Yes, my friend, the FBI in New York has its sources, too. We know you are not a 'Zolli', and we know that if necessary, you will give your life for Peter. You will be pardoned after the war to return to Monterey, or anywhere in America, to begin a new life. Both you and Salvatore, true Sicilian brothers, deserve peace and freedom for your loyalty and patriotism to Sicily, Italy, and America. Survive with Peter what you are about to undertake. Each of you three exudes valour extraordinary and truly heroic. You will not be forgotten, even if you do not return by us, the Supreme Headquarters of the Allied Expeditionary Force."

With that, Clark and Bann stood up, signaling the end of the meeting. And, amid the extensive handshaking engaged in by all the participant, Peter stepped forth and inquired if upon return of his mission he and Antonello could visit with Aliandra's youngest of two brothers, put Allesandro Largomarsino serving under his command in the U.S. 5th Army.

"Lieutenant, if you return safely from your mission, and notify my headquarters where you are, I give you my word that I will personally drive you to his whereabouts. Meanwhile, give my G3, Brigadier-General Brann, his full name and other personal data to assist searching our records."

"For that promise alone, General Clark, I will return."

With that, Brann spoke up,

"Gentlemen, step to my right. I have for each of you a 7.62mm automatic pistol Berretta; small, powerful, easy to conceal, probably the best of all small weapons in this war."

"And, men," added Clark, "as you adjust to them, let me say one last thing to you three before being escorted to your sleeping quarters for this night. By the time you awaken, my staff and I will have disembarked off the central coast of the mainland, between Anzio-Nettuno and Lido-di-Romo and Ostia. While you're having breakfast, I'll be at my Allied SHAEF, Supreme Headquarters, Allied Expeditionary Force, headed by Eisenhower, although Ike is still in London about to transfer his SHAPE, Supreme Headquarters Allied Powers in Europe to Paris. Remnants, isolated, but well concealed and camouflaged of the German-manned Italian torpedo boats and a dozen or so fighters of the 19th Luftwaffe Field Division hidden in the caves of the Lombardia Casimaggiore hills."

"And, as I mention 'Air Force', tuck this fact somewhere in your memory vaults: Should you, God forbid, be captured by Italian fascist or German SS Troops, always search for an officer wearing an irregular, atypical uniform. It'll stand out as 'strange' beside SS black and fascist gray. You can't make out its rank or nationality. But the officer wearing it is on our side, vehemently anti-Nazi. He'll be wearing an all-forest green matching jacket and pants, long-sleeve shirt a shade lighter than the forest green. An orange marchese crest on the right side where medals are usually worn. He will be one of a hundred aide-de-camps to the Italian King, Victor Emmanuel III. He's ceding his sovereign rights to his only son, Crown Prince Umberto. Although a virtual abdication and Mussolini long gone, that royalty still impresses the Huns, Hitler in particular. We'll learn instantly where they are taking you, unless it's to Berlin where hopefully you'll not be hung or shot but can sit out the war. If you are sent to a camp in German occupied Northern Italy, the aide-de-camp will arrive at the camp gate with a truckload of fascist-looking police and demand you three, or whomever among you is there, be released. Crown Prince Umberto, the new king of Italy. Every Italian and Sicilian of worth is on our side and have been since the war began. So, men, always, always be alert for that crest which, Lieutenant, I'm sure Antonello and Salvatore will draw for you so you recognize it."

"Now a final note, which deals with a hero to all of us, even the Italians. That man, of all men, is, believe it or not, the comic strip Buck Rogers of the 25th Century! Ike reads all the western novels of Zane Grey, Charles Stewart White, among others, while many of his generals follow America's favorite funnies in 'Stars and Stripes', our daily army newspaper. Buck Rogers is always boldly fighting evil, getting captured, being rescued, or manages to escape. Every day, it seems, he is exposed to execution."

"Well, hero Toscanini, you, within hours from now, will be fighting evil. Yes, be bold, be somewhat daring, but never reckless. Do not get captured. Avoid it at all costs. Read your orders. Antonello and Salvatore will follow your orders but will not know of the mission until the end. No man can withstand the torture that comes with capture. If they don't know where they are going or what they are supposed to do, they cannot reveal information, even if cut open. Upon reading the mission orders, burn them, or eat them, or throw them overboard to disintegrate in the choppy Mediterranean."

After a moment of reflection as he looked down at his feet, his right hand fingering his chin,

"Oh, and know that you three are to stay away from the eastern parts of Italy, Venice in particular. The city is suffering under a catastrophic flooding. High tides have put the canal city in a state of emergency. God help you all if you get caught in an inundated devastation while the Gestapo is at your necks."

Smiling broadly, Commander Clark looked into the eyes of the three men,

"Your sleeping quarters will be in the big executive cabin suite reserved for admirals and Mussolini when traveling the surface. The pantry attendant is preparing a quick supper, and it's probably waiting on the burners now. The bunk in my office will do for tonight. We're making a quick sprint of only 230 nautical miles, north by northeast, which, if no interruptions, will put us off Nettuno north of Anzio. A small caravan will pick us up for a coastal drive up to the small Ostia port at Lido di Roma.

"Now, go eat men. Sleep well, then, in the morning, eat fulfilling breakfasts for you will begin the journey to what my advisers believe is virtual sudden death."

"You won't forget my request to locate Allesandro Largomarsino?" Peter reminded Commander, softly.

"I'm on my way to the ship's radio room. If I get a report back before disembarking, I'll slip it under the cabin door. If not, when I learned you returned, and where I will honor my pledge and drive you to him. Now, get something in those stomachs, and close those eyes!

CHAPTER TWELVE

Disaster!

Long after dusk had deepened over the Mare Meditterraneo, and the low, sleek shape of the "Mario Sonzini", with increased speed, slid through the choppy waters, Peter stood stalwartly at the deck railing of the stern gazing into the void of midnight.

Although the hefty furred collar of his double-breasted pea jacket braced the Lieutenant's head and neck against the strong Tunisian northeasterlies, he shivered. Less than ten feet behind him was access welcoming the flagging man to an aft stairwell leading down to the Officers' cabins and the Admiral's suite where Antonello and Salvatore had long since succumbed to deep slumber.

"How I hanker for the warmth under thick, full, Navy-blue woolen blankets," he smiled a bit. "I'm so tired. Heck, how many hours was it been since I boarded that plane in Monterey"

Peter was too weary to sleep. He was fevered with thoughts and emotions, the feelings passionate, but controllable and all acquiescing to sensibility. Hours gradually passed in thoughts and half-thoughts. He wondered and wondered until he was near buckling in wonderment, his only solace Aurora, the Roman goddess of dawn, was on her way. Later that day, he would be allowed to rip his top-secret official communique from his chest and learn his mission.

Meanwhile, despite the late hour, the deck was a scene of utter din and confusion. Used primarily as a troop and a merchant vessel transporting munitions and supplies from Trapani to the port facilities of Napoli, Lido di

Roma, and Livorno, every inch of boat space including the decks, were occupied with stores and supplies, boxes and crates, motorcycles and other small vehicles. Since the southern Mare Tirreno waters between Sardegna and the mainland were considered safe from attack, the only foreseen danger was the turbulent weather. Reverently, it seemed to Peter, the petty officers and man clad in khaki uniforms, dungarees, and other light work clothing, totally oblivious to the chill, were at work alongside of welders and shipfitters, with cutting torches, gunners, mechanics, including yeomen, cooks and mess boys! Floodlights illuminated the areas of labor.

Despite the deck activity, Peter mused over all that Salvatore Giuliani had revealed regarding his knowledge of the famed Largomarsino family in Monterey, California. As a Chief Petty Officer and several yeomen carried in and set up two makeshift beds, the bandit king smiled, Peter recalled, chuckling to himself, and said, with Antonello translating,

"Certo. Sei un vomo splendido--coraggioso e coraggioso. Sei un vomo quadranto."

"He says...," interpreted Antonello, turning to Peter, "... certainly because you are a most splendid man, a 'square' man. I think he heard G.I.'s talking about a soldier being a 'square' type of man. That is a high compliment, Peter. I doubt if he pays such compliments to others."

The lieutenant had reached out and shanked Salvatore's hand, nodding and adding,

"Tell him I appreciate being acknowledged as a 'square man'. That's very kind of him. But he meant 'squarest' type of man rather than a 'square' man. Please tell him to continue and that he can trust me with what he says."

"Si, si," countered Salvatore, interjecting, "I understand you. I trust you, Peter Toscanini. You are brave and courageous, *coraggiso e coraggioso! Mi fido di te.* Musso is out and a temporary democratic government is in, wants me dead and sent an expeditionary force out to kill me, but they couldn't. The American Ambassador in Rome is a friend and sympathizes with us who want our own state, and, with cooperation by all, with the United States. Last week, before you two arrived, I wrote to President Truman for aid under the Marshall Plan."

"I tell you all this, Peter Toscanini, to help explain I have my followers all over America, in every state, in every large city in California, too. What unifies us as one party, one group, is that we hated Mussolini, the Mafia, and those who claim individuality when there is none. We want out of Sicily and we want it now."

"I know the people well in Monterey and a committee reports back to me once a month by secret means, which I will never tell you about for their safety. My leaders in Monterey are Elio, Giacomo, Ugo, and Torquato. It's not necessary to mention their last names. They all live within a city street or two from the Largomarsino house."

Peter, impatiently, an edge of irritation in his tone, "Yes, yes, Salvatore. But it is Aliandra and Mama and Papa that affects me. How and what and who do you know about these who are so dear to me?"

"Pazieza, pazienza, mio amico, eroe di Guerra, ispirazione per tutta la vita. Vi dico subito. Patience, patience, my friend, war hero, and lifelong inspiration. I tell you now," Salvatore smiled.

"Our Sicilian people of the separation movement who live in Monterey work at the Pacific Seas, same as Aliandra. One, the second in command of the committee there is also a member of the California Fish and Game Commission. It is this Committee of three; Elio, Giacomo Ugo, and Torquato who rule all the Sicilians of the Central Coast of California. If a young man or woman, boy or girl, becomes deviant, it is the Committee of Three that decides the punishment. The committee runs the Santa Rosalia Festivals, agrees on engagements and marriages and supervises the baptisms. The Committee runs both the Sicilian-Italian fishing community, but also the fishing industry. Even Orazio Anastaio Danta, the Sicilian business agent of the American A.F.&L. reports to the Committee."

Peter nodded somberly as Antonello grinned.

"But there is one man there the Committee meets with and reports to. That man is the head, the leader, the chief and commander, and no one knows who it is, although some suspect. The name of that elder, that overseer, that ultimate authority is Pietro Largomarsino, the father of your beloved Aliandra. And, in that family, the two sons don't know, Mama feels it so, but never speaks of it. The only two who know are Uncle Pasquale and Fausto. Fausto, a cousin on Mama's side, is the shadow of Pasquale, rarely does he say anything, even when his son, 'Ronnie' went missing, presumably killed.

Last year when Americans landed with the British at Salerno in September of 1943. Pasquale, the godfather of Ronnie is still adamant Ronnie is still alive, which he may well be."

Peter studied Salvatore, steadily, hanging on every word. Antonello was suddenly alive with interest, hearing aspects of the family he lived with for more than a year but knew nothing about.

"Peter, your future father-in-law is a most honorable man. He despises the Mafia as much as he scorns the Germans. Few hated Mussolini more than he. To this day, the Largomarsino name is held in reverence in western Sicily, his grandfather remembered and highly regarded. I have heard Pietro is a kind, generous man, but as a leader of his community, he can be ruthless.

You have come late into the family, so I have heard nothing yet. Me? I say you go into a fine family. They, in turn, get a fine, new son."

At that point, Peter, relieved by the account, walked over and did something he had never done before his in entire life. He put his arms around the Bandit King and kissed him on the cheek. Antonello exploded into applause, beaming. With only a smile, the Lieutenant's eyes radiating in joy, looked into Giuliano's, who returned the moment of gazing, and no words were needed between them. Peter turned away, touched Antonello as he passed him on the way to the door where he exited without glancing back.

On deck, Peter, having relieved the discourse, one of the most critical of life, was enlivened with thoughts and reflections, Aliandra at the core of every one of them. Since he was suddenly cheerful, albeit restless, he suddenly felt an overwhelming urge to write a short, heartfelt note to his finance. Since his mission was designated "most secret", he was forbidden to mail any correspondence anywhere. He would simply fold them over and carry them in his pocket. If he was killed and his body found intact, the folded note-sized pages with the Largomarsino address attached would be found and sent by personnel of the War and Navy Department V-Mail service. If he survived, he would hand them to her face to face. Among the brief letters would be several to his parents for her to personally deliver.

Using the handrail as his writing board, Peter, pen in hand, wrote under the dim but nonetheless illuminable deck lights in the pitch blackness,

"Christmas is soon upon us, my Aliandra, and I would gladly give a limb for a six-day leave to come to you. Flying thousands of miles would be worth an hour sitting next to you on Christmas Eve dreaming of the years to come with our little ones."

"Sadly, I cannot look into your eyes and talk to them, nor can I send you a postcard with a sentence or two, let alone a letter, dear Aliandra. Urgent wartime secrecy requirements necessitate no communication between us, or any of us at war who love those at home, lest words or even whispers be read or heard by those who would harm of good men and women and ships. Therefore, what I feel I write and pocket to present to you when I stand before you when this horrific war is over."

Pausing a moment to peer into the vacuousness, Peter noted the weather had weakened, causing the Sonzini to pitch in the increasingly rough water. The calm sea was now smacking stinging slaps against her hull to the point angry geyser-like columns of water gushed high and over the deck with cannon-like thunder.

"Whoa!" the lieutenant grinned. "Feel free, ship Sonzini, to roll, rumble, rat-a-tat-tat, rub-a-dub-dub, all you want, but I'm writing to someone more important than President Roosevelt and your winds, wafts, and whiffles, wags, wavelets, and waves, may break my bones, but will never stop me."

Again, studying the void of darkness for a moment, Peter watched his hand and their fingers holding the fountain pen, begin to write from a subconsciousness hitherto unrealized, despite his comprehension of personality theory.

"Forgive me, my wife-to-be, if I sound sickeningly maudlin, syrupy, and overly hyperbolic. But I struggle to find the right words to compose sentences reflecting what is so deeply heartfelt."

"From this moment in the near freezing blackness of night, I promise, no, vow each and every day to form notes how my whole being soars in gratitude and happiness by just whispering 'Aliandra'--this to bridge the distance between us. Whether I am deceased or can hand them to you with a smile having survived the largest war in World history, the writings will be folded over in my front pocket. All deal with your largeness of spirit, your smile, the joy you bring to all you encounter. The notes will be you."

"Now, well past midnight as I write at the railing of the ship sailing me to a mission of extreme danger, I am nonetheless filled with elation as I hold your hand, looking into your beautiful eyes, envisioning our journey through our lives side by side with our children in hand. Aliandra, my darling, with my good night for this day, let me say this: I am no special warrior. I've never faced an enemy soldier up close. I'd kill him, if I had to, to save one of my own, or myself. Yes, I could do that, I suppose. Yes, I know I would, without question, to return to you."

"So, my sweetheart, I say to you as I enter my most dangerous assignment with the same words I've heard so many of my friends, my fellow soldiers, young men exactly like me, normal, ordinary, decent boys from small and big towns across California, across America, say, 'Please, you and your wonderful family, don't pray only that I will return safely, pray that I have the courage that I do my duty. I will…'"

Then, in less than a fraction of an instant, a lightening-like blinding reddish-orange flash followed by a deafening explosion erupted with a towering geyser of sea water up the height of the Sonzini foremast.

From somewhere in the increasingly broken waves of the Mare Tirreno, either a long, cigar-shaped, self-propelled, explosive-laden underwater projectile or submarine mine, but more unlikely an aerial torpedo from a German Heinkel bomber, slammed forward of midship below the quarterdeck level. Puncturing the three gray belts of armoured steel plated protecting the ship's hull, the Sonzini began immediately listing starboard.

Peter, meanwhile, instantly hurled across the deck by the impact, reeled with ears splitting, stumbling headfirst into the bulkhead of the stairwell leading to the officer's quarters including the Admiral's where Antonello and Salvatore had been startled awake. Banging his head against the cold steel, Peter turned unsteadily and, attempting to stand erect, toppled over semiconsciously at the base of the watertight, fireproof boxlike No. 3 gun turret barbette.

More giddily dizzy than seriously brain-injured, lightheaded concussion, Peter struggled to regain both his balance and consciousness. In doing so, he was vaguely aware of human howling from pure anguish, clanging of alarm bells, a bugler bellowing out general quarters, the bosun shrilly piping, 'All hands to battle stations', 'All hands to battle stations'; the nearby deafening bang-bang-bang of 5-inch, 20 mm A.A. guns firing into the void of night; feet dashing, none walking; more deck orders being shouted, someone screaming to someone atop the Captain's bridge, "No warning, a direct his at point-blank range. We were doing 18 knots, now down to four. Sitting duck for a U-boat."

Scurrying by as the dazed Lieutenant whom they believed had been killed by the massive explosion, corpsmen, doctors, petty officers amid officers of all ranks, ranger finders and signalmen, yeomen, clerical freeholders, mess boys, and other seamen, sailors, and marines were totally oblivious to an inert lump of flesh. Crawling and dragging himself along the smooth No. 3 turret substructure support, Peter seemed to be seeking a place of safety to snuggle in. Fragments of smoke, smell, and shouts in incomplete sentences, isolated words aided in regaining a semblance of sensibility. Of particular concern to himself, as well as Antonello and Salvatore, who were emerging into greater clarity, was a brief agitated conversation between three sailors, a petty officer and two doleful "dockwollpers", hefty mizzenmast mechanics of seagoing turbines.

With the three at the ship's guardrail, their heads looking overboard searching the hull for the detonation point, one of the experienced specialists commented,

"List is increasing. Won't be long before we're under. The VIPs are being evacuated in one of the forward lifeboats. Distress SOS signals through this sea. God help us if we're hit again."

"Grit, man, grit. Show your resilience," his fellow "dockwollper" commented.

The petty officer mused,

"The U-boat either had broken our Allied code to obtain knowledge of the VIP general on board, where he was going, and waited for us, a highly unlikely possibility, or the enemy sub merely moved into a firing position and waited to attack when we sailed by, or when the first convoy came by from North Africa or Palermo on its way to Northern Italy. The Germans wanted to sink our boat to drown General Clark."

At that very instant, the lookouts who only moments before had dashed to their after-guntub stations, began shouting feverishly though megaphones,

"Rippling, agitated surface movement coming toward us! Rippling, foaming starboard beam! Starboard beam! Torpedo! There! There! Fire at will! Fire! Fire!"

Elevated at too steep an angle to fire effectively, the 152mm (6 in) guns, as well as the 150mm/53 cal automatic "rifles", all arranged in four twin centerline mountings, two forward and two aft, in turrets of rectangular flatforms, were virtually useless. The antiaircraft 40mm automatic and

13mm machine guns, aimed upward had insufficient time to shift and pitch their powerful barrels 45-to-90-degree angels.

Suddenly, a dull, deaden underwater thump less than 100 yards off the bow detonated a wide tumulus of drenching spray. The jolt, in addition to vibrating the entire Sonzini, triggered a tidal wave deluging, almost inundating, the listing vessel.

Peter, meanwhile, had managed to upright himself on his knees against the barbette-parapet of fixed armor protecting the big-gun turret. Bracing himself by placing his two hands against its steel side, one flat, the left clenched tightly, Peter heard one of the dockwollpers shout to the other,

"The moderate swells are sure to sink us now that we've been smacked by that tidal."

"Are we taking on water? Feels like the list is increasing," asked the other. "At least the mine or torpedo didn't hit or lift us."

"Who knows what's going on below decks," he responded, then gestured to his right. "Look, his staff is evacuating General Clark into the midship VIP lifeboat, all told six or eight of them. We better see if we're needed in any way. Or, head for the aft life preservers, a boat, dingy, anything of buoyancy. Yeah, I feel we're about to capsize. If the tidal wave of water cascading over the ship didn't turn us over, another torpedo will. Let's go!"

"Wait. We gotta help the sailor out of sorts leaning shaken against the gun wall. Looks like an officer. Yes, Navy 1st Lieutenant by officer rank badge."

Peter turned to the two men seizing his arms and shoulders and smiled,

"Hello, fellas, seems we're in a heap of trouble, right?"

"Yup. And "Abandon ship' calls are about to be ordered."

"Was that a second torpedo that hit us?"

"No. A near-miss that exploded in the sea off our bow launching a big wave at us. Fortunately, it had no real force, although it's increasing our angle of rollover. We're headed for the fantail and hopefully, a lifeboat that's already in the water. Pray we make it before we bounce again."

Under the cold bright moonlight, Peter, hobbling along the increasingly crowded, noisy deck, in the middle of the two dockwollpers, his arms around their necks, muttered,

"My two friends asleep in the officer's cabins, the admiral's suite. I have to go back and get them. And General Clark, too."

"You're quivering from concussion shock. You're not shaking violently, but you are quivering, lieutenant. You can limp along with us, if held up, but you are impaired enough to not go below looking for friends while a ship is sinking. Once you're safe in one of our launches or lifeboats, I'll dash back to see if anyone is still alive, below deck.

"LIST TO STARBOARD INCREASING! LEFT TO RIGHT, LEFT TO RIGHT FACING BOW!" shouted dockwollper No. 2.

"I know, I know," responded his fellow turbine mechanic, "especially now that we're dead in the water."

"LOOK, MAN, LOOK!! A LAST DINGHY, EMPTY FOR MAN, ENOUGH FOR THREE MORE!" shouted the partner.

"MAKE IT FOUR!" shouted the petty officer, rushing up behind them.

"HENRY!!! We gave up on you! Where have you been?"

"Ran forward to help General Clark's staff lower the 10 metre diesel covered launch and get the commander aboard. Just made it. General got away. When I turned to find you fellas, the ship's forepeak was submerged and the sea flooding the bow. Now, I'm right behind you men."

Peter, appearing dazed as he was being roped in preparation to be hoisted to the sea, asked in bewildered wonder,

"If we're at a knot or two, and a hole in her side, how long will it take for a 6,000-ton boat to touch bottom?"

Both dockwollpers looked up in astonishment.

"Good question, lieutenant, good question. I'll let you know once we've entered the 'Pearly Gates'."

"Darn dinghy looks dingy and dismal."

A voice from behind shouted,

"Unless you want to waste time looking around for any remaining 10mm motorboats, you better haul that man down here and jump in yourselves! She's an 8 metre 'unsinkable' pulling boat the Italian Navy has sworn by for years. From my angle down here adjacent the stern anchor hawsepipe, I see the whole forepeak and, under it, the quartermaster's stores under water!"

"In a moment! In a moment!" shouted dockwollper no. 1.

"NO TIME! DROP HIM! DROP IN!" The forward superstructure is tilting. You don't drop him right now, we're not going to have time to get away from the suction as she drowns!"

Finding himself strapped into a waist harness by handrailing rope and dangling over the stern two stories above the pulling boat, Peter, as he was being lowered, noted the throbbing hulk breaking up. Just then, the dominant, tall, superstructure began its wrenching collapse, the straining screeching, high-pitched sounds commingling with the screams, yells, and cries of those still at their posts and stations in the conning and gun director's towers, radio rooms, rangefinder units, chart and wheel houses, crashing to their deaths caused Peter to faint.

As the sole occupant pulled the limp, incapacitated lieutenant to the floor of the wobbling boat, he gently turned the toppled officer over on his back in the short aisle, buffing his own overcoat as a cushion under his head, and extended his legs. Noticing his right arm was inching over its body to locate an opening between the pea coat's buttons as if in search of something, the occupant immediately unbuttoned the hip length, double-breasted jacket. The officer's eyes closed, his mind semi-conscious, he nonetheless was probing himself something vital and important.

Then, as the two dockwollpers and chief petty officer, all three of whom jumped overboard the two stories to plunge into the sea less than 10 yards from the unsinkable pulling boat, the occupant turned away to assist the three crawling into the 8 metre craft.

Soaked and shivering, the three covered themselves with readily available blankets.

"We've got to get away. We'll be sucked down but thank God she's taking her sweet time about sinking," said one of the three.

As the three began rowing frantically, the Sonzini, forward peak pointed down more than 40 degrees, the sea having reached mid-ship, the occupant returned to attend to Peter, who was now fully cognizant.

"Thank you, man, but help me get back aboard. My friends, I'm sure, are trapped on the lower deck. The cruiser is about to go. Please help me."

"Did you find and secure what you're looking for?" asked the occupant.

Peter didn't answer. After blinking in considerable pain, he closed his eyes and was asleep, allowing who appeared to be an American soldier to search and examine what was under his shirt. Unbuttoning the pea coat, the boat's occupant saw that the lieutenant's long-sleeved Navy shirt was partially opened with his right hand flat across the chest. Fingers wide apart as if in protection of something of value and importance, the man in the boat saw that an official letter had been double-taped to his flesh.

Rising to stand before the quiescent Navy man, the occupant noticed his left fist clenching an item so tightly the hand was a shade of blue. It was hard to discern what was so important that he would fight to his death to protect it.

"He won't even allow me to pry it out of his hand," the occupant mused, turning to the three oarsmen.

No one responded as they frantically rowed away from the sea's suction area. Light waves left from the surface vacuum of the Sonzini's sinking had already reached them, lapping gently the little getaway craft. Their lives were no longer at stake, having evaded the sucking force of the vortex, and the four could now search the cold, choppy water for additional survivors.

With the first hint of dawn and scant visibility, the three seamen and soldier managed to haul aboard four additional survivors. Peter was carefully lifted into a sitting position between dockwollper no. 2 and the Army man who had placed his own blanket over the soaked and now shivering lieutenant. Slowly regaining consciousness, he slowly smiled as he glanced around. Despite the increasing breeze, mist hung so low, less than a hundred feet, he could see nothing in the distance.

Then, frowning, he asked worriedly,

"Anyone see Antonello or Salvatore?"

No one said a word as all waited patiently for rescue. Peter, shaking under the two blankets, lowered his head and wept openly and softly. Troubled, and with his muscle strength relaxing, an apparent crumpled thick piece of cardboard or paper fell from his tight grasp, landing near the brown leather boot of the soldier. As Peter instantly bent over to reach for the mashed wad, the soldier, who appeared at first sight to be Asian, picked the lump up. Two words caught his attention as he smiled, handing the folded-over three-page letter back to the lieutenant,

"Dearest Aliandra…"

CHAPTER THIRTEEN

Rammed!

Dousing the bright stars while increasing the chilly winds, the gray drab of dawn creeping over Mediterraneo's Mare Tireno was upon the survivors, suddenly.

By now, seven survivors sat in silence in the rosy light of the cold morning. Peter, as the others, was not only dealing with weariness, but also suffering in despair. The maniacal face of Death had undoubtedly claimed Antonello and Salvatore, and most certainly was nearby to call on him.

But it was Antonello, and Salvatore, too, who consumed his thoughts. God, through Junipero Serra, had sent him to the Post Graduate School in Monterey, California, where, a few blocks away, he met his special friend and Aliandra, his wife to be. Both had opened his heart to the highest forms of friendship and love and now one was gone, until they met one day beyond.

For Peter, who was beginning to slowly regain full consciousness, a feverish passion and longing for Aliandra consumed him. Regrets followed, pouring over his entire being, increasing a depressive pain. But under no circumstance would he unleash pent up tears before men he didn't know.

To quell the gnawing, Peter raised his head and asked softly to no one in particular, yet everyone in the boat,

"If no one picks us up, how far north are we to scull our way north to Sardinia's Gulfo di Cagliari?"

No one responded.

Meanwhile, visibility was unlimited under yet another amazingly clear sky over an increasingly choppy sea.

"Where are the search planes and rescue ships? Nothing on the southern sea horizon above Sicily expect an obvious large convoy headed east toward the Italian Peninsula. The black smoke is a dead giveaway. No German Navy or Airforce down here now except for the U-boat that sunk us," the lieutenant ruminated softly, knowing full well no destroyer protecting the herd of troops and cargo ships would break away to dash into the area searching for survivors, especially if an enemy submarine, or God forbid, a wolf pack or flotilla surfaced simultaneously to loosen torpedoes in every direction within the thick group of ships.

With seawater sluicing off the lifeboat sides in the oily swells, Peter, sullen and shivering, gazed upon the Asian-American who sat on the flooring at his feet smiling up at him. As he returned the friendliness with a nod, the Lieutenant for the umpteenth time ran his fingers over the waterproof envelope taped to his chest. For some unaware reason, he recalled the words of Sigmund Freud, one of the three pioneers in psychoanalytic theory he admired most,

"Any period of a mind's incubation frees the person of gloomy fixations, somber depressions, and dormant fears, anxieties, psychological pain. Emerging from the unconscious planning that goes on during quiet repose, or torpid state of unsocial withdrawal, one sees the future with fresh eyes, summoning strength, faith, bravery, resolve, tenacity, singleness of purpose, gameness and optimism coupled with stamina."

Peter smiled more to himself than the soldier he was gazing upon,

"I'm such an oaf. I always get in trouble when I psychoanalyze myself too deeply. Yes, I won't let my country down, nor you Aliandra, my parents and yours, my wife soon. I am free of gloomy fixations, depressions, fears, pain. I am ready to go forward on my mission. I will read my orders as soon as we are rescued."

Peter, who had again turned his gaze to the southern horizon, returned to study the still-smiling Asian soldier. Smiling himself, the lieutenant said softly,

"Whether you like it or not, soldier, you and those two turbine-mechanics sitting behind us are now my friends for life. I'll talk to them soon enough."

The soldier who sat quietly, his arms wrapped around his knees, nodded in appreciation.

"Are you Nisei?" Peter asked.

"Yes. My parents, grandparents and entire family; uncles, aunts, cousins, are interned at the Topaz, Utah, camp," the soldier responded.

"I'm an Italian-American Naval Lieutenant on special assignment. My entire youth revolved around the Nisei kids in South Stockton, California. Less than four months ago, I was at the Rohwer Internment Camp in eastern Arkansas on the Mississippi River. I've always considered myself half Nisei."

The handshake that followed between the two of them was sincere and heartfelt.

"Now," Peter said laughingly, "Tell me your name."

"My name is Private Kojii Kondo. I'm 21 years old, from Turlock, California, and a bazooka-man with the Japanese-American 100th Infantry Battalion somewhere in the Southern Bologna vicinity. I was scheduled to disembark with the General Clark staff at Ostia near Lido di Roma. I was already on deck and noticed you when you walked up from the officer's quarters. I helped lower the launch because I was strolling past it when the torpedo smacked us."

"Why were you with his staff? You must be a VIP of some sort."

"Yeah, I suppose I am," Kojii laughed, self-deprecatingly.

"How so?"

"Well, I was awarded the Distinguished Service Cross for extraordinary heroism in action on the Fifth Army front. I was scheduled to be flown at noon today to Livorno, then driven to Firenze, and picked up by one of General Patton's staff members and escorted to my unit."

"With M.M. Tozier, Chief, Reports Division of the Department of Interior's War Relocation Authority. They sent me to various cities to tell my story, except places in California. For the first time in my life, walking down the city sidewalk, pedestrians made way for me, seeing my medals and that I was some kind of war hero and being escorted by a small retinue of white officers. Before volunteering for the 442nd and 100th, whites expected me to step in the gutters to make way for them when there was plenty of room for me to simply walk past. In basic training in Arizona, I often heard 'Dirty Jap', 'Remember Pearl Harbor', 'Chink-a-link' by white unable to distinguish Japanese-Americans from Chinese-Americans. Whether I was alone or with other JA soldiers, we heard time and again while passing white males, mostly young men not in the service, say, rudely, almost angrily, 'You Japs, when you see us coming, pass to the right street-side. We Americans pass on the left.'"

"How did you earn the DSC?"

"Well, I was also given a Bronze Star for heroic action under fire and a Purple Heart for wounds received in combat."

"Wow!" exclaimed Peter, eyed widening in awe and respect. "If we get pulled out of this, I'll personally campaign for you to get another one for saving my life. What was the heroic action under fire, and where?"

"After our landings at Anzio, in a place called Frascli on the road to Rome while engaged in a divisionary movement. For my inconvenience, I received a 25-day furlough. Went up to surprise my family at Camp Topaz."

"That's another story I want to hear all about. They must have been so surprised and startled, especially when they saw the Distinguished Service Cross pinned to your chest. Now, again, and don't be so modest in telling me!"

"Aww, it was nothing. I was about 25-30 yards away from a German self-propelled gun which had reached our 100th Battalion sector."

"How'd you get so close to it?"

"I crawled."

"With the bazooka on your back?"

"Strapped over my firing shoulder for quick removal to fire. I was able to fire three quick rounds, knocking it out, and setting its position on fire. Other bazooka men and rifle grenadiers had tried to stop the advancing enemy gun but couldn't. The brass and my fellow 100th battle mates gave me an ovation for my deadly accuracy. After the battle ended, we counted 14 German dead."

"I understood from having spent some time at the Schofield Barracks in Hawaii that the 100th Battalion was made up entirely of Americans of Japanese ancestry from Hawaii. You're from Turlock. How'd that happen?"

"I was a supplement, with about 150 others from the 442 Regimental Combat Team, during the Battle of Cassino. Originally, the 100th was made up of the 299th Hawaii National Guard Unit that during the bombing of Pearl on December 7th, they were sent out to help patrol and guard the beaches of Honolulu in case of a landing."

"Ah, yes, I remember that…", and in mid-sentence, just then, one of the silent, sullen dockwallopers sitting in the back of the swaying, slightly pitching boat stood up pointing out to sea behind him shouted, "LOOK! LOOK!"

Everyone, Peter in particular, instantly swirled around to scan the horizon pointed to. Simultaneously, all seven survivors recognized the unmistakable web-like conning tower of a German type VII U-boat maneuvering directly from astern to aim her bow straight at them. Identification of the submarine was distinctly recognized, due not only to the short distance, but also its one-of-a-kind distinguishing German Naval features including the swastika flag of Nazism.

Under light clouds with ceiling and visibility characteristically unlimited, the lifeboat's occupants stood awestricken mixed with sudden fear. Despite the wind force, choppy sea, and perpetual whitecaps, the shape of the submarine that bore the number 74, a knife wire-cutter on her bow, powerful appearing artillery on her forward and aft decks, as well as all the usual make up, such as the snorkel in a retracted position and aircraft "Kill" markings on the bridge, was on route right toward them!

"Where are our search planes?" yelled the chief petty officer. "The rescue ships, our destroyers?"

"Undoubtedly looking elsewhere," responded Peter. "My guess is that he has been zigzagging all around us for hours, waiting for a cruiser or at the least, a destroyer to stop dead in the water, making for a perfect sitting duck. My guess is he's now less than several thousand yards. He's not going to waste a torpedo on a little boat with a handful of poor survivors crowded in it."

One of the dockwollerpers interjected,

"He's closing fast, and no splash yet."

"And no incoming wake from a torpedo," echoed Peter, "but he's altering his course slightly to come at us. No evasive tactics and closing. Distance must be three to five miles. We're a juicy target, that's for sure."

Seven men stood erect, motionless, silently waiting as they tensely studied the rapidly approaching submarine, the intensity replaced by agonizing suspense.

As she raced forward on the surface, she left a trail of dense brownish exhaust smoke. Because it was easily tracked, the U-boat appeared to be attempting to outflank the lifeboat on the starboard side for a submerged position.

"The lieutenant is correct," interjected the chief petty officer. "Once she gets ahead of us at starboard, she'll dive, return submerged, and await a rescue ship to launch her torpedoes as did the Sonzini followed by a coup de grace artillery barrage after a quick surfacing. The dirty, filthy…"

Then, for some reason, U-74 changed her course and instead of making for the starboard side of the lifeboat she turned her bow widely again, steering a straight course toward the hapless survivors. Apparently, during the sinking of the Sonzini around 2:30am, the radio operator repeatedly transmitted distress messages requesting air and sea protection in addition to search planes to locate the position of the motorized launch transporting General Clark and his staff to Anzio.

"The Krauts picking up our SOS's must figure we have a dozen ships and torpedo planes heading our way. That submarine is not coming to pick us up, but to crush and drown us, then skedaddle."

Peter muttered, "Well, there's absolutely nothing we can do expect wait in the morning sunshine. No artillery flash, no torpedo wake. He's going to ram us or pick us up. We'll know the answer in less than five minutes. If it's a ram, it'll be a group death, bound together, a common identity. No frenzy, men, stand and stare. Jumping overboard is of no use because of the sub's crashing into us, rolling over us, or simply passing by allowing the water from its track to drown us."

Initially patrolling the Mare Tirreno at 15 knots, and assaulting the Sonzini cruiser at 21 knots, the submarine, running silent, had reduced her speed to 10 in order to ram the lifeboat more effectively. Four Germans suddenly appeared on the stern deck hurrying to mount a maneuverable MG 34 type German machine gun on a portable tripod.

"Look at the Huns," shouted one of the dock wallopers, "getting ready to shoot any of us surviving the ram, struggling not to drown in the wake. The setup is perfect."

"No fear," countered the petty officer. "We'll all be sucked under the debris after our boat is split apart."

In overwhelming intense pain, Peter flashed on Aliandra and said softly to her,

"My wife for eternity, I stopped struggling the night of the afternoon I first met you on the tennis court of trying to find new words for what you might mean to me! And, now I may be leaving to wait for you to meet me in the future beyond. But know I will be with Antonello and our new friend,

Salvatore Giuliano. I say this, Aliandra, with all the love a man is capable of."

A moment passed in mesmerizing dread. Then, Peter shouted, "HERE SHE IS, MEN! BRACE YOURSELVES! COLLISION!"

Seconds prior to ramming, with the U-boat's bow-point aimed directly at him, Peter stood sternly resolved to encounter it face-to-face. With fists clenched, and a sneer of open defiance edged with contempt, he cared naught, not an iota that she was slicing her way through the ungenial sea fortified by 1,051 tons of brute force steel, including 22 torpedoes, minus the three recently spent.

What happened next in sound and sight was beyond even the excessive verbiage of an imaginative wordsmith.

Less than 15 yards from the target, at 18 knots, meant impact was NOW! But just then, an ever-increasing, powerful bow-wave swelled toward portside jouncing the submarine slightly toward the lifeboat's brow.

The violent collision, a hard, heavy blow accompanied by a blunt, dull, indescribable crunching-grinding noise catapulted most of the survivors in the lifeboat in all directions. Strangely, the sound of crushing steel ripping through flimsy layers of wood glued together triggered a concise thought of conduct among psychologically healthy humans: certain death is not without hope when accompanied with the fierce resolve to live.

CHAPTER FOURTEEN

Exposure and Starvation

With the churning foam of the bulky U-boat's trail, Peter, in a subliminal daze, felt himself slowly sinking shoulder-down to the dull-green, bottom of Mare Mediterraneo's Tirreno Sea.

Having been flung into a submerged freefall with a mildly delirious mind, his only concern as he began to suffocate in the increasingly darker and darker immersion was,

"Water's rough, not too choppy, but certainly freezing cold. Wonder if one of the Mediterranean's man-eating tiger sharks will chew me, like they do helpless Egyptian fishermen in the Red Sea. If not, wonder what marvelous ancient Roman secrets the lowest depths have to offer." When Peter stood defiantly, with fierce resolve and utter contempt, to face the submarine's perforating bow aimed straight at him, he and the survivors lurched forward when a strong splashing, sinuous swell pitched the floundering lifeboat slightly ahead of the collision point, causing a glancing blow rather than a direct hit. The U-27's right projecting hydroplane sliced the small wooden craft wide open, the sub's tonnage splintering most of the stern of the launch into a million pieces.

Miraculously, the only wounds of the powerful jolt to Peter was a momentary moderate concussion and, to his light-bronzed body, a series of thin slits over both thighs; a bluish ridge of welts across the entire width of his upper back, and a nasty gash below his right armpit.

Just now, Peter, submerged and dizzily careening to unknown depths, was vaguely aware a pure animal instinct had kicked in and he was no longer breathing freely. As he plunged backwards, face up, daylight from underwater was all at once cloudy, and within a few seconds, no longer translucent. Lieutenant Toscanini's world had become diaphanous, serene, ghost-like, and silent as a tomb.

With the chill of the icy water startling him back to a semblance of consciousness, Peter felt the initial sensation of suffocation. With oxygen so indispensable to his respiration, and his lungs now demanding satiation, he ached to breathe. He craved to live. He would resist to the bitter end entering the Sea of Lethe, the dreaded waters of Oblivion, if only oxygen and opaqueness prevailed.

But as much as life persisted within his mind, heart, and soul, Peter continued to drift downward in the strange, thickening darkening immersion. With, perhaps, less than a half dozen seconds left to live, regardless of how much life begets life, Peter, in anguish, flashed on Aliandra. With clenched lips hinting a smile, he thought,

"I tried, my love, I tried so very, very hard to survive for you and the young ones of ours to be. I go now to wait for you. And, I go with my fondest images of you, and I know them all, the image that is truly you to the core, the image of what God has to have made as the example of a woman for all women--the image of you, my dearest one, one an afternoon side street in your neighborhood of Monterey, bending over, then kneeling face to face before a little girl strolling with her mother visiting a neighbor around the block. You didn't know either one of them. But it was your instinct to stop, introduce us, then, with every precious impulse of your soul's love, you ever so gently reached over and with three fingers stroked her golden curls. Of all you are and have been, that moment tells the world and the only God who conceived the woman you are of the warm, radiant heart and mind that is. That very, very moment, of all the countless others, I cherish in me until…"

Then, with the movements becoming increasingly constricted, his consciousness again beginning to fade, and vaguely recalling that gasping would allow water into his lungs, Peter, barely able to hold his breath, felt his body twitching in the throe of suffocating strangulation. He felt like he was already dead by asphyxiation.

But, strangely, the young lieutenant was somehow sedated by it. The black stillness of the sea seemed soothing, even welcoming.

Then, suddenly with a violent jerk by the thick collar of his life preserver, Peter blinked, then glimmered in the spume and froth of the vortex, legs kicking, one arm swinging, the other clutching the "Mae West" preserver and yanking him upward. Believing he was already dead, the commotion hovering over him had to be an activity from the hereafter. He seemed to hear gurgling sounds in the action, the exertion, the performance. It all spoke of life, not inescapable expiration. Most of all, it meant 'HOPE!', despite the promise of Mediterranean miasma, the thick, noxious vapor, brackish bubbly smell of underwater decomposing human flesh.

'Ah, 'HOPE!'

Billowed by a swelling mass of craving to live, with a hither-to-unrealized exigency to breath, Peter aided the barely outlined form jerking him upward with the only strength he could muster, a feeble, pathetic threshing. Although saltwater had begun to flood to his lungs, drowning him, he resolved to endure another six to ten seconds with the same vim and vigor, will and determination, the undefinable, undeniable resolve he enjoyed in tennis tournament tiebreakers. He would face the Angel of Death in the next century, if necessary, even then. His debts to the Almighty, and especially

Junipero Serra he owed so much to, would have to be postponed. Damn it, he would LIVE!

Whomever it was, the uncouth turbulent human form that had so crudely, violently gripped his life preserver, then handclasped him tightly, stroked upward. The rescuer as rough and scabrous as he was, was thankfully employing the carry-stroke taught all military personnel in basic training. Although seemingly an eternity, the lieutenant's entire drowning episode lasted less than 45 seconds, partly due to the strength of a heart and mind that reverted to instinct from over three decades of physical exercise and endurance.

With the brightening of water above him as he opened his eyes again, the two broke through the choppy waves of the Mare Tirreno, both men, especially Peter, gasping, choking, racking with mouths wide open, sucking in as much oxygen as humanely possible. Panting heavily, and in vehement desire, each struggled to catch his breath. As he opened his eyes in the core of the plume, Peter found himself within a wide sea circle of lifeboat splinters, fragments, shares and shives, most toothpick sized. Although the wooden debris was flung thick and wide, nothing was burning. Sadly, however, he noted several bluejacketed corpses facedown, three of which he instantly recognized as the chief petty officer and the two navel turbine engineers who had originally saved him.

For Kojii, the perilous task of keeping Peter afloat face up, then, quickly lifted atop flotsam from the sunken cruiser Sonzini sufficiently stable to support at least him, would be just as formidable. As he scanned the surrounding water for anything afloat, Peter again passed out, adding to the Nisei soldier's challenging resolve to save him. Noticing a low, jagged protrusion in the sea, the only safe harbor for miles around, he saw there was no choice but to head for it.

As Kojii swam in its direction with one arm, while the other pulled Peter face up by the collar, the lieutenant awakened vibrating in complete consciousness, eager with new energy. Pointing skyward toward the sounds of steady droning, he said excitedly,

"Look up there, friend Kojii, see the Army Douglas Dolphine amphibious flying boat? Undoubtably looking for Mario Sonzini survivors. The Dolphine RD-4 is strictly a search-and-rescue float plane. He'll spot us now and come down and pick us up! We'll be going home, Kojii, we'll be going home on 30-day furloughs after short stints in the Naval Hospital in Bethesda, Maryland. From there, five hours by PBY to San Francisco Bay! But now, it wouldn't be too selfish to indulge in doughnuts, sandwiches, mincemeat pies or even Spam, washed down with oranges, a chocolate or two, then gallons of milk, gallons of coffee."

"Sounds good to me," he exclaimed amid short puffs.

But Peter was wide awake, well aware, that what he had just envisioned was unlikely. Now, his life depended upon this young, brave Japanese-American soldier, and he hoped the rather thin, less than six-foot tall man's muscles held for wherever he was being pulled to.

As for himself, the near-freezing cold water had drained all his physical strength. His hands were incapable of grasping. Cramping pain extended the lengths of his arms and legs, every muscle in his tight body ached, and, he clearly knew his life now depended on a man he barely knew. "Fortunately," he managed to smile, "he's Nisei and I know his inherent heroism. No man on earth is so naturally loyal to assisting the helpless. He'll keep us afloat."

All at once, pulsating, trembling, and quietly pressing urgently, he turned amid the broken billows and rolls to see a low, unobtrusive bulge, partly protruding, mostly submerged in less than a foot of water.

"This will have to do," Kojii whispered weakly, as he reached for, then clutched a torn, jagged edge of the balsawood lifeboat that had been ripped through and apart by the U-boat forward hydroplane.

"Would rather have a light rowboat, or even rubber dingy. Even a small scull could work for us. But with those unavailable and no raft-like debris in sight, let's settle for this," Kojii said softly as he pulled Peter forward to the floating object.

"Whatever," Peter returned, "at least it's morning, clear vision all around, sun shining on us, and we're alive."

Shivering, numb, and weary, Kojii somehow managed to jostle and nudge the heavily breathing lieutenant onto the partially immersed wooden cowling, or nacelle, an enclosed convex curvature fitting snugly into the curving bow. Removeable, it housed first aid supplies, rainwater catchments, cork belting replacements, the main canvas top covering, and the like. At impact, the swinging doors had swung open, spewing the contents within the radius of the razed lifeboat.

Fortunately for Peter and Kojii, the cowling, joined solidly to the undamaged laminated timber layers within the near vertical bow, fashioned an odd, but useable buoyancy, although partially awash. Once pulled atop the wide metal keel, an inch or two underwater, riveted to the hull's main stanchion kedge anchored to the lifeboat flooring, the lieutenant was hauled upon the Nisei's back in a slow, amble over the four yards to the base of the hollow bulging bow protruding six to ten feet above the sea surface. Angled at some 20 degrees, it appeared an unsinkable floating concaved fortress.

Sitting Peter down, Kojii hurried back to where the stern had been attached to the keel in search of one of the lifeboats' footing planks or Bollard Board to assist him in sliding Peter higher up the thin layers of strengthened tropical balsa that comprised the bow's bending façade. If reclined on the sloping curvature of the bow façade in the warm sun, Peter would be in near-perfect position to rest and heal until rescued, hopefully, that very day.

To ensure added heat for the lieutenant's frazzled torso, Kojii removed his Army-issued windbreaker-jacket, squeezed as much of the sea water out of it as he could, then bent over to place it from Peter's chin to his belt. As damp as it was, it would have to do. Seeing Peter was breathing hard, his eyes shut and face bruised, although no apparent head injury, Kojii had to cloak him even better. Taking off his long-sleeved Army-issued shirt, he added it too, over the slumbering body. Then, he pulled off his white undershirt, squeezed it as dry as he could, then folded it under the lieutenant's head for added comfort. With that done, he again surveyed the surrounding sea for the canvas cover that had been ejected from the cowling when U-27 ripped the lifeboat apart. Spotting it unwrapped in the distance, Kojii instantly dove for it with only his pants and Army boots on. Fetching the canvas meant protection from the cold, wind, possible rain, and winder sun at its zenith. He simply needed it for his fellow American and new friend.

Later that afternoon, Peter awakened to Kojii bare-chested bent over him, smiling.

"You warm?"

"I'm so warm with all this stuff on top of me suffocating me more than drowning," he chuckled. "Where's your jacket and shirt?"

"On top of you."

Peter returned the smile, then was silent a long time. Finally, he spoke, slowly and deliberately,

"I'm surprised they haven't found us yet. We'll have to spend a cold night on this crazy hodge-podge jumbled mixture of wood, barely floating."

"It's saving our lives, sir."

"Yes, friend Kojii, of course."

"When the sun goes down, we'll wrap ourselves in the canvas, one at each end. But no food, no water. But we'll make it, lieutenant."

"Look, I'm okay now, no longer shuddering and turning into ice. But you are. Here, my warm-hearted brother, your life preserver, windbreaker, and shirt. Put 'em back on."

For more than an hour, there were no words between them as the float bobbed in the increasingly swirling sea. Finally, Kojii said quietly,

"Rainproof canvas and South American lightweight balsa to keep our new home upward rather than downward, we'll be fine."

Peter, thoughtfully responded,

"You know, Kojii, I have no right to be alive. You saved me twice. But my two best friends are gone, Antonello and Salvatore, and I'm still breathing. Not fair, not right. I can't bear to think they are both gone. I have to think about them later. Not now, or inexpressible grief will consume me. But I want you to know that I know that if it hadn't been for you…"

"Look!" exclaimed Kojii, pointing to the southeastern horizon. "Barely visible, blurred, but not black smoke. A ship, it has to be a ship, but not headed in our direction. It looks like it's fading rather than getting stronger. While you slept, I saw what looked like specks circling the area down there…"

"And it'll soon be dark and stormy, I'm afraid."

Suddenly, for the first time since coming face to face with drowning, he felt for the sealed envelope taped to his chest. Yes, it was still there, taped securely. And, the letter he had been writing? He searched his pockets, and yes! It was in his front pocket, neatly folded by Kojii. Both were waterlogged, early that morning thoroughly soaked, now partially dried but damp.

Kojii smiled, watching Peter.

"Not for a second did you relax your grip on that piece of paper you were writing on. I had to walk you erect from where I pulled you up onto the keep. You were in pain so excruciating I though you would pass out with every step forward. I had to keep you afloat because if you fell back into the sea unconscious, you would surely have drowned. Then, we need food, soon, or you won't renew your strength."

Peter pulled himself up into a sitting position, looked up to watch a solitary search plane more than 2,000 feet above him, circling to the southeast. He knew that no one on board could see them from that height and distance. He had to resign himself the two would spend a miserable night under canvas without dinner.

Nonetheless, he scanned the horizon for a rescue launch. Just as the sun began to sink, two "Wimpeys", British Wellington aircrafts flew directly overhead at about a thousand feet. Surely that low the pilots or someone on board had to see them! Peter watched the Wimpeys fly on, waiting for them to swing around to better study the weird object protruding on the surface below them. But they did not. They had been carrying out a routine check for remaining floating survivors from the Sonzini. Peter and Kojii waved frantically, to no avail. There was no doubt in either mind that the Wellingtons were returning to base south of Rome to report that only wreckage debris were left after the survivors had all been rescued earlier in the day.

As the dimmest part of twilight turned into night, Peter felt intensely lonely. Kojii was enormously comforting, yet his yearning for Aliandra, coupled with death staring him in the face, intensified what he felt back on Pavuvu Island only months earlier. Sooner or later, he would die. But in this way, floating on a piece of balsa wood, hungry, instead of what he prayed for, instantaneous death, not the lingering kind. He had led the life he wanted for the most part, and now, for the first time, was certain he wouldn't survive.

Then he felt the first droplets of a suddenly fast-moving rainstorm descending from the British Isles, crossing southern France, and now inundating the vacuous skies of Mare Tirreno.

"Well," Peter coughed huskily, "what else should we expect in early winter? The usual huge Mediterranean moon, I'm told, so bright and beautiful to gaze upon, especially by lovers and poets, disappears regularly in late November through February, leaving the sea as black as a nun's frock. Kojii, help me stand up. I'm man enough to reach up and push the ominous black cloud cover over past Spain and back into the Atlantic."

Both the stranded men chuckled, Kojii adding,

"At least no fear from any U-boats tonight."

"Yes, unless one surfaces directly beneath us!"

With the sea rising and falling in the increasing swells due to the encroaching furious squalls, the frightful anxiety of a thousand nightmares kicked in. Because the heavy layer of clouding was less than two thousand feet, the rainy night's visibility was nil, if not eerie, especially with the sounds of the initial gusts of the mournful winds. Now, all that Peter and

Kojii could do to bide the incoming fury was to seek cover by draping the lifeboat canvas covering over themselves.

"Nothing to do but wrap ourselves in the canvas and sit down at the most comfortable spot on the slight slope of the 15-degree angled hull."

First, despite the strong winds, a soft, rustling rain began, followed by a more propelling, heavier type, then the more horrific teeming kind, one downpour after another, straight through the long hours of the cold wet night. Peter wasn't a hard man, and neither was Kojii. Sitting back-to-back for human warmth, their faces were pale, and they were plenty hungry. They were physically miserable in the near-freezing conditions and forlorn about surviving on their skimpy raft which appeared from a distance to be a long-handled cuplike spoon bent at its neck.

At midnight, weather conditions worsened. What began as a mean storm transgressed into a violent tempest, further diminishing their prospects for survival. Although it blew cascades of rain across the entire Mare Mediterraneo, Peter and Kojii agreed it was targeting them personally. Accompanied illuminating the turbulent waves, furious blast after furious blast after furious blast rocked, jolted and lurched the barely buoyant balsa float with high winds, heavy rain, and hearty hail.

"Kojii, if we don't survive this, I want you to know how much I owe you for saving my life, twice. And, I'm disappointed in never having the opportunity to repay you with lifelong friendship. I truy wish my Aliandra could have met you."

"Peter, and I presume at this late moment you'll allow me to call you by your first name rather than 'Lieutenant'," Kojii breathed heavily, "let's go down laughing and whistling in defiance of what Mother Nature had in store for us when we didn't do anything to warrant dying in a cold bath."

"Agreed," Peter chuckled.

At around 4:00am, the winds abated, the rain became an early morning mist, and Peter and Kojii crawled out from beneath their protective canvas. Bright starlight greeted them with the promise that by daybreak the last vestige of the terrifying tempest had evaporated. Then, hungry and shivering from both the surface temperature and soaked clinging clothing, the two, with the canvas cover pulled around them to their necks, they observed the first ray of sunlight streak through the breaking clouds.

"Well, Kojii with the waves having simmered down, we can say we safety made it through. I'm sure today we'll be picked up and I can get on with my assignment," Peter smiled, lying down and pulling the cover over his head again. Kojii nodded, and, other than a grunt, followed suit. After ensuring the envelope with his assignment was still taped to his chest and fingering the letter he had been writing to Aliandra before the Sonzini was sunk, he lay awake a moment longer, watching the thin ray of sunlight widen into a fully illuminated world, warm and peaceful.

With their bare heads resting upon their outstretched arms, the two slept straight through the morning. By 9:00am, Peter awake and full refreshed and energetic, lay under the canvas, his hands folded behind his head. Kojii's head only inches from his, snoozed on silently.

"Oh, for coffee, bacon, and eggs fried over easy, toast to dip into the hot, soft yolk," Peter grinned ruefully. "Wonder if Aliandra will cook them the way mother does. Why, of course she can. One more minute or two and I'll get up to search the skies. Bet it's a fine morning."

However, the one or two minutes lengthened into more than an additional three hours as he drowsily wilted into a deeper slumber. When he leisurely lifted his eyelids, he peered reposed and unstrained out from under the canvas covering initially, all was reverie, he believed, due to his growing famine. Slowly, to his surprise, he saw he was face to face with one of the thickest fogs he had ever encountered. Having been born and raised in the San Joaquin Valley of California, where heavy ground vaporous mists often lasted 25 days or longer, he instantly understood no search boats or planes would activate until the low Mare Tirreno fog burned off.

Sadly disappointed, his hope blighted, Peter weakly emerged as quietly motionless as he could from under the canvas as to ensure Kojii's continued sleep. He struggled to stand without assistance, then balancing himself by extending his arms sideways. Adding to his vexation, he noticed that their pinnacle-appearing raft which had been partially inundated throughout the long hours of the night was beginning to disintegrate.

"What else could we expect from hurricane force deluges of hard hail, teeming rain, powerful winds? Can't ever remember anything like this happening. With our only safety about to go, I hope Kojii will be less skittish and restive than I'm' sure to be today. In what direction are we supposed to swim or paddle?"

Somewhat inured to the ever-present uncertainties of death, Peter yawned, rubbed his eyes, and attempted to peer deeper into the utter silence and stillness of the surrounding sea.

"Nothing, absolutely nothing, other than the gentle lapping wavelets against the like wood of a once-upon-a-time lifeboat."

Pondering his dismal fate while staring into the nothingness, Peter was electrified to hear what sounded in the deathlike silence like a muffled bell similar to those aboard boats marking the periods of a watch!

Instantly, instinctively, he shifted, feebled, at an angle to squint for the possible source. Amid a slightly louder rhythmic splashing, gently and smoothly, against something not wood, perhaps metallic, Peter's eyes slowly dilated, wider and larger by the second.

Disbelief merged into mortification as he gawked stupidly, his mouth a bit ajar and beginning to drool. The thinning fog some 20 yards away began to yield the unmistakable shape of a fog-wreathed submarine, large black lettering painted on its gray bridge identifying it as the U-27 which had sunk him and the Sonzini in the first place.

Even more shocking as he began to survey the scene where black-suited sailors manning 2cm and 3.7cm antiaircraft guns, mounted behind the raised conning tower aimed at him. It was only then he noticed halfway in the sea between his slender-spired raft and the U-boat, four additional Kriegsmariners in a rubber dingy, one cradling a heavy German MP-40 machine gun rowing headlong toward him.

CHAPTER FIFTEEN

Steering his U-boat's sizable rubber dinghy up to what appeared to be the bow of a protruding capsized lifeboat, the German coxswain shouted, first in Italian, then in English,

"Come! Come! No time waste! Hurry! Fog thin! Fog thin!"

Then issuing commands to the rowers in his distinct Teutonic language to cautiously inch the rubber craft to the jagged edge of the bizarre-appearing raft, he turned to the bewildered, misfortunate survivors gaping at them in disbelief.

Easing from his strain and anxiety, Peter returned the bellow with his own, "Darn! We were hoping you were American, British, Itilian, or even Hindu. But you'll do. We're ready."

Hearing the shouting, Kojii awakened and peered out from under the canvas cover. Rubbing his eyes, he emerged, and stood next to Peter, noting his stunned demeanor. The steersman angrily repeated the command,

"COME! JUMP! JUMP!"

With the light skiff bobbing and the raft pitching in the choppy sea, the transfer was perilous.

Arm in arm, Peter and Kojii hobbled the few yards over to the raft's edge, and, assisted by the coxswain and machine-gun-bearing sailor, jumped in. To break the impact in the short, clefting waves, a boat-spike was cast into the balsa-cork protruding hull, piercing its exterior sufficiently to fasten the dinghy. Once the two unshackled Americans were seated beside each other, the open skiff metal line was released, and the rowers began paddling fiercely back to the submarine.

Cold, shuddering, and calculatingly all around him, Peter suddenly felt the impact on his back from a thick blanket thrown by one of the sailors behind him. Turning, he weakly waved, then threw it over Kojii, who was trembling as well. A second blanket was passed to the lieutenant by one of the lead rowers.

Smiling at Kojii, who grinned back, Peter whispered,

"Never thought we'd be captured by an enemy whose submarine sawed us in half."

"Better than then winding up on the bottom of the sea. To tell you the truth, although I wouldn't admit it at the time, I was at wits' end about the sharks circling the raft."

"I didn't notice any," Peter pondered.

"There were there. Best I keep my mouth shut while you slept through this morning. We've made it. Any POW camp will do, since the 442nd will soon take Northern Italy."

"Wonder why they saved us? It'll be the first thing I ask when the U-boat's captain invites us to dine with him at the table."

"Hope he serves us a glass of red wine," chuckled Kojii.

Overhearing the barely audible conversation, the coxswain turned from the front of the rubber craft, and said in surprisingly near-perfect English,

"War is almost over. My Navy knows it better than the Army. We strive to show more mercy so as to not be accused of war crimes. Do not forget the officers and crew of U-27 saved you from the fish."

"If so," Peter shouted angrily, "why did you run over us, killing all in the boat except us two?"

"You ingrate swine! I will swat you back. It was night, no? You had no light, no? When you were seen, we tried to turn. For me, I say in French, which I presume you Americans know better than Deutche, 'C'est plus qu'un crime, c'est une faute!' What happened was worse than a crime, it was a blunder! We did not turn in time. Then we waited underneath to see if a rescue ship or plane come to save you, then, as they help, we would sink the boat or airplane. When no one came in the fog, captain say to surface and save you. Now, we hurry, fog sweep away. Soon, we put you in sick bay, shower new warn clothes, then you eat."

As the undulating dinghy neared U-27 in the evaporating fog, Peter was astonished to see how weather-beaten the boat was.

"Is that piece of scrap metal what sunk us? It's worse than what we just got off of. I'm not getting on that."

Surprisingly, the coxswain roared with laughter, as Kojii chuckled.

"Maybe you know how to walk on water to Italy, huh?"

Peter himself had to smile as he surmised the effects of long underwater cruising, exposure to sun and rain, and overall general fatigue.

"Yes, she is new, and our snorkel even more new. But she fight and drill all day long, every day, all over the Atlantic Oceans."

"To me, the boat looks surreal, the new movement in art where the workings of the unconscious mind are painted. Acclimatized, the bridge and conning tower colors alone will scare off a cruiser or destroyer. Their protective orange undercoat paint is smeared into the shards and slivers of the dull gray surface paint so the whole U-boat appears a toughened, tanned pile of aging fecal matter."

Glancing at the coxswain who once again turned in anger,

"I know not those words, but they not good. That I know," he said loudly as the sailors continued rowing.

Peter, feeling somewhat exuberant, shouted,

"No offense! No offense! I just feel sorry for her hardened, overworked physical condition, what with rust streaking all over the steel gun barrels, the foredeck, and hull. In fact, fecal matter is a compliment in English and when I say, 'It's a pile of it', that's high praise!"

"I ask the captain. And, there he is, coming down from the bridge with the First Seaman's Mate to greet us."

"*Schnell einsteingen!* Quick, get aboard the boat! *Sich beeilen!* Get a move on! The corona of the sun is coming through the fog. The fog will clear."

With the afternoon waves growing increasingly turbulent waves smacking violently against the hull, the crewmen struggled with the sub's portable hoist, lowering the large boat-hooks to the rubber rowboat, then lifting it with Peter and Kojii seated in the middle, tightly-buckled to the main deck. After long, hurried minutes of jouncing, the dinghy, with Peter and Kojii still seated and relaxed, rested on the main deck between the forward hatch and tower compartment.

"Take them to the sick bay," bellowed the captain auf Deutsch to his seamen, while signaling his First Seaman's Mate to sound the general alarm to dive. As the alarm bell was sounded, and all on deck scurrying for the hatches, Peter and Kojii were led down the tower ladder to the Chief Warrant Officers' washroom and sick bay where they were to be physically examined for injuries.

"Shower them, change their clothes and I'll have lunch with them in the Captain's Nook," he ordered his Seaman's Mate.

A swarthy, morose corpsman trained to administer first aid and apprentice medical treatment greeted the two survivors with a scowling look. As Peter and Kojii stepped across the threshold to his pantry-size dispensary-infirmary-sickbay, he grunted,

"You in pain?"

Neither of the two responded.

"So, when we ram your boat, we toss you into sea, eh? Now we jump to save you. The captain not murder mad. Our lookouts only see the lifeboat seconds enough to turn, but we smack the boat. Then we wait for ship to sink when cruiser or destroyer come to rescue you. But no one come! It does feel good, however, to see you both hale and hearty, yes half-drowned and near-starved, dehydrated, barely able to walk, all the same. So, come in here, I will examine you and see you well when you leave our boat. But don't forget when the war crimes trials begin; no artificial respiration needed, the crew of U-27 saved you. Now, take your clothes off, put fresh crew clothes on. Then you go eat, drink water and hot coffee."

"Thank you," Peter said thickly, but sincerely.

"Thank you," Kojii echoed, nodding.

"Well, warriors of America, I speak a little English, somewhat. I lived and learned medicine in Germantown, Philadelphia, Pennsylvania, 1937-1939, then ordered home to Berlin by Herr Hitler."

As the two slowly undressed, Peter oblivious to the long-forgotten envelope, unopened and surprisingly dry under waterproof clear tape attached to his chest, suddenly realized for the first time since the sinking of the Sonzini the folded sheath had become so integral to his anatomy that it was unnoticeable.

What orders, what secrets, did it enclose, if any, that could help the enemy, costing American lives?

Glancing up at the corpsman, Peter saw the somber medical technician notice his consternation and break into a broad grin.

"Oh ho, no, no, no, no. Put hands behind the head. Put all from your pockets on the table."

Then, he motioned to the sailor standing with a Luger in the doorway to rip the envelope from his chest.

"Maybe, it's a Christmas card to the German military! Let me see!" he joked.

With Peter and Kojii standing virtually naked in the small room of several blanketed cots and where medicines and first-aid treatment were available, the Lugar-pointing guard walked over. Fingering the end of the tape, he instantly ripped the entire waterproof envelope from Peter's chest leaving him bleeding around the rectangular skin area where it had been so securely affixed. The pain was so excruciatingly painful that for a moment Peter, wide-eyed, appeared to be fainting. In fact, the intensity of it erased any awareness the U-27 was in the mode of crash-diving, the loud sounds of clang-clang-clang commingling with straining engines, shouting, and overall adverse action activity obliterating Peter's calming return to normalcy.

When the captain had issued the order for "Alarm! Alarm! Alarm!", comparable to the U.S. Navy's "Dive! Dive! Dive!", Peter had been impressed with the crew on watch tumbling down the aluminum ladder and hitting the deck plates, jolting violent, yet balanced. The continuous clanging and shrieking throughout the length of the U-boat muffled his own sharp yelp of injury from the guard's brutal yank. To Peter's chagrin, he may as well have taken a bullet from the German Lugar less than a foot away from his stomach.

"'Oh ho,' I say again. This no Christmas card to the German military. It is for the eyes of the captain only. What say you about this order? Most impressive indeed. And, why you so special for this assignment? You that important? Eleven words?"

"I haven't read it. I was supposed to only on board at sea, but we were sunk, and I forgot all about it," Peter said in truth.

"Guard will watch as you take shower and change, then escort you down to Captain's Galley."

Meanwhile, all the crewmen who had been on deck above had tumbled through the hatch and slammed the lid shut, with the sea crashing literally upon and over the U-27. It had dived in just 22 seconds, leaving a margin of safety of at least 12 seconds. Although neither aircraft nor boats nor the horizon had been sighted with the evaporation of the fog, the captain was taking no chances and ordered the sub to remained submerged for 60 minutes. At the moment, it was going nowhere; he studied the horizon but spotted nothing other than at short intervals dazzling flashes of lightening. Peter had to smile, as he said to Kojii,

"You have to hand it to our enemy, the Germans. A merciless fury can be unleashed upon them and yet they go about running their submarine amid laughter, whistling, and singing despite what's happened above the surface. We're lucky to be on this U-boat, even if it did try to kill us."

Showered, issued freshly washed seamen clothing, albeit enemy-style, Peter and Kojii presented worthy appearances as they were presented to the Captain seated in his nook, sipping a metal cup of steaming hot coffee; in front of him a platter of pastry.

"Ah, ack so, there you are! Supper and wine later, now after hot shower and change from wet to dry clothes, you are ready for German paste to dip in a stein of Arabian coffee."

Without a further word, both Peter and Kojii began consuming confections of jellylike consistency cut in cubes dusted in sugar.

"For now, sweets. Later, meats, potatoes, and vegetables washed down with thick German-style seafood soup. Fresh bread the dessert."

As Peter and Kojii relished their hot coffee and refreshments, the captain smiled,

"Lieutenant, we are trying to crack the code in your love letter to an 'Alian...' somebody, presumably a woman because no normal man writes such mush. Only poets. And, you do not look like a poet. But the wet piece of paper, folded neatly, but very wet, is not of our concern. It is your instructions we took from your chest. Only 11 words long, it says to me, confirmed minutes ago, I take you immediately to La Spezia. The order say in only words:

'Go to Kesselring immediately. Arrange for surrender of all enemy armies in Italy, and cessation of hostilities. By order of the joint chiefs of staff, endorsed by the President."

CHAPTER SIXTEEN

Provincia della Spezia

Peter was perplexed.

"What?" he pondered. Although seated, clutching a metal stein of steaming hot coffee and a large platter of freshly baked German gumlike confections on the nook's small table in front of him and Kojii, he felt he was reeling.

Noticing the American's frozen bewilderment, the captain questioned titteringly,

"Shaky sea legs, or do you need to use the toilette?"

Although Kojii chuckled, Peter, in stunned silence, saw no humor in the commander's response. Suddenly, he was sickened. The striking disclosure of his assignment was real, and the ultimate of all American military leaders, the Joint Chiefs of Staff, expected him to do his duty and fulfill the high mission without direction.

"Ah," Peter said weakly, almost in a whisper, "reread the order. Unless I was brevetted to an upper nominal rank, am I the one for such an undertaking?"

"Perhaps I surface and you walk off my boat?" the captain laughed convulsively with no effort to suppress. Kojii had to turn away with his chuckling lest he insult his new friend.

"You, dumber idiot. You assigned to end war in Italy," the captain snickered. "You like Field-Marshal Kesselring, best of the Schweinhund's military minds. You fail, I personally come and find you, put bullet, maybe two, up arsch. Now I go see if we leave hatch open and water come in and sink my boat. My adjutant, wonderful *Leutnant* Helmuth Weichold, *'der Pavian'* as crew refers him, tell the rest of your story, ah, that's it, unless you want *steig von meinem* boot."

"No thank you," Peter replied irritably. "I don't want to get off your bucket of rust jewel of a boat. And, what does *'der pavian'* mean?"

"Fat, fierce dog-faced monkey of German East Africa."

As the captain rose from his bolted-down aluminum chair, he grinned,

"Delicious seafood supper tonight. Don't be late. Meanwhile, stay seated, under guard. No foolish! Helmuth sit now and tell all we know."

With that, he offered a half wave, turned, and started to exit the Captain's Nook, straddling the armed guard and a lieutenant who so obviously was the "*pavian"* referred to.

One glance further nauseated the *leutnant*. His sweeping two-second survey startled a near-vomit. The German lieutenant was an ugly mortal, appearing more anthropoid than earthling.

"My God," Peter thought, turning away, "this guy has the most repulsive countenance I've ever encountered, at home as a kid, out in the Pacific at war. Large head with dull red eyes as if emerging from a dead black pool of water in a swamp, the long bristles about his fat snout was enough to scare our troops into winning the war, quick! Can't see behind him, but I bet he has a long reptile tail, lizard-like. So much for Hitler's superior Aryan Caucasian race."

Meanwhile, the crash dive was nearing its completion; the whole operation required less than 30 seconds by the obviously well-trained crew. The alarm bell that had been shrieking throughout the boat had ceased. Peter heard the *leutnant* say in German that the depth-gauge needle was gyrating at 40 meters and was now balanced out on even keel. So smooth was the diving maneuver that not a single item, food cans, personal belongings, boxes, utensils or equipment, all that had not been fastened or attached, had crashed onto the steel-plate flooring and rolled down the center aisle. Nothing had failed. The electrical lighting hadn't blinked even once. Not a drop of seawater had penetrated a single valve. And neither had a gauge stuck, nor a battery lost an acid, poisonous chlorine fume.

"No question about it, Kojii, these sailors are as good as any of our boys," Peter whispered.

Seating himself where the captain had been dining on the jelly tarts and strudels, Helmuth Weichold, the "dog-faced monkey of German East Africa," overhearing the remark, responded in near-perfect English, with a surprisingly pleasant rich and resonant voice,

"Yes, lieutenant, keen observation. But that was only drill. If enemy appears overhead, we go to water in less than 20 seconds. We 'alarm' dive now because fog cover evaporates, exposing us on surface. We stay submerged for limited period of time until we need air. Now, we return to near surface at periscope depth until dusk, then stay up all night."

As he shifted his hindquarters into a more comfortable position, he judged the grossly looking officer to be in his middle 40s. That he was highly articulate was obvious, with intelligence and education not far behind. Undoubtedly a man of no nonsense, of himself and most certainly the underling in his charge, it was no wonder he was nicknamed "The Beast" by his crew. Peter sensed there was a streak of human kindness and decency in him, and was proven correct when "Der Pavian" smiled,

"So, Lieutenant Peter Albioni Toscanini, USN, Medical, on special assignment, you are the chosen savior of the world. Well, don't forget your friends and the captain, and I are most certainly on your side now that the war is ending and we Germans have lost."

Peter, in utter amazement, asked,

"How did you identify my full name?"

"Oh, we know all about you. Most impressive what you did on that island in the Pacific Ocean, then in the military prison. As you heard, I even called you by your middle name."

"How did you know it?" Peter asked, still somewhat dumbfounded. "I only use the initial 'A' when I have to include it. You knew it in its entirety."

"We have our sources. Upon reading the document affixed to your stomach, we messaged Naval Headquarters in Berlin. Within minutes, we were informed by the highest authorities there to deliver you both hastily to La Spezia southeast of Golfo di Genova in Mare Ligure. There, south of Chiavari, at Sant' Agonello, a boat will come out to pick you up. You will be detained and confined until the General Headquarters of Field Marshal General Kesselring decides if he will see you. If so, they come by to get you. If no, you will be taken to a prisoner of war camp."

It slowly began to dawn on Peter as he watchfully listened that he just might be among anti-Nazi officers! For the captain to refer to Herr Hitler as a "*Schweinhund*" would get him shot on the spot if an SS man or member of the Gestapo overheard him. And, for his adjutant, Lieutenant Weichold, to talk so openly to the enemy about military decisions and their locations would be sufficient cause to immediately ship him to the eastern front. Certainly, such an epithet as "pig-dog" for the führer signaled anti-Aryan doctrines and German fascism principles.

In the short silence that followed, all three men, the captor and his two captives assessed each other, each with the bare hint of a smile on his lips.

Although the Germans were displaying unusual respect to their nemesis, with the gift of refuge, Peter would remain prudent. They knew his identity and mission which meant for Peter intensified watchfulness, listening and thinking.

Helmuth suddenly leaned back, placed his hands behind his head, smiled, and said without caution or restraint,

"For us, the war is lost. Most of Italy is already in Allied hands. In Europe, it is rapidly moving to a close. A few more months, the Russians will overrun Germany, the English over Holland. We fully expect Admiral Doenitz to order all German submarines and surface-ships to cease operating and surrender."

Again, a silence followed between the lieutenant and Peter. Kojii, as usual, followed every word intently. Then, Peter, in an unusually brusque mood, asked curtly,

"Are you still bound to National Socialism?"

His tiny rose red eyes in wide white sockets seemed to shine with a gleam of passion, his swollen face a corrugation of deep creases and furrows. He responded,

"In Italy, now that the war has ended for most Italians, Fascists become anti-Fascists. In German, with the Americans and English crossing France and entering Germany, the Nazis will become Anti-Nazis. Everyone is out to save his own skin. And, don't forget, American, you believe in democracy because you grew up in it, went to school in it. We grew up, went to school with National Socialism. Your heroes were George Washington and Abraham Lincoln. Our heroes were Adolph, Hermann, Heirnich, and Joseph, all who will soon be shot on sight unless they put their Lugars in their mouths and pull the triggers. Yes, I was Nazi once, but not now. But none of us who changed overnight will be thrown into a tomb, buried alive, or put against a wall.

Peter extended his hand across the table and shook that of 'der Pavian'.

"Yes, I understand, *Leutnant* Weichold. We are still at war with each other, but once it is over, I will tell the world how you treated your prisoners, the two of us, anyway."

It was true. Peter and Kojii were well-treated and fed. Since they were well behaved, they would be allowed to move freely about the U-boat. Helmuth was pleased to say that during their 36-hour cruise to their rendezvous off the coast of La Spezia, they would not be treated as ordinary ship-sunk prisoners of war. The *Leutnant* added, "When we surface, you will be called to the bridge to enjoy the late night, early morning air. Just remember, if we detect a convoy; American or British or otherwise, we will sink as many of those ships as possible. We are sorry for what we have to do, but until ordered to stop sinking ships by the German High Command, we will continue our course and duty. But, as for you two, we trust you as American warriors and gentlemen we offer this, we believe this, as gesture of courtesy. In the summer of 1939, the Schweinhund meant to push countries, and their political leaders around at Munich. But now, as a result, he is being shoved against his will to the Luger at his bed-stand or on his desk."

Where U-27 had wallowed, rolled, then surged in the strong head sea most on that windy afternoon, it slowly emerged into a calm, sparkling twilight. Visibility extended to Bastia and port Vecchio, the busiest port cities of southeastern Corsica. And, further east, the enthusiastic American onlookers could barely detect the subdued island lights of d'Elba. Nearing midnight, a wireless signal was received by the captain to "Arrive and assemble for delivery of the guests off a point at Rapallo on the Riviera di Levante", a strip of the Mediterranean near Chiavari.

As expected, the bridge was crowded with officers and lookouts when Peter and Kojii emerged through its open hatch. A quick glance of the rail told each there was plenty to see. Even in the black of night, the prevailing weather conditions allowed unlimited clarity under the Mediterranean canopy of indefinitely bright stars.

Joining them, *Leutnant* Helmuth Weichold, 'der Pavian', said quietly, despite the monotonous tone of the diesel twin screws,

"Look to my right, bright flares have just opened up and we can hear, if you listen hard, the opening of your Naval gunfire near Pietrasanta, probably our important defensive position at Aulia."

For more than half an hour after the German submariner returned to his duties below deck, Peter and Kojii observed the death and destruction of an ancient Italian costal town. Peter, sickened, turn to the nearest officer and asked, "At what latitude is La Spezia?"

Without so much as a swift glance away from his night binoculars, he responded, "44 degrees N, 9.82'E, I think you say in English. In Deutsch, we say 44, either freinheit, Die Breite, or 44 Vierundvierzig."

Peter, blinking to hold back a tear, triggered by so much senseless death and destruction as World War II was drawing to a conclusion, nodded,

"Yes, eight degrees northern than my Monterey, California. The latitude and longitude coordinates of my little city are 36 degrees, 36'N and 53'54W. That's where my Aliandra lives. We are eight hours ahead in time. It is probably a little before noon there."

By 2:00am, Peter and Kojii were so cold and weary they retreated from the bridge's observation deck to the warm bedding of the crew quarters adjacent the petty officers' sleeping area. The two slept soundly and undisturbed past a perfect daybreak.

Submerged since sunrise, U-27 cruised below the surface at periscope depth for hours as Peter and Kojii snoozed comfortably. Not once had an alarm been triggered. Nearing the western fringes of the destination area, the Chief Engineer positioned at arm's length next to the captain ordered the engine room crew to disengage the diesel engines from the propeller shafts and switch to the sub's electric motor propulsion. Leveled off at the desired depth between 230 and 300 feet, U-27 arrived in the outer waters of ancient Varese Ligure villages off the northern coast of La Spezia.

By early afternoon, the rusty, dilapidated-appearing U-27 making 14 knots surfaced. Having alerted all German coastal sea and air defenses of its presence in a special mission, the captain was the first out of the tower hatch and on the bridge. With other officers and lookouts following, Peter and Kojii were last up the ladder and into the fresh southern Golfo di Genova air.

Helmuth, 'der Pavian', at the elbow of his captain, immediately walked across the bridge,

"We are safe now. We reach our drop-off destination in one hour, you go off, we go to the boat docks at Chiavari. Field-Marshal Kesselring moves his headquarters frequently to keep the partigiani, of Provincia della La Spezia, especially those in the hills and mountains of Cinque Terre and the Portovenere towns and villages from attacking his bodyguard and killing him."

"Where, exactly, do you think?" Peter asked, his curiosity now piqued. "I make out large metropolitan centers to the north. What cities are those?"

"Rapallo and Chiavari, the important cities. They serve all the inhabitants of the towns, villages, and communes in the 1,000 square miles of the province."

"Where is Kesselring? Point it out to us."

"No one knows, not even his commanders, let alone us. Only those in the lead car of the armed convoy on the road at the beach off the highway connecting La Spezia with Genova. Those in the motorized boat who come out to our U-27 to take you off and ashore don't know. Instead of Rapallo and Chiavari, it could be one of the most beautiful villages in all Italy, Brugnato, Montemarcello, Tellaro near Varese Ligure. But, for us now, we have reached the protection of our people. While most of our boats are strewn at the bottom of the Atlantic and now the Mare Ligure and Mare Tirreno, we still float."

In the fading light of winter's dusk, Peter felt a grin cross his lips, "All this hassle means the mission may be coming to a head, which, hopefully means I'm a step closer to reaching the arms of Aliandra. Or, it could all mean I'm a step closer to imprisonment or being shot or hung."

Yet, for whatever reason, Peter was pleased by the prospects. He and Kojii might come out of this well. Everything, he hoped beyond hope, might just be right with the world.

CHAPTER SEVENTEEN

The Night Before…

As shadows of the purple twilight moved swiftly across Golfo di Genova, the rust-blotchy U-27 anchored off the tiny port of Aulia a few kilometers northwest of La Spezia.

Earlier, after surveying the southern Riv. Di. Levante coast, the captain had turned from the attack periscope in the shaft compartment to the radio and sound room in search of any last-minute communiques from Field Marshal's war center.

"Here's one, Justin!" he announced to Peter and Kojii. Not from the general, but from Admiral Karl Doenitz who rose to the German Navy almost two years ago, end of January 1943, I believe. This is top secret, from as close to Hitler as anyone can get. He told Herr Hitler, as we all know, 'We lost the Battle of the Atlantic because our scientists have no answer to the very long rang airborne radar the Allies started using last year!' Let me tell you directly what he had ordered for you two on your secret mission."

Peter, of course, knew all about the Gross Admiral Doenitz since he took charge of the new U-boat arm of the German Navy in 1935. The American Joint Chiefs of Staff know him well since he boasted openly that Germany's main plan for winning the war against Britain was further developing the XXI advanced all-electric boat three times the speed of U-boats like U-27. Churchill openly admitted what feared him the most in the war was the German Navy's ability to surround Great Britain and her sealanes. No, there was a reason Doenitz had been chosen by Der Fuhrer of the Third Reich, the

Chancellor of Germany, to name him the Commander-In-Chief of the Kriegsmarine. He is smart, that's why.

"Go ahead, captain. We're listening," Peter said, controlling his excitement.

With Helmuth having joined them and was now reading over his superior's shoulder, the captain again perused the lengthy wire, then smiled at Peter and Kojii and said,

"Well, first of all, I am proud to say, the good Admiral has congratulated me and my crew for what his Central Command in Berlin not far from the Herr Hitler's Chancellery. You understand why it is, of course, I keep referring to him as Mr., don't you? Because he doesn't even deserve that distinction. In any case, with Hitler's approval, we will be further acknowledged for our 'astonishing feats of navigation' getting you through the Mediterranean seas of proximity mines."

"Then, Doenitz gives me the precise position fix where in one hour and seven minutes from now, a German 'subchaser', as we call them, will come alongside the U-27 and haul you to shore and a small convoy of safeguard officers and troops in trucks will transport you to General Kesselring's headquarters. He does not say where that is, and it is none of our business. Soon, you will be ashore, headed to his presence. I now wish you both well as the *Leutnant* will also wish you his best. As for me, I must lay down, not sleeping for more than 31 hours without it."

At 1475 on Friday, December 6, 1944, having fueled to her full 3,750-gallon capacity, the converted Italian subchaser Scire II, confiscated by the German occupying forces, cruised gracefully toward the starboard side of U-27 to debark Peter and Kojii to shore.

Observing her clean, sleek lines coupled with a high box and unbroken sweep of well-groomed deck lines, Peter, at the railing of the bridge with Kojii and "*Der Pavian*", exclaimed,

"What a craft! Only imaginative, experienced Italian shipwright-craftsmen out of La Spezia could have built that. And, they constructed her with rare seasoned juniper wood."

"Yes. She was the Italian pride, tried and true, her lines 'salty'," agreed *Leutnant* Helmuth Weichold. "The Italian Navy was going to scuttle her last year when Italy surrendered in the Armistice. They didn't want her to fall into our hands, but we managed to save her in time. We employ her as a small passenger boat, ferrying our men to and from larger ships. Small car go, too."

"I like how she's armed, a 3-inch gun mounted forward, two heavy machine guns midship, and twin depth-charge racks at the stern."

"Yes, my friend. Well, there she is being moored for your transfer. You two must go now. There is no threat at night to our boats, but you never know what the partigiani are up to. They have been known to imitate the Italian Navy's Tenth Light Flotilla, two frogmen pitting themselves carrying demolitions against a single ship. Time bombs placed underwater on hulls of unsuspecting ships. Sometimes one single frogman against one ship. They wait now, go. And, maybe we meet again. Maybe after we surrender, we can be friends; you come to Germany in the Rhineland, me, I come to America. We become lifelong friends."

"Yes, Helmuth, after the war. But for now, lest I forget, you and crew here sunk 17 ships. How many lives? Who knows. But I am here thanks to you, the captain, and the crew. I am also here to improvise a plan of peace. Until then, my friend, we are deadly enemies. After the war, if you get to

California, remember I am in Monterey, California, south of San Francisco, if I survive. I will know where to find Kojii, and we'll share a bottle of cabernet sauvignon, homemade Sicilian-Genovese style."

With that, after shaking hands all around, the two Americans left the bridge and descended the tower to the deck of the U-boat for the transfer to the Scire II. Nary a word was spoken by the crewmen to the new passengers and before Peter knew it, with the two below deck in the Captain's lounge guarded but relaxed and comfortable, the converted subchase had entered a dark port facility in the black of night. Cruising slowly and conservatively, it inched its way along, from gulf buoy to buoy, by their numerical numbers. Plodding past shoals and coral heads, it entered an enclosed manmade basin of a small naval operating base. All was dark and silent. After a few minutes of searching with her 16-inch quay on a short pier to dock. Peter whispered to Kojii,

"And, all that to ease into a mooring without the benefit of any help or supervision. These Italian Navy men sure know how to sail."

With the bridge and engines secured, the gangway watch stationed, and all hands turning below to their cots, Peter and Kojii were hastily escorted off the ship to the middle staff car of an Italian three-car convoy. Against the shiny blackness of night, the convoy departed brusquely.

Replicating the silence of the crew aboard the subchase Scire II converted to ferry shuttle, the Kesselring-ordered bodyguards of elite Italian troops, all experienced veterans, uttered nary a single grunt let alone word.

Through the side of his mouth, Peter whispered,

"These warriors opted for fascist dictatorship under Musso and Herr Hitler rather than fight for freedom and democracy with us and the British. Or, as most Italian soldiers, returned to their farms and crops to eke out a living. Look around you, in the cars, on the roads, no one smiles, no one laughs, no merrymaking, no joy. Everyone is bleak! Only stone, cold, cemetery-like silence. Well, Kojii, I'd be silent, moody, dejected, even oppressed. They know they lost the war, especially when their nearby countryside defenses, villages that billet the enemy are shelled by our Navy less than a mile or two offshore and there's no retaliation, I'd be crestfallen, too."

"Yeah," murmured Kojii, steely-eyed.

Even as pitch-black as the night was, glimpses of moonlight broke through the rolling rainclouds revealing mountains of rubble clogging the otherwise neatly maintained roadways and well-groomed vegetable and fruit fields. Armored German tank columns and the three-car convoy took turns passing each other on the partially blocked two-lane highway. The foul smell of smouldering reeked within the military-painted sedans.

"We must as well snooze, Kojii. We're obviously headed north since Mare Ligure over there to the left. I figure Kesselring's headquarters is certainly north of La Spezia, somewhere south of Chiavari, and west of Pontremoli. We'll roll up in the blankets they put with us here in the backseat."

As the three-car convoy rumbled on through the night, never exceeding more than 25-miles per hour, they were constantly stopped at impromptu checkpoints the specially trained partisa-guerrilla fighting units of the German armies were famous far. At such traffic stops, a dozen or more pro-fascist Italian security, machine-gun pointing troops emerged from the shadows to surround the convoy for a thorough verification of its travel papers as well as a complete search. At each halt, Peter and Kojii had to exit the back seat of the middle vehicle "hands up."

After each time-consuming occasion, Peter had time to study the numerous small, concealed, well-camouflaged quays and wharves of hasty concrete and stone construction hitherto probably unidentified by Allied Navies. Then, with no communication whatsoever, everyone returned to his car where the two Americans promptly returned to their dozing as the slow, dismal journey continued.

Well past midnight, after traveling more than an hour over a winding coastal cliffside road, the convoy chauffeuring Peter and Kojii, both sleepy-eyed, to a surprisingly large hotel.

Peter, of course, had no idea where they were, and he refused to ask. Because the environment appeared urban enough, the town might well be Pietrasanta. Glancing around all about him, he noticed how seamy the surrounding neighborhood was. Even at that late hour, men in a variety of Italian Army and Air Force uniforms, some from World War I, appeared to be milling about.

Meanwhile, the Italian officer sitting opposite the driver on the passenger side of the staff car nodded to who appeared to be a German colonel or major assigned the receiving end of the escort. Standing behind him were Italian police officers of varying ranks. Italian troops encircled the solo structure in what appeared to be a vast garden.

"In a strange way," Peter whispered, chuckling, to Kojii, "There seems to be a festive feeling in the air. Is it because the war is concluding, or due to our arrival?"

"Or," added the 442nd trooper, "because they are still alive after the steady stream of Navy gun shells last night."

"Certainly nothing elegant about any of this," Peter responded in a low tone. If there's time in the morning, I'd like to look around and meet my fellow Italians, that is if the Genovese geography reaches this far south."

With that, the Italian officer sitting on the passenger side rolled down the window and shouted to the officer starting to double-step toward him,

"Quanto dovro aspettare? Sono stufo. How long should I have to wait? I'm fed up."

The officer responded,

"Cosa dice mi! You don't say. *Va! Va!* Go, go! Fai presto, make it snappy."

As Peter and Kojii climbed out of the staff car, whose motor was still idling, he noticed the approaching "German" officer was indeed Italian as well. His cap insignia identified him as a senior officer, perhaps a Lieutenant Colonel of the Italian Regia Aeronautica Air Force's 87th Torpedo Aircraft Squad.

As the convoy zipped away without so much of anyone waving a goodbye, the officer hurrying toward him smiled, and in perfect English, cried out,

"Ah, there you are. We wait, and wait, and wait! Then, word came from the boat you are alive and well. Field Marshal Kesselring waits, too. I'll tell you all about it, later. Now, I will take you to dine, we talk, and then to bed for you both. We leave immediately at 11:00am tomorrow for our 3:00pm meeting at his headquarters nearby."

"Where are we now?" Peter inquired, as he again scanned all around them, standing on the concrete sidewalk before the hotel entrance.

"Near the A12 motorway which connects the province with Genoa and Livorno and A15 which connects La Spezia to Parma. We are just on the north edge of Brugnato at Vara. All the villagers here all whisper the rumor that you come here to stop the war. No secrets among the people of these parts of Italy. No secrets. They hear, they tell anyone. No, they see you in Perso. Soon all the Liguria towns spread the word you are here."

Peter smiled at Kojii.

"Now," continued the Lieutenant Colonel, "My task is to feed you, put you to bed, then, tomorrow, drive you to the Field Marshal's headquarters center. So, come forth. We eat."

And, did they ever!

For Peter, the hotel's famous meat sauce atop a huge serving of Tagliatelle, flat narrow spaghetti-type pasta, pan-fried chicken drumsticks, oven-roasted cabbage, artichokes, tomatoes, freshly baked garlic bread, all washed down with two age-dusted bottles of house made il vino was simply sumptuous. Nodding to Kojii who was hungrily devouring his supper as enthusiastically as himself, Peter pausing in between his steady swallowing, grunted,

"Simply to die for, Kojii, to die for."

"What's for dessert? And, maybe, real, real coffee?" asked the 442nd combat veteran, half-kidding. "Sorry, boss, I have no time to sleep just now."

The acclaimed hotel on the highway between Genova and Rome was the "America, America," certainly the favorite of American tourists, relatives, and visitors on business or official business, Italians, who could afford it, enjoyed it as all, especially the old-world aristocracy, nobility, state dignitaries, functionaries, bureaucratics, and even Roman Royalty. Built only two stories with a superb view on a clear day of the Mediterranean and its coastal towns from Rapallo to Viareggio. Built in the traditional 29th Century bastardized Italian classical style, the interior was patterned in all-things New York. Prime ministers, foreign ministers, and diplomats loved it, including the German Navy until the 1943 Italian Armistice gently forced the slowly sinking Kriegsmarine and its favored staff out.

Peter, with Kojii at his side, was enthralled with the contemporary American decorative style dominating the wide lobby and delighted by the brightly lit, big, warm, and comfortable appearing separate bedrooms. Bowls of Northern Italy's winter flowers were placed throughout, including the bathrooms.

After the Lieutenant Colonel of the Regia Aeronautica led them to the balcony off Peter's room to experience the night view, he said,

"Gentlemen, I must sit you down for a few minutes to lesson you about the situation in Italy today and the Field Marshal you meet tomorrow afternoon."

As exhausted as both Peter and Kojii were, they eagerly pulled up chairs in front of the officer who sat back on the bedroom's couch.

"Where to begin? Well, I begin by saying that we Italians have enormous respect and admiration for you allies, your accomplishments together that achieved such tremendous and decisive results against our superior number of Italian and German divisions. But your genius during war and intimate brotherhood in arms won out. You, Americans, British, New Zealanders, South Africans, British-Indians, Poles, Jews, Brazilians, with strong forces of liberated Italians in North Africa, all in high friendship and unity fighting for freedom and delivering of mankind. Oh, how I wish I were with you from the beginning, me and my squadron of good men who have hated Mussolini and Hitler."

After a pause, during which he looked past Peter and Kojii across the bedroom through the window and into the night, he resumed.

"Instead, we, the Italian and German armies of our dictators, brought incalculable awfulness to much of the world, but the Huns brought even more to Europe and Russia. Yes, Hitler won the battle for France in 1940, then he lost his grip on the faltering Wehrmacht in 1941, all of Stalingrad in 1942, El Alamein in 1943, and Normandy in 1944, followed by endless Russian counterstrokes throughout all these months of 1944. By October of this 1944, it was clear to your generals and our German and Italian generals that the Allied hope of damaging our armies and pushing us across the Po River to the north was fruitless, at least in 1944. Your troops taking Sicily, Naples, Salerno, Rome, Florence and heading our way began to wear out despite the constant replenishing reinforcements of men, munitions, and materials. But they halted at Bologna. We intercepted a message from General Clark's headquarters saying the 5th Army was stopped below La Spezia on your left flank, not because of weak obstacles or particular defensives, but because his men merely ground to a halt, they could fight no more."

Again, a short pause, but one in which he studied Peter's face intently. Then, without turning away, he said quietly,

"Field Marshal Kesselring has personally guaranteed Hitler that our current position can be successfully defended to give his Fuhrer the time and opportunity to conduct his war free from any danger that your Allied troops will break into Germany from the south. Tomorrow, Lieutenant Toscanini, you singlehandedly can stop the senseless slaughter of troops on both sides, including innocent civilians. The true peace-loving peoples of Italy and Germany, Russia, and France, all nations were killing continues will know you, your name, your reputation, your courage and heroism, forever. So, sleep well tonight, on two of the best mattresses of the entire hotel pulled into your two bedrooms. I tell you, sir, the whole La Spezia coastline and hill towns and villages know you are here, why you are here. All German troops on this side of Italy knows it, too."

With that, the Lieutenant Colonel pulled himself up from the soft, coil-springed sofa, and started for the door.

"Good night, friends. No later, absolutely no later, stand at the entrance downstairs to await us."

"We'll be there, waiting. 11:00am. After breakfast, hopefully in the hotel dining room, we would like to walk around Brugnato at Vara. Should we have an escort?"

"You will have two tonight, one guarding the hotel, the other guarding the room. IN the morning, the same two, but with six rested elite, how do you say them? 'Snipers'? will be watching your every muscle movement. Now sleep, sleep well. 11:00am in front, tomorrow morning, I leave you a sheet of information about Albert Kesselring so you know who you are dealing with tomorrow. Read it before sleep, read it upon awakening."

"We don't even know your name, Lieutenant General!"

"Not important, not important," he waved as he reached the bedroom door. Opening it to exit, he turned with a broad grin,

"Oh, you meet at 3:00pm tomorrow because the general has three special gifts for you. As I speak now, they are being wrapped in special boxes and sent to his headquarters, so you'll have them by suppertime tomorrow night for your return to General Clark Headquarters in Rome. Field Marshal has searched hard to find the gifts to show and prove his good faith to Mr. Clark, the President of the United States, and the American people. He hopes you will be surprised and like them. It was very hard to find special treasures presented to you in the good name of Germany."

CHAPTER EIGHTEEN

"Meet Albert Kesselring..."

That night as gray clouds which had been accumulating since midafternoon opened up, Peter sat in the dark for a silent hour on the bedroom's comfortable couch and pondered the occurrences of the past four days.

How was it that so many friends and enemies knew so much about him?

Neither his weariness nor the grandiosity of the place, food, drinks and dancing band whose lively music sounded from downstairs interested him in the least. Whatever "treasures" Field Marshal of all the German and pro-German/Italian armies in Italy, General Albert Kesselring had mustered up was surely stolen loot which he would pass onto the proper authorities rather than the Joint Chiefs of Staff and President in Washington DC. Whatever "peace" his common sense dictated would have to pass muster with both the German and Allied authorities.

With a cold, steady rain gently drumming in the bedroom window and Kojii snoring loudly in the room adjacent his, Peter still keyed-up, turned his attention to the man who would determine his fate, perhaps the fates of hundreds of thousands of military men and women, if he crossed the Rubicon, the taking of an irrevocable decisive step or decision. Was he on a path of doom?

Perplexed, Peter fingered the one-page sketch of Kesselring the Lieutenant Colonel suggested he peruse prior to meeting the field marshal. Should he read it now when he was starting to wince from lethargy?

That the elite of the Allied military cliques picked Albert Kesselring as the puree of Hitler's military leaders was irrefutable. Some even believed that Ike, Alexander, Monty, Patton, and a host of others, including Mark Clark, couldn't hold a candle to his peerless administrative leadership. That he was the only major commander to maintain incumbency at one of the der Fuhrer's highest, most trusted posts suggested he feared little for limb or position when arguing or disobeying the *"schweinhund"* hog dog, as the captain of U-27 openly referred to him.

Peter knew nothing of the Field Marshal's distinguished trajectory into the top echelon of the Third Reich's military strategists. General Clark had mentioned Kesselring in a tone of respect, describing how as an army officer form Bavaria he joined the Luftwaffe in the mi-1930s, achieving the position of Goring's deputy and supervising the air squadrons bombing France and Great Britain in 1940 and 1941. He and Rommel teamed up to terrorize the British in North Africa in 1942. In 1943, he was assigned Commander-in-Chief of all German and Italian troops in Italy in 1943-1944. Kesselring's imaginative defense of the Italian Peninsula, after successfully withdrawing all his troops from Sicily in secrecy after the Allied invasion, was considered by all a masterpiece of intuitive strategic thinking.

Peter was especially intrigued how in mid-September of 1943 Kesselring proclaimed all Italy a war zone and occupied the landing fields around Rome because German intelligence informed him that an airborne assault was pending. Furthermore, Berlin was sending him an additional 25 divisions, more than 400,000 troops to stop the Allies advancing up "the boot". After the Americans entered Rome in early June of 1944, the Germans under the Field Marshal's critical eye established the Gothic Line.

But the Allies under Clark pushed on with determination in order to kick the "smiling Albert" as the Americans nicknamed him, over the Alps and back to Bavaria. With heavy casualties all around din front of the Gothic Line, the Germans and the Allies dug in for the winter. That was when Peter was ordered to make haste, get to La Spezia and negotiate a German surrender so the slaughter would not resume when winter's mud dried.

Well-fed, the soft sound of pit-a-pattering of light rain on the window, and welcoming warm blankets across the room atop a comfortable appearing feather bed were enough for him to strip down to his shorts and slide in between. Within seconds of his head hitting the Italian style, double pillow, he was dead, in a sleeping condition, to the entire universe.

Just after dawn and a good night's sleep during which he sunk a full foot into the amazingly comfortable feather bedding, undoubtedly the prized mattress of "Hotel America-America", Peter awoke with renewed vigor and the firm resolve to end the war. Upon awakening Kojii, the two walked down the staircase with three Italian members of the military police into the dining room. There, Peter insisted upon two tables being pushed together to serve breakfast for five unassuaged hungry men. Upon consuming platters of baked eggs, meats and pastries slashed down with steaming hot coffee, the five exited the hotel and began strolling the half mile to the Brugnato Varese Ligure Central Plaza and Main Square.

Peter, well rested, was completely at ease and happy with his lot as the five enjoyed the calm air and warm radiance of the rising sun. Entering the outskirts of the small town, Peter, pleased, sensed a buzz of excitement and expectancy. Passers-by paid no heed to the obvious Italian bodyguards but slowed to scrutinize Peter and Kojii in the center of the group to see if they were the exalted or bemedaled persons, heroes, or officials expected. Upon seeing the tough-appearing escorts, some of the onlookers even raised their hands in either the Nazi or Fascist salute. One unseen person, either in deep sincerity or outright sarcasm, began chanting, "Du-chay! Du-chay! Du-chay!" although Mussolini had been thrown out of office by the King of Italy's Grand Council in July of 1943 and arrested by General Badoglio government.

Nearing Brugnato's main square, as word spread, the crowds thickened, many from side street hotels rushing out in civilian suits to see the VIPs. Peter chuckled to Kojii,

"Some sensations we two are, eh PFC 442nd?"

Most of those milling about in furtive harmony were ordinary townspeople mixed with businessmen, merchants, civic officials, laborers, market farmers, fishermen, pimps and prostitutes, and a combination of German troops, recently released Italian prisoners of war, and pro-fascist, pro-Nazi Italian troops.

For more than an hour, the group ambled down narrow streets between or behind ancient stone structures housing crowded apartments, then strolled through the more tasteful luxurious neighborhood before drooping into a cozy café for hot coffee.

With that enjoyed, they returned hastily to "Hotel America-America" where the same three-vehicle convoy and drivers awaited, the motors of the automobiles running. Without so much as a word, the Lieutenant Colonel motioned for Peter and Kojii to climb into the third vehicle rather than the second. Once seated, he signaled for the convoy to begin its journey. Of course, Peter had no idea in what direction or where they were headed.

During the Allied Naval bombardment a few nights before, several shells supposedly aimed into the interior had fallen short landing between the central plaza and the hotel. One of the stately stone structures was demolished to a smoldering rubble. Toxic fumes reeked over the neighborhood. Although comfortably seated in the third of the three staff car convoy, the strong, unpleasant smell was so offensive Peter coughed well into several minutes.

As the convoy slowed to less than five miles per hour to negotiate the rubble-strewn and shell-cratered thoroughfare, it passed Italian Army trucks with firefighting equipment dousing debris scattered about anti-aircraft detachments, hospital ambulances, and civilians by the hundreds assisting troops in controlling the few remaining flames were dispersed about.

Making a left turn on Vernazza Strada at the corner Villa Giulia, the cars drove around evenly-distanced bomb craters to approach a slope past a large equestrian statue of Mussolini with his controversial sword of Islam. Further along the descent, the passengers enjoyed their turn toward Lungo Mare, a fine the Castello, a find old ancient fortress on a tree-lined avenue skirting the Brugnato to a pleasant coast road to Manarola, a dozen or so miles north of La Spezia shining with white houses, winter bougainvillea, open-air cafes, a cinema, and small shops full of wartime European goods.

From there, the convoy traversed the main seaport with Genova, then followed a narrow, unpaved road paralleling it in the same direction.

"Well, I suppose we're near," Peter said aloud.

"Si, si," responded the Lieutenant-Colonel. "His headquarters moves frequently in case either your paratroopers learn where he is and want to pay a visit, or the partisans sneak through the hills to enter from the back door."

"You think the bombardment the other night was aimed at the Field Marshal?"

"No, no, especially when everyone knows you're coming to make peace. And, look up there," the Italian officer pointed. "See the well-camouflaged 'Schwerer Gustav', the mobile railroad artillery gun? If we thought your naval bombs had been aimed at our prized general, the Gustav would have unleashed a torrent of shells at your ships. It is the biggest gun ever used in battle. See it? It is meant to protect our general.

Peter indeed spotted the single cannon atop at least a dozen attached flat railroad cars.

"Oh my God!" Peter exclaimed breathlessly. Indeed, both he and Kojii stared transfixed. Peter, catching his breath, gulped, "How far can she shoot? And, the weight of her shells?"

"Perhaps 47,000 metres, or 43,000 yards to be truly effective. One round every 45 minutes. Only two built. The other is in France on the English Channel at Calais. Each projectile weighs more than 10 tons."

At that point, the convoy drove past the remains of an ancient Roman City and a large amphitheater, then through an avenue of poplars.

"It was once an important trading post for the people along the Ligurian coast between Viareggio and Savona west of Genova. Everyone traded here because La Spezia was so wonderfully naturally protected, with its safe harbor in front and high mountains behind it. Name them, the Phoenicians, the Tripolitania, the Sabrathans, Egyptians, Libyans, Ethiopians, Cathagians and others used to come for Italy's gold in exchange for ivory, slaves, exotic foods, and wild beasts," smiled the Lieutenant Colonel.

"Excuse my history lesson then and now. But I love dipping into the past, a moment of thinking Mare Ligure antiquity, so full of life, imagination creativity, killing, death, and destruction, especially today. Lieutenant Toscanini, a good, Italian-American boy, you must be bringing peace here!"

Then, at the first major motorway junction a mile or so beyond the ruins, a seam where several ancient but useable roadbeds intersected. Directional signs had long since been removed.

"To confuse any attacking forces," admitted the Lieutenant Colonel. "We now enter Liguria's rural towns and villages, a place the world has not heard, where certain people still live who no one, even in Italy, has everyone heard of. The German High Command in Berlin has chosen this place for two reasons: one, to ensure Field Marshal is protected from sneak paratroopers, and, two, the best hideout to command the Gothic Line, our series of fixed defenses against your Fifth Army. The Gothic Line, as you may know is stronger than the Gustav Line. It is our last protection of Northern Italy. We feel the war of movement is over. You try to breach it, breakthrough, America, and Britain will pay dearly in the blood of young men. Very, very dearly."

Peter, without comment, continued to gaze upon vertical cliffs the convoy was driving through at reduced speed. The earlier horse and draft animal wagons, carts, and carriages were no longer evident on the increasingly steep grades, although occasionally single official staff cars and patrolling military horsemen made way by pulling off the often-cobbled road. On the summits of the mountains and hills through which the three cars were traveling were high observation posts and antiaircraft guns. In every village and town, naval and military officers were noticed strolling about. Artillery and gun emplacement, most concealed, proved to Peter the Germans were making serious attempts to stop the Allied advance toward Germany once and for all. Battled, deadly and costly, were destined for Liguria's Maritime Alps. The unequal struggle of overwhelming Allied airpower against less formidable German ground forces and their meager and sparse air defense batteries meant the slaughter of defenseless inhabitants and the utter annihilation of the scenic towns and villages.

Peter pondered softly, "So, so senseless, this horrific waste and tragedy."

"All because of the lunacy of a World War I corporal who is determined to fight to the bitter end."

In virtually every hamlet, small town, or narrow roadway thoroughfare, there was a barricade of hastily built shelters for eventual enemy heavy hire. Most were built of concrete, logs, boards, sandbags, barbed wire, etc., often with, obvious to Peter and Kojii traps and mines. Without so much as slowing down, the convoy sped through, the machine-gun-carrying guards waving in delight.

"They all know it's us. They, too, for the best, the end of the war."

Continuing their ascent, the three vehicles had apparently made good time.

"It's almost 2:00pm. In less than 25 minutes we will be in Field Marshal Kesselring's Headquarters. Perhaps even in his private garden he loves so much. The mansion he has chosen to command the German armies in Italy is perched atop a palisade from where on a clear day you can see across Golfo di Genova and see the palaces of Monaco. The name of the village is Apricale. Like most of the mountain towns in the secluded and remote nook and niches of the Alpines around here, it looks ungrande cuoco, a grand chef, had come out of the kitchen and poured a thick minestrone soup down the steep side of a hill."

"When you look up from the main square below, it appears to be un grosso miscuglio, a huge mishmash of from what all villages and towns are made, ancient brick rectangular roofed cigarette cartons all smashed together, most left natural, some new, either brown and tan, or white. Dismal damp alleys and at least half a dozen churches, open air markets, year-round flowing water fountains, several mountain brooks snaking their way through to the sea breaking up the medley, the chaos and confusion of squashing homes, apartment buildings, all in bella chaos und confusion."

"Sounds like a sheer paradise to me," Peter smiled, beguiled. "I'd like to be Chief-of-Police of that peaceful community, an autonomous community that could become known as an art hamlet of poets, writers, painters, sculptors, musicians, cinematographers, all seeking the gentle, quiet life. Any criminal activity could be handled by me and local leaders."

"Si, si."

"Aw, I'm just kidding, dreaming actually. Maybe something I'm unconsciously yearning for."

"Ah, me as well."

"For me, Lieutenant Colonel, because of my Aliandra, I would never leave this paradise, perhaps writing romance historical fiction unraveling man's higher nature through a natural woman."

By now, it was well past two o'clock. NO point that day had his thoughts become desultory, although the intensity of his alertness was becoming somewhat wearisome. Although the geography of Ligurian coastal hills and low mountains had been favorably compared to those of Northern California, every patch of land the convoy traversed, no matter how dull and inhospitable, held his full attention. Someday, he prophesied, he would lead his Aliandra and their children over these very same hillside terraces, narrow cobbled roads, crammed-together houses.

Having negotiated the winding, twisted main thoroughfare of Apricale without a single stop, the convoy exited the town only to be challenged by an even steeper road, absent of a single structure that soon led to a prettily wooden flatland. Here, whole stretches of forest had been cleared for a series of heavy anti-aircraft cannons. Passing through them, a number of single-post signs then greeted them, reading in German, "Go Slow", "Heavy Traffic, Turn Left," "Visitors to the Right".

Branching to their right, the convoy turned into a long avenue with the large 700-year-old monastery attached with a recently completed soft Gothic-style chateau. Under the shade of the trees were numerous German staff cars, lorries, and field kitchens.

The three vehicles entered the grassy, flower-encompassed yard before the white-painted chateau and pulled into the designated parking areas for the protective garrison and arriving visitors.

Upon pulling up and parking amid a well-groomed copse of leafless trees and evergreen shrubs, an Italian staff officer in the initial car of the three jumped out and trotted toward the well-guarded entrance. The dozen or so machine-gun carrying guards nodded as they passed, insinuating they were well-aware of the convoy's mission. Meanwhile, the arrivals sat back and snoozed, except for Peter, who perused the entire compound searching for sentries and machine gun nests posted and built to guard against danger.

A minute later he hurriedly emerged with one of the most unpleasant, unprepossessing human beings Peter had ever observed. Following him down the entrance steps in a relaxed, ambling pace, a countenance of vicious foreboding scrawled across his bull-necked, tallowed face, was an obvious adjutant dressed, surprisingly, in the black uniform of an SS officer.

"Huh?" Peter grunted in a ton of irony.

"Yes," responded to Lieutenant Colonel, sarcastically. "All Germany knows Hitler places SS officers next to military leaders of importance to keep a watch on them, lest they plot to kill him."

"Ah, one of the aftermaths of July 20, 1944?"

"Si, si."

As unctuous and nauseating as he appeared, Peter was surprised how mild-mannered the Teuton turned out to be. Reaching the Lieutenant Colonel's staff car, he smiled weakly in decent English,

"Ah, is that him?"

"Si."

Through the rolled-down window of the back seat, the German offered his hand.

"Welcome on this warm sunshine day. We wait for you. Come, the general is in the garden hearing the mountain birds sing. The general eager to talk, while surprise gift is near, coming in an hour. You take it back to America to show Germany is good people, want peace now. No more killing."

"Yes," Peter responded, "Let's make peace while we listen to the mountain birds sing in the garden."

"Sehr gut. No need the shells with our names on them need to be fired."

As Peter and Kojii with the Italian Lieutenant Colonel in tow walked past innumerable quiet, watchful armed guards on duty, several hundred observing eyes studied them. Peter, marching somewhat formally up the chateau appearing structure, was mesmerized,

"None of these in California. Sumptuous villa, if it is one."

"No, it cost the German people an unthinkable number of lire to build it. When the SS took it over, they stupidly kept the same cooks in the big kitchens, same workers in the laundries, and gardeners in the gardens, all Italian of Apricale."

Lowering his voice to a whisper, he deliberately mumbled indistinctly,

"While at work, those workers who understand German hear many things, much information, important and useful, which they bring on their way home in Apricale to leave with the partisan families for pick up. The overheard news and knowledge is often urgently needed and used in their raids and assassinations. Our headquarter for the Gothic Line is in the heart of the partisan den of Liguria. Is that not the height of insanity? And everyone on our side wonders why we are losing the war!"

Meanwhile, entering the impenetrable chateau, within, more a country house than a feudal residence of monks, Peter felt a thrill of excitement. Numerous officers with briefcases or folders were scattered in small huddled groups, single officers walking the hallways solitarily. Here he was in the heart of the command center of one of the most holy of holies military strategies of World War II and he had not a shred of insight of what he was going to say about enemy armies in the hundreds of thousands about surrendering.

Led by an SS adjutant who didn't bother to introduce himself, the small assemblage made its way down the main hall past a series of palatial rooms and highly ornate staircases into a large domed rotunda which led down several corridors to various halls, bedrooms and suites. At numerous intervals along the way, the SS man had to show a pass.

Peter's heart skipped several beats as the group made their way down the final 100-yard long passageway to Kesselring's west-wing residence/office/map room overlooking magnificent gardens. All along the way were vaults and arched columns.

"My goodness," he thought, "the whole 15th century or so structure is a monument! Look at all those cabinets stuffed with ancient documents and papers. Would love to stop and browse through them. Not a single person pouring over drawer after drawer, file after file, all pure history. At least the Germans are respecting them by leaving them alone."

Although there was activity in every arcade, passageway, hall, and gallery, many areas converted into makeshift, stopgap offices, counters, and cloakrooms. Midway down the passageway was what appeared to be an open arsenal workshop, lined racks from floor to a half-dozen feet high, filled with varying firing weapons, most of the latest automatic German industry was capable of manufacturing.

Nearing the field marshal's inner sanctum and its adjacent communication and private rooms, huge corridor wall placards demanding SILENTIUM in large bold black lettering were prevalent.

"The only levy he makes on all his subordinates," the adjunct whispered.

A deathly calm seemed to hover over Kesselring's entrance. No fewer than six hefty, heavily-armed, black-uniformed fascist officers stood rigid and erect before immense double- wooden doors, each sculptured in 17 century hunting motifs. All three black shirts on each side of the doors, wood shining glassy from heavy polish, studied the unarmed approaching entourage with pallid eyes, emotionless metal-appearing faces voice of human expression. Without a nod or word, the sullen adjutant, filled with self-importance, walked past them and shoved the wide doors forward, allowing the small party to follow him in.

Finding himself and the others in a narrow chair-less chamber before the only admittance into what was obviously the heart of the Gothic Line Headquarters that supervised all the German Armies that had retreated into Northern Italy and reorganized into the 10th Army Group to fight or die before the Po River Valley, Peter was a bit giddy. Behind this single entry, he pondered, "Smiling Albert" commanded more than a quarter million

German and Italian troops in nine armies, 17,000 military vehicles, and some 1,100 tanks of varying types. Heinrich Gottfried von Vietinghoff, second in command, was situated in the emergency replacement headquarters on the outskirts of Ravenna on the opposite side of Italy anchoring the Gothic Line at the Western shore of the Mare Adriatico.

Patiently waiting for a response from the adjutant's soft knock on the inner sanctum's door, Peter, as usual, automatically memorized his surroundings in the empty antechamber. Two additional guards; tall, young, Aryan-appearing Germans, stood at the door of Kesselring's sanctuary.

Arms folded, semi-automatic OUR Modello Berrettas belt-holstered, their physical heights enhancing the appearance of foreboding, they, too, gazed upon the expectant group silently, without comment, and, if anything, with the hint of fierceness in their eyes. Although wearing the same long-sleeved black shirts as the sentinels posted outside the chamber, theirs bore embroidered gold emblems of two lions standing upright facing each other on guard over their hearts. Again, for Peter, an atmosphere of deadly calm pervaded as no one uttered a sound.

Then, suddenly, the plan door to the field marshal's strictly private retreat flung open and a middle-aged, gray-haired woman stormed out, wearing the very same black fascist shirt with the embroidered gold emblem. In three strides, she stood before the small assemblance, and, without so much as a glance at the adjutant, beckoned,

"Come!"

Peter's instant impression was expressed in a low whisper to Kojii,

"The militant heart of feminine Fascism. Loud, arrogant, blowy, no nice lady for certain. How would you like to be married to that?"

"No Nisei, not a single one like her. We don't make crusty, sulky, spinster types who resemble offensive weapons that look like battle-axes."

Peter laughed. "She was obviously a Nazi concentration camp guard before this job, Hitler must love her."

Although she was yards away, she cast a nasty glance at Peter as she hurried back into the open-doored sanctum.

"Come in! Come in! Make haste! Make haste! No time for courtesies or introductions," she bellowed from well within the suite. "You follow the aide-de-camp into the private compartment for visitors over there by the fireplace where there are chairs. Come along! Come along! "

In doing so, Peter, et al were startled with brilliant sunlight streaming into the Kesselring offices from broad floor-to-ceiling windows. Peter was forced to blink, thinking he was in a dream instead of the second most vital war center of the Nazi empire.

As the adjutant wordlessly waved the group forward into the drawing room, Miss Crusty Sulky, as Kojii minted her moniker, walked across the large map room and through the suite's open doors onto the first story veranda and to its railing. There, she blew a piercing shrill on her whistle and began waving her arm in a circular motion. Two men, one bearing a submachine gun; the other weaponless, wearing a single white tee-shirt and white sorts with a black swastika printed just below the left pocket, waved back. The one wearing the white shorts with the official emblem of the Nazis and the Third Reich ceased his stretching exercises in a small meadow surrounded by a sea of winter hellebores, muscari and emerging red peony foliage. Native Fritillaria imperialis extended from that border to the edges of a short bluff and headlands.

Meanwhile, instead of following the small entourage to the seating area before the fireplace of the visitor's drawing room, Peter, unnoticed, remained behind to breathe the air of the high-command. First and foremost, more so than the innumerable posted maps in varying sizes of battle sites along the Gothic Line, extending over 800 miles between La Spezia, through the Apennines Mountains and Foglia Valley to the Adriatic Sea, was General Kesselring's open desktop. Near one of the large windows overlooking the well-groomed landscaped gardens, Peter, dying to inch toward it, began to salivate.

As he slowly, nonchalantly, stepped toward the broad windows behind the desk, Crusty Sulky reentered from the veranda and, in her strident voice, shouted,

"Other way, peacemaker, other way. Get close to the desk and I shoot you dead. Best you try to memorize the maps if you intend to spy on our defensive bunkers, anti-tank ditches, air defense installations, machine gun emplacements, all 3,000 of them, 10 miles wide. I enjoy placing Luger bullets in heads."

Startled, and somewhat disconcerted, Peter looked into her savage, fiery eyes, and said softly, an angry edge in his tone,

"I had no idea I was in the presence of Himmler's whore."

"No!" she retorted, without a tremor in her voice and fingering her holstered Berretta, "Heydrich's daughter. And, I assure you, American, a woman of the New Order does not fear death. Heil Hitler!"

With that, and a final sweeping glance around the War room, Peter headed for the drawing room, noticing it was the massive conference table he was passing that atop contained neatly organized paperwork, files, drawings and sketches. If only...

Just then, a booming voice of a man who appeared to be an athlete entering from the veranda exclaimed fervently.

"You are a brave little Nazi, Ingrid. All of us National Socialists love you. I wish I could find someone who loved me as deeply as you love the Fuhrer."

"Oh, but I do, Albrecht. You know I do," Crusty Sulky said softly, gazing at him with a wistful smile as he rounded his desk and with arm extended for a handshake, smiled,

"The peacemaker, I presume."

Ingrid grunted, then turning to Peter who stood transfixed as he raised his hand to the approaching field marshal, announced in a formal diplomatic tone,

"Lieutenant Peter Albioni Toscanini, US Navy Medical on Special Assignment, meet Field Marshal Kesselring, Commander-in-Chief in Italy. And, if I may add a personal note, Adolf Hitler's most trusted, favored general."

CHAPTER NINETEEN

Unwilling to believe it…

"Yes, yes, I know all about him! And, anyone who would dare call you, Miss Nazi Party 1938, Himmler's Whore has my added attention, especially that he was sent by the Americans. As I usher our guest into the visitor's room to talk peace, Ingrid, put Verdi's opera 'Macbeth' on the phonograph to relax us. Also, bring us two bottles of Pino Noir from the Luxembourg Six Yellow Chrysanthemums Vineyards and Winery."

Turning from Crusty Sulky to Peter, the Commander-in-Chief of all the Axis Armies in Italy, winked,

"You want good red wine in Italy, go to Luxembourg, buy it by the case, and bring it home!"

With that, he impulsively grabbed the lieutenant's arm and said, "Follow me. We eat and drink before we talk heavy. You choose, either drink German beer, Luxembourg wine, or real French caffe doppio coffee service with Italian cream buns."

As the two slowly ambled toward the ongoing fireplace simmering or smouldering blaze, Kesselring chuckled half-apologetically,

"I hope you don't smell my perspiration from noontime stretching exercises, almost an hour's worth. Some of my subordinates prefer to run, box, hike, or swim for their exercise. I select stretching, especially the way we do it at home, with long rubber bands made for stretching legs, back, and arms. That exercise is good for all the 600 muscles in a man's body. His joints, his heart, his mind."

As Peter was pointed where to sit next to Kojii, he had no time to judge Kesselring intuitively. The Lieutenant Colonel and his escorts had been dismissed only moments before. Now, only he and Kojii remained, both assigned the comfortable couch before the fireplace. On the Axis side, six sat in semicircle assigned seats, the field marshal's pivoting the others. Peter noted the unique furniture had been designed at the Bauhaus in the 1930s. The five supporting Kesselring, the sixth being the general himself, consisted of the general's SS adjutant, Miss Nazi Party of 1938, the general's official stenographer, and two military officers serving him as aides-de-camp.

With a double nod to Kojii as he sat back on the couch next to him, Peter's spirits were high, feeling neither fatigued nor resigned. With curiosity, he watched the movements of all prior to the matter of business at hand. One of the aides replenished the logs in the fireplace while the other poured everyone a glass of the red wine. Ingrid, meanwhile, had switched on the ancient phonograph which began reproducing from a large disk recording of Verdi's opera 'Macbeth', one of his most splendid orchestral works, the daunting music.

"How does one not want to live a thousand years in a thousand-year Reich when there is such sound. The chorus, the melodies, the tenors, baritones, sopranos, all resounding beautifully. My Germany never produced a Shakespeare nor a Verdi. Where the subject is so grim, the music is all heroism, inspiration to fight. I listen to it twice, sometimes three times a day. My skin always tingles with shivers of delight. I am always awestruck," Kesselring said quietly.

Peter, hearing the opera for the first time, nodded his approval.

"Please, if it's not too much, let's listen for a few more minutes, then we'll make peace, so apropos, as you say in American, us Germans the Lady Macbeth, the name of overweening national ambition."

In the few minutes that passed as the assemblage listened, pretending mutual appreciation, Peter had moments to gaze upon the extraordinary man who, by accident, happened to be a field marshal.

Studying Kesselring's demeanor as he closed his eyes, then gently almost unnoticeably, shivered as he emotionally absorbed the uncanny sounds of a soprano unleashing her vocal fury, Peter intuited the Commander-in-Chief was the most Herculean of all Hitler's generals and field marshals. Such passion, so loving and devout, was one of the surest signs of personal strength and psychological healthy imaginable. "Thank God this guy is sick of killing and wants peace."

"Smiling Albert" was a year shy of reaching 60 years of life. His father was a schoolmaster and town councilor in Bayreuth. In World War I, Kesselring served as a balloon observer, during a period in which he established a lifelong friendship with Hermann Goering. For his friend, he established a close tactical air support technique called the "rolling attack", a strategy that became the model for the US Air Forces' "carpet bombing".

Against Holland and Belgium, Albert earned his reputation as an outstanding air marshal. Because of his growing likeability and fame, he was appointed Oberbefehlshaber, Chief Commander of all German land and air forces in the Mediterranean. Although he disliked Rommel, Kesselring maintained a respectful and semi-friendship with the "Desert Fox".

Two days after the Allies landed in North Africa, Kesselring became Mussolini's military deputy and commander of Italian forces in addition to Air Fleet 2 and Rommel's Panzer armies.

Now, with the most important military challenger of his career, the field marshal was forced to defend the indefensible, the so-called Gothic Line, regardless of the number of tanks, machine-gun nests scattered across the five-mile width, anti-aircraft guns, and quarter of a million troops, to say nothing of the winter mud.

Although Peter appreciated the biographical information the Lieutenant General had provided, he was interested in sizing up the personality rather than counting the legend's medals. Now, with the opera's first act's tensive arias and melodic stanzas concluding, Kesselring seemed to awaken from a dream, smiling at Peter.

"I'm so sorry, but I pray I have an imaginative, cultured partner who also loves finely rendered artistry."

"Oh, I do," responded Peter with an equally wide grin. "I never, ever heard 'Macbeth' before these past minutes, and I thank you for the introduction of such rich tones. Being Italian-American, you can imagine my sub and unconscious connection to all the composers of Italy."

"Ah, yes, yes," the general reached over and shook Peter's extended hand.

Then, he abruptly stood up, and without a word or nod to Peter or Kojii, called for Ingrid and adjutant. As the two reached him, Kesselring led them a distance out of earshot range and by his finger-pointing gesticulating, seemed to be issuing orders.

Watching this, Peter leaned back on the couch and began rehearsing the Germans' anatomical physical and psychological for his presentation to General Mark Clark of the 5th Army upon his return to Allied lines. There was no doubt Clark would want a full report considering he had been halted by Axis forces before the Gothic Line with the field marshal supervising direct masterful delaying actions, thwarting Clark's orders to advance to River Valley.

In reciting Kesselring's anatomical features, he listed a long, muscular, athletic torso, a fire, virile face with high cheekbones, blue eyes, capped with thinning light gray hair, all told, a man neither handsome nor gruffly or brusquely appearing. Peter sense he was a man of passion and deep emotional feeling who seemed to radiate an animal charm, a certain magnetic warmth. Somehow, that trunk, including the head and face, exuded a solemn determination while simultaneously exalting invincibility.

To Peter, who liked the field marshal instantly because of his open naturalness, saw that he did not possess a shred of truculence and cruelty, personality traits most, if not all, Nazis had. That being the case, he would not be governed by anti-Jewish feelings, which were so dominate among the German officer class. Yes, he had been completely disarmed by Kesselring's informality and bluntness.

As for the general, he seemed to embrace the "peacemaker" the moment he jogged up the veranda steps from the gardens and through the doors leading into his inner sanctum. It was as if Albert had known the young Naval Lieutenant all his life. With their mutual feelings for one another, Peter was certain peacemaking was viable. After all, the field commander for some unknown reason, hailed Peter has a Heaven-sent savior. No, he reiterated to himself, his equal in surrender negotiations, was no surly brute, loud-voice evildoer.

Meanwhile, those who remained in the drawing room were quiet, the intensity between them growing. Their silence continued to ensue, deeper than before, as Kesselring further instructed his two closest subordinates in an obviously important matter. Neither of the three were smiling.

Perhaps as many as a dozen minutes passed before the field marshal waved his adjutant and Himmler's whore away and returned to the seated assemblage.

"Excuse me, Lt. Toscanini and others, I had to handle the arrival just now of three lorries, the largest in our Armies, which happened to arrive within minutes of each other from varying camps in Northern Italy beyond the Po. As we talk, the three parts will be cleaned up, brought here all shined and sparkling and you will be surprised and happy, as will be General Clark, the President of the United States, and the American people. This is my gesture, no, no Deutschland's gesture, to show them and the world we are more than 'Krauts', Huns, beats of torture and death, sadistic reptiles."

Peter nodded, refraining from smiling, swallowing all words he thought of expressing. Kojii remained as wordless and stone-faced as ever. Kesselring beamed as he gazed upon the two.

Finally, Peter offered weakly,

"If it required three trucks to bring whatever it is here, is it too large for one of our heaviest bombers to transport it back to the states? Maybe my aide here and I could help escort to Washington DC and eke out a few days home on furlough. How large would you say it is?"

"Although I haven't seen the three individual pieces, let alone assembled, I'd say they are as large as life itself," he roared with laughter. "And, lieutenant, if you like, I'll pen a few words to my nemesis, General Clark, or even General Eisenhower, that you did such a wonderful job that you deserve a special leave to spend with your fiancée, Aliandra, at home in Monterey, California!" again accompanied with resounding laughter.

Peter was so electrified by the mention of Aliandra's name and that of Monterey, he catapulted form the couch into a standing position, shocking all, and surprising Kojii, who was the only one who noticed Peter's clenched fists.

Too stunned to speak, he only blinked in surprise, then awe.

As Kesselring continued to rejoice in the moment, Peter, relaxing his tightly gripped hands asked, "How do you know that…?"

"Listen, young officer," he responded, suddenly turning somber, "we have our means and methods. Once the war is over, all will be known. And, you and others of the military will learn how deeply our spies penetrated your most strategic offices and positions. A few more years in preparation of our forces, and with our people so well hidden, normal Americans of every stripe and in all capacities, would have taken American and Britain down, which would have meant the fall of Stalin and Russia. But our 'brilliant Fuhrer', who knew better than all his best warriors combined, was impatient. Consequently, we lost the war, which leads me into the message I will not put in writing, but only in words for you to deliver in person, with Germany's gift to you, him, the President, and the American people. If he accepts my proposal for unconditional surrender, he is to broadcast a phrase in my care, publicly, for all the world to hear. The moment it is broadcast, I will issue unequivocally, clear and concise, unqualified and unmistakable, the order for all German and the Italian troops still fighting for our side to lay their weapons down and, with hands behind their heads, to surrender by standing before their gun positions. Any holdouts, any resistance, any defiance on our side will be met with instant execution by hanging or firing squad."

As Peter sat back down, he offered a half smile, and asked softly,

"And your SS units, Gestapo and other secret state and terrorist secret police forces, diplomats, Navy and Air Force personnel?"

"All, my friend, all."

As Peter pondered the message to Clark and Eisenhower, Kesselring continued,

"We will act fast. Within the hour, you and your gift will be loaded back on the lorries which are being gassed up as I speak, and you'll be driven across the line, now in a truce mode, to where I understand General Clark is waiting for my words at Massa above Pietrasanta. From there, you'll accompany him to the Via Reggio airfield for a waiting plane to fly you to London where Mr. Churchill and General Eisenhower are waiting for your verbal report. Should our elaborate espionage system in Rome or London get wind of my proposal, the SS divisions in Northern Italy will be dispatched to Apricale to make very fine chopped meat out of me. A tasty dish, I might add, mixed with raisins, apples, spices and suet and tallow," he again laughed heartily.

"And, if we're stopped along the route? How do I explain me and my assistant, and the gift, whatever it is?"

"Not to worry, Aliandra's future husband. And, I do intend to get you married off soon. Everyone, German, Italian, American, and British, and I might add, Private Kojii, the 442nd Regimental Combat Team guarding the lower motorway, know you will be coming through between the hours of suppertime, 6:00 and 7:00pm. My guess, you'll be having a late dinner with Mr. Churchill by 10:00pm tonight, seven hours from now."

"So, we'll be heading down the A12 motorway which connects Genova, La Spezia with Livorno."

"Yes. So, let me repeat what you must repeat from memory. Nothing written. You will only carry with you two items, the gift and the crumpled letter, water-damaged and all, you were writing to your Aliandra at the time we expertly sunk the Sonzini."

"Yes, let's go over the message. Kojii, I want you to listen, too, in case I miss a major point or two when explaining, because you will be at my side every moment of the way. Now, repeat it, General Kesselring."

As the field marshal leaned back in his comfortable chair, and one of the aides stoking the smoldering, glowing embers in the fireplace to feed wood chips, then half-logs, the field marshal reiterated what he offered earlier, unconditional surrender of all the combined German and Italian armies in Northern Italy.

"Outside, beyond the garden, partially hidden in the lower landscape is a tent city of over 2,000 wounded German soldiers. They can't be moved; the wounds too severe. They need the attention of American doctors, American medicines, American hospitals. My troops are ready to fight. They number almost 300,000. But they are tired and in pain from fighting and killing and marching up and down and across Italy and Sicily, then Calabri, Basilicata, Salerno, Cassinos, Abruzzie Molise, Tosca, and now Lombarda. Our uniforms are worn, our tanks and lorries decrepit, our horses and mules scraggy. We have lost World War II and my men, those who survived, want to go home now. As for me, it makes no difference. Shoot or hang me. But let my boys, most younger than 17 years of age, go back to their mothers."

Peter gazed upon Kesselring with genuine sympathy. As the general compressed his lips and stroked his chin, Peter waited for him to continue.

"And, I want you to convey to the good General Clark that although the Hitler cronies henchmen at headquarters in Berlin won't admit it, the Italian SOE agents and partisan forces throughout Italy impacted our movements.

Genuine, organized resistance also conducted so many raids, guerrilla ambushes, horrific reprisals to which our troops were often subjected."

After a pause, he continued,

"Unconditional surrender on our part, with your forces conducting orderly withdrawals from our Gothic Lines into the prisoner of war camps we used before the armistice. The moment I hear this refrain, we stop shooting, lay down our weapons, and be sent into the captivity of the Allies. You will leave here the moment the gift arrives in my office."

Just then, stirrings accompanied with low murmuring was heard within the main office area of the field marshal. As second later Himmler's Whore, Ingrid, boldly burst through the drawing room door and hastened up to Kesselring's ear and whispered loud enough for Peter to overhear,

"Die Schenkung ist hier."

Having taken Elementary German in high school, the lieutenant understood the four words to translate as,

"The present is here."

The general paused, then smiled and said,

"Before we dismiss to view the unwrapping of the treasure, let me encumber you both with the passage to trigger the surrender. Memorize it since not a single hair will be surrendered unless the full verse is heard and confirmed by myself. The verse will be memorized by you and transmitted by the signal operators of Clark's staff. As I said, the moment the passage is heard, surrender take effect. Now listen and memorize this passage from Eleftherios Venizelos, the Greek poet who served as prime minister of Greece from 1910 to 1916, and again from 1928 to 1932. He was the strongest, most powerful and influential leader in modern Greece. Ten times the man old Musso was while in power. Listen:

'A power pushes me toward a purpose I do not know. I shall be invulnerable until the moment I reach the goal; if I am no longer indispensable to it a fly will be able to overthrow me!'

These words of the Great Napoleon fit perfectly to the mystical faith that I have in my mission to bring peace to Italy, first, then Germany, and the rest of Europe. Do you understand this? If so, we move on! I now take you to the gift, the present, and you take it immediately across the line into secured Italy.

The Lieutenant Colonel who brought you up here will take you down, the gift next to you in the convoy for General Clark and Mr. Churchill."

"Now, Lieutenant Peter Albioni Toscanini," Field Marshal Kesselring whispered in a Bayreuth brogue, a dialect pronunciation in high German that Peter had never heard before, "Go, go hard, go fast, and go with the fates of countless men, young and old, citizens and country folks, all innocent, on your head. You must not fail, my friend, you must not fail world peace."

Struggling a moment to stand from his comfortable chair, he lifted himself and said, "Follow me for your gift, our present, to show the German people's good faith."

Crossing the drawing room threshold where Himmler's whore and the nameless adjutant stood formally, expressionless, Peter noticed the conference map room was beginning to crowd with varying officers, clerks, typists, military civilians, undoubtedly Gestapo, sentries, etc., all greeting each other, most standing with glasses of effervescent French and Italian white wines.

Glancing at the stone-faced adjutant, Peter confessed to himself that he had taken a liking to a man who was no more than a fixture. It flashed on him that it was probably the last time he would see the short, fat German with a pink white complexion and frozen sullen, scowling look. To the lieutenant's surprise, the black uniformed man gave him a knowing wink.

Entering, Peter blinked. Not only was he dazzled by the attempt to take stock of who it was that warranted an invitation to an apparent historic turning point in the World War II, but also by dusk's Mediterranean golden sunlight. Somewhat blinded by the bright golden yellow dusk light streaming through the floor-to-ceiling French windows overlooking the gardens, Peter had no interest in distinguishing by rank, then gauging the personalities of the officers and high command staff attending the gathering. Seen against the background of window light, the silhouetted military members all looked alike, despite most being German and some Italian.

Standing for a long moment, allowing his eyes to adjust, Peter whispered to Kojii, "If they give us any kind of a gift or present, you handle it. We'll carry it to the car, put it in the trunk, or take turns resting it on our laps to meet with General Clark."

During this time, Kesselring, Ingrid, and the adjutant managed to meander their way through the milling crowd without commotion. Peter noticed three figures across the room gazing through one of the windows nearest the office exit to the broad balcony, appearing to revel in their natural beauty. Nearby, in the nearest corner, were two additional black uniformed SS men, in addition to the adjutant. The lieutenant's attention drawn to barely formed men was partially diverted by so many who seemed to be scrutinizing him. Consumed by committing to memory all that the field marshal had offered in unconditional surrender terms, dazzled by the room's electrical illumination commingling with the day's last rays of high mountain sunlight, to say nothing of the drama of a temporary cease-fire, and the hope he and Kojii would dine with Winston Churchill and his inner circle in the War Room Westminster, King Charles Street, left him unsteady, if not outright frivolous.

Then, without hearing him approach, Peter casually turned to find the Italian Lieutenant Colonel who had delivered him to the Kesselring headquarters face to face with him. Kojii was equally surprised by the officer's stealth. Before Peter could greet the surreptitious fascist, he smiled,

"Staff car motors running. Then away you two. We must go now, right now, this very minute for the three and a half drive, perfectly coordinated through the lines. A light bomber awaits your arrival to fly you to England. No wasted words that can wait to be spoken on route. Now, I am told your gift to be taken to General Clark is waiting for you by the windows there. Come with me and get them, then we leave."

Bewildered and yet indifferent, edged by a hint of respectful beneficence, Peter turned to where the officer pointed. He would do as told, behave as a goodwill ambassador, and make the most of the surrender. He liked Kesselring very much, his high quality of body and brain, his surprising abundance of piety, his innate compassion, empathy, and humanity. Peter would do all in his power to assist the good German achieve his vision of peace. The field marshal might occasionally garb himself in the Mussolini black shirt uniform, but somehow he was describing himself in the secret code he chose to defy Hitler and order absolute unconditional surrender: The words of Eleftherios Venizelos, "A power pushes me toward a purpose I do not know--I shall be invulnerable until the second I reach my goal…"

It was Kojii's stinging yelping cry that instantly returned the Navel hero to reality. Before Peter could learn its significance or look where his friend was pointing, he heard astounding words that had no reference, no meaning,

"Unbelievable, absolutely incredibly unbelievable. Peter…look…"

As he did so, the moment mushroomed into the second most momentous of his life, the initial being when he first saw Aliandra and knew she would be his wife.

Struggling to regain a semblance of social consciousness, Peter strained to illuminate the gloaming of twilight that engulfed the vague forms against the windows. He ceased to see anything else. Neither did he hear a sound. He knew he was no longer in a illusional temper and had to focus then converge on what Kojii considered to be so "…absolutely incredibly unbelievable".

As he felt himself beginning to amble in a loose, easy gait toward the windows, the vague forms began to contour into three human beings, their backs to him, as they gazed out the casement windows. Were these the three gifts the field marshal had so enthusiastically promised? A sudden hush inundated the crowd since all knew what was happening.

Then, as Peter was within some twenty feet of the trio, the three simultaneously turned away from the windows, aware of the sudden silence, but oblivious that someone had approached them from behind.

The eyes of two from the three widened as they faced Peter transfixed and motionless, they were as impaled and thunderstruck in astonishment as the lieutenant. Not a sound was uttered by anyone, those of the crowd or the three involved participants.

Peter, so shocked, so emotionally, knotted and disoriented, struggled bravely to remain erect. So happy had he come in less than a minimalism of a second that it seemed impossible that anything could match its increasing depth and force other than the future births of his son and daughter.

For it was that standing before him, face to face, were Antonello 'Zolli' Audisio, Salvatore Giuliano, and Aliandra's youngest of two brothers, Allesandro Largomarsino.

To be continued in

Volume 5, "Rome Nocturne 1945 - - Fighting the Nazi Gestapo, Mussolini Fascists, and the Camorra, Sicilian, and New York Mafia"

MEET THE AUTHOR

Don DeNevi

Don DeNevi was born in Stockton, California, where his father ran a hardware store. Seeing the Stanley Kramer film "My Six Convicts" at the age of 14 incited a life-long fascination with the psychology of imprisonment and the viability of rehabilitation. In the late 1950s, he interned as a teacher at a prison near Stockton before graduating from College of the Pacific with a B.A. in History. He continued his education at U.C. Berkeley, from which he received his Ed. D in the early 1970s, and has since taught classes such as Criminal Profiling, Organized Crime in America, Classic Crime Cinema and Understanding the Criminal Mind at multiple colleges throughout the Bay Area. In addition, Don was Recreation Director at San Quentin State Prison for 15 years, where he introduced a comprehensive recreation program and built the prison's first tennis court. The author of dozens of books, Don is a prolific writer and a fan favorite for many readers.

THANK YOU FOR READING!

If you enjoyed this book, we would appreciate your customer review on your book seller's website or on Goodreads.

Also, we would like for you to know that you can find more great books like this one at www.CreativeTexts.com

www.ingramcontent.com/pod-product-compliance
Lightning Source LLC
Chambersburg PA
CBHW072354020726
47506CB00004B/1105